SON OF A WITCH

A WITCH SQUAD COZY MYSTERY

M.Z. ANDREWS

Son of a Witch
A Witch Squad Cozy Mystery: Book #2
by
M.Z. Andrews

Copyright © M.Z. Andrews 2016

ISBN: 9781687321435
ASIN: B07WSCYVTP
VS: 02.08192019.01

Second Edition
Cover Art by: Arrigo Verderosa
Contact email: verderosa.arrigo@gmail.com
Editing by: Clio's Editing

CONTENTS

COMPANION AUDIOBOOK

Son of a Witch, narrated by the talented Lisa Cordileone, is available to listen to in audio!

US Store Link
UK Store Link
FR Store Link
DE Store Link

PROLOGUE

The heavy beat of rock and roll music filled the empty spaces of Jimmy Spencer's small darkly lit tavern. Jimmy towel dried two glass mugs and carefully placed them behind the counter before acknowledging the customer waving to him at the end of the bar.

"How ya doin'? What can I getcha?" he asked expressionlessly as he flipped his long wavy brown hair out of his eyes and stashed it casually behind one ear.

The stocky man in front of him looked at his date. "What are you drinking tonight, sweetheart?"

"I'll have a cranberry vodka," the leggy blonde said to her date but kept her eyes trained on Jimmy.

Jimmy's eyes scanned the length of the attractive woman. She wore a tight red dress that hugged her voluptuous body in all the right places. Jimmy gave her an appreciative little nod and then glanced at her date. He was a stocky fellow with a puffed-out chest and big beefy arms. The way that the man was standing with his arms out convinced Jimmy that he wanted people to think those arms were all muscle, but Jimmy knew the only reps that guy was doing was with a burrito.

"And you?" Jimmy asked the man.

"Just gimme a beer. Whatever you have on tap."

Without acknowledgment, Jimmy turned and began to prepare their drinks. As he moved around behind the bar, he could clearly hear their conversation.

"I'm glad we got a room upstairs. Now we don't have to drive anywhere tonight. Seven hours on the road is too much for one night," said the man.

"Oh, babe, but it's going to be worth it. You'll finally get to meet my parents," the woman cooed.

Jimmy turned around with the cranberry vodka in time to catch the woman clinging to her date provocatively. He grabbed a mug from under the counter and held it up to the tap as he poured the beer.

"You'd think they could have come to see us," the man grunted.

"I didn't want them to come see us, silly. I haven't been home for years. I'm dying to see my old room."

Jimmy handed them the drinks. "That'll be eight bucks."

The man handed Jimmy a ten-dollar bill. "Keep the change," he said.

Jimmy glanced over at the woman curiously. "You say you're from Aspen Falls?"

Her face lit up. "Yeah, I grew up here, moved away about ten years ago."

"Huh, I don't think I recognize you. I've lived here my whole life," Jimmy told her. "What's your name?"

"Harper. Harper Bradshaw and this is my boyfriend Vaughn Carlisle," she said with a smile, revealing her perfectly straight teeth.

Jimmy's eyes opened wider. "Sergeant Bradshaw's daughter?"

"Yeah, you know Daddy?" She cocked her head to the side curiously. She obviously didn't recognize Jimmy.

Jimmy shrugged and slid the ten spot off the counter and shoved it in his pocket. "Sergeant Bradshaw is a regular in here. He and a couple of guys have coffee here in the mornings. I've known him for years. But he always talks about his daughters like they are little girls." Jimmy's eyes rested on Harper's cleavage for a split second. "You're not quite the little girl I envisioned."

Vaughn slid a protective arm around Harper's waist. He didn't seem to appreciate the looks Jimmy was shooting his girl.

"Oh, that's my daddy," Harper said with a little giggle. "He never wanted me and Elena to grow up."

"Come on, doll, let's go shoot some pool or something," Vaughn said. Gripping her hip, he guided her away from the bar.

Harper turned around grudgingly but managed to give Jimmy a fluttery wave of her fingers before he pulled her away. "Well that was rude, Vaughn," she mumbled to him under her breath.

A ringing of the bell above the heavy wooden front door caused all seven sets of eyes in the bar to swivel to see who had come in. A tall, dark and handsome stranger stood in the doorway wearing black Army boots, black jeans, and a black leather jacket over a tight burgundy v-neck. With a backpack slung over one shoulder and a duffle bag in his other hand, he took one step inside the bar and stopped to scan the joint. Two couples on a double date were talking quietly in a corner booth while Vaughn and Harper had just picked up a set of pool cue sticks. Behind the bar, Jimmy was assessing the stranger as he did every other stranger that walked into his bar.

The man ran a hand through his thick black hair before noticing he had caught Harper's attention. She smiled at him much to her boyfriend's chagrin causing the stranger's mouth to curl up in a tiny acknowledging grin and give her an ever so slight nod.

The stranger caught Jimmy's eye and made his way to the bar.

"What can I getcha?" Jimmy asked him.

"I saw your sign out on the highway. You got any rooms left?" the man's deep voice asked. One eyebrow cocked itself up, and he tipped his head slightly to the left.

Jimmy grabbed a small binder under the counter. "Just gave the couple over there a room, but I think I've got one left." He flipped a few pages in the binder. "Yeah, one left. How long do ya need it for?"

The man shrugged. "Not really sure how long I'll be in town. Does it matter?"

Jimmy shook his head and stuck out his bottom lip. "Nah, not so much. Give me a day's notice before you check out, and we're solid. Forty bucks a night and I need a credit card on file."

The man pulled out his wallet and slung a card down onto the counter.

"I need your name for the book too," Jimmy told him.

"Name's Reign Alexander."

Jimmy scribbled the name down in the book. "Top of the stairs to the right," he said handing him the key to room 203.

"You serve meals here?" Reign asked, scanning the bar for signs of food.

Jimmy nodded. "Bar food – wings, burgers, fries."

"I'm going to go throw my bag down in the room. Mind starting me a burger and fries? I'll be right back."

"Sure thing," Jimmy agreed.

Jimmy was alone for only minutes before the devilishly handsome man with the five o'clock shadow was back at the bar. "I'll take a bottle of Sam Adams if you've got it," Reign asked.

Jimmy nodded and grabbed a bottle from the cooler behind him, popped the top off and slid it down the bar to Reign.

"Something bring you to town?" Jimmy asked him.

Reign took a long slug of his beer before setting it back down on the bar half empty. "Family stuff. I didn't catch your name?"

"Jimmy."

"Jimmy, I'm gonna need another one of these," Reign said and polished off the rest of the bottle with one big swallow.

"Long day?" Jimmy asked him with an amused smile as he handed him another bottle from the cooler.

"Long life," Reign sighed.

"Food's up," said a voice from the kitchen behind the bar.

Jimmy turned around and grabbed the basket and sat it down in front of Reign.

"Put it on my tab?" Reign asked as he scooped up the food and the fresh beer.

"Yeah, no problem."

"Thanks." Reign stood up with his meal and carried it over to a booth next to the pool table Harper and Vaughn were playing on. He plopped down with an audible sigh and made himself comfortable.

Harper took the pool cue stick from the side of the table

and made a show of leaning over the table. She made sure Reign got a nice view of her cleavage while Jimmy got a clear shot of her rear. She giggled before taking the shot, wiggling her rump in a way that clearly begged all the male eyes to look at her. Vaughn grunted in annoyance.

"Knock it off, Harp. Why you gotta embarrass me like that?" he asked her gruffly as he moved behind her, so her rear wasn't as openly visible as it had been.

"Oh, Vaughny, you're so boring. I was just moving to the music. What's the harm in that? Can't you ever just have a little fun?"

He rolled his eyes. "What's the harm? You've got half the eyes in this room on you. You think Daddy Bradshaw would be happy to know his little girl is making a fool of herself at the local pub?"

Harper stood up and shot Vaughn a menacing glare. She strutted back to their table and downed the rest of her drink. "How about you just zip it and get me another one of these."

"You're a real piece of work, you know that?" he grunted at her. "Bartender. Another round over here."

"Jimmy!" Reign hollered from his booth. "Put their drinks on my tab and bring me another beer too."

Jimmy nodded his head and set about getting their drinks.

"Ohh," Harper cooed, leaning over Reign's table. "That's so sweet of you! I'm Harper." She extended her red fingernailed hand to Reign.

Reign's left eyebrow shot up with interest as he took her hand, giving it a little squeeze. "Hey. I'm Reign."

"We don't care," said Vaughn as he stood up from taking his most recent shot.

Harper gave Vaughn a disgusted look. "Don't mind

him. He's got a pool cue shoved up his...hey!" she squealed as Vaughn reached around Harper and pinched her backside.

Vaughn glared at Reign. "You can't find anywhere else to sit?" he asked, looking around the bar. Aside from the two couples in a booth in the far corner, there were at least a dozen empty tables and half a dozen empty booths in the bar.

Reign gave him a cocky half smile and nodded towards the pool table. "I was hoping you'd invite me to play."

Vaughn glared at him in annoyance.

"Sure, you can play!" Harper said excitedly. "We just started. Let's start over, Vaughn." Before her boyfriend could object, she ran around to the other side of the table and grabbed the two balls that had rolled into the pockets on the two far corners and tossed them onto the table.

"Ugh, Harp!" Vaughn groaned as Jimmy set the mug of beer and the cranberry vodka down on their table and handed Reign his bottle.

"Look, if you don't want me to play, it's fine," Reign said after thanking Jimmy.

Vaughn looked at the drinks and rubbed his forehead. "Oh, fine. You and I'll play. Rack 'em up, Harp. You can break for us."

Reign took a swig from his third beer and then scooted out of the booth. Harper gave him a once over as he stood up. His broad muscular shoulders tapered down to a slim waist and a nicely shaped bottom. Harper took an extra-long glance at his backside.

"Where y'all from?" Reign asked.

"Well, I'm from here originally, but Vaughn and I are living in Connecticut right now."

"You're from Aspen Falls? Ya don't say," Reign said as

he leaned on his pool cue while Harper loaded the balls into the rack on the table. His eyes traveled the length of her body appreciatively, watching her every move.

"Yeah, my dad is kind of well-known in the area. I've been gone for awhile. Haven't seen him in two years," she admitted with a hint of regret apparent in her voice.

"You haven't seen Daddy in two years, and you're back in town playing pool at the local tavern? Why's that if I may ask."

Harper's bubbly demeanor suddenly quieted as a dark cloud seemed to float across her face. She shrugged before answering him. "My mom's not going to be very excited to have me back," she admitted. "I know Daddy will be excited to have me home, but in all honesty, I didn't exactly tell him I was coming. And...we rolled into town kind of late. I didn't want to go over there at this time of night and be like 'surprise!' or anything."

Vaughn looked up at Harper sharply. "You didn't tell the Sarge we were coming? You said you ironed all that out!"

Harper grinned nervously. "I didn't want you to back out. I couldn't face them alone..."

"You know how they feel about me. About us. You don't think they would have appreciated a little warning that they were finally going to meet me?"

She shrugged and scooted over to the front end of the table. She put the cue ball down on the table and lined up her shot. "It'll be fine. I'm sure Daddy will just be happy to see me, that's really all that matters." Her cue ball barely broke the triangular figure. She stomped her high-heeled foot down on the ground petulantly.

"If you say so," said Vaughn. He then stepped forward, leaned over and took a shot. A striped ball sank into a side pocket easily. He stood up straight, puffed his chest a bit and then took another shot at a striped ball. It came close to falling in but bounced and rolled away.

"So, what's your story?" Vaughn asked Reign as he walked back to his table to take another drink.

Reign scanned the length of the table, looking for a good shot. "No story to tell," he said then leaned over, pulled the stick back and launched it, sinking four solid balls into four separate holes. "Visiting family in town, same as you."

Vaughn's eyes widened as the balls all dropped. Harper clapped while bouncing on her toes. "Wow, Reign, that was awesome! You should give Vaughn some pointers!"

Her boyfriend shot her an angry glance as Reign leaned over to take his next shot. "I'd be happy to give you some pointers, man." Reign took another shot and sank his last three balls.

Vaughn's face dropped. "Nah, man, I don't need any pointers. You a hustler or something?"

Reign laughed as he leaned his pool cue up against the table and returned to his booth to grab his beer. "Did I ask to play for money?"

Vaughn looked at Harper nervously. "Then what's your game?" he asked.

"No game. I've been on the road all day by myself. I just wanted to have a little conversation. How about you two join me. Next round's on me again?" Reign suggested easily.

"Ooh, I better finished this one then," Harper giggled, taking a long sip of her rose-colored drink.

"Jimmy, hit us all with another drink. In fact, throw one at those four too. On me," Reign nodded towards the couple in the corner. They all smiled and waved at Reign.

"Thanks, man!" hollered one of the men in the group.

"See, no game," Reign said with a little shrug. "Just being friendly. I'm gonna go throw some money into the jukebox over there. You two wanna hear anything special?"

"I'll come with you and help you pick!" Harper said excitedly.

Vaughn rolled his eyes at her. "Harper, he doesn't want your help."

"I don't mind, come on, sweetheart. You can choose them all," Reign told her with a sexy grin as he extended his elbow to her.

"Ugh, Harp," Vaughn growled and threw both hands up in the air.

"You got a handful right there," Jimmy said to him from across the bar.

Vaughn looked at Jimmy and nodded. "Yeah I do."

CHAPTER 1

I smoothed out the wrinkles in the slinky little dress Holly let me borrow and looked down at myself self-consciously. "You really don't think this is too...I don't know, revealing?" I asked, spinning around in front of the full-length mirror.

"Duh, that's the point," Holly said as she adjusted the strap on my right shoulder to lift my chest up higher. "It's unfortunate you don't have bigger boobs. These will have to do, I guess."

"You look hot, Mercy, Smokin' hot! Houston won't be able to resist," said Jax, my tiny pixie of a roommate.

I took a good look at myself in the mirror. I barely looked like me. Gone was my ratty old AC/DC hoodie, skinny jeans, and the Converse sneakers I usually walked around in. Who was this girl in the mirror? I certainly didn't recognize her. Even with my black framed glasses on, I looked like a fake glamour version of Mercy Habernackle. My long auburn hair wasn't in my usual side braid because I'd relented when Holly offered, pleaded really, to curl my hair. Now it bounced cheerfully around my shoulders and with the makeup she'd held me down long enough to put on, I looked like, ugh, a girl.

I shrugged. "I guess I look okay. I just don't think I look like – me."

Jax squeezed her petite arms around my middle. "You look like you, Mercy. You just look like the date version of you."

I peered at myself again. I didn't necessarily care for the date version of me. This was my first college date and in reality, my first *date date*. Not that I would admit that to the girls. They didn't really need to know that I was freaking out inside. Houston Brooks had sort of tricked me into going on this date with him. He'd helped the girls and me when we'd gotten into a sticky situation, and I'd promised that I owed him one. Little had I known that he'd have collected by asking me out on a date.

"Thanks, Jax. What do *you* think, Alba?" I asked the tall, sturdy girl who lived down the hall from my dorm room. She was Holly's roommate and the two couldn't be more opposite – physically and mentally. Holly was a klutzy buxom blonde with vanity issues and Alba was tall, dark, and grumpy, in the nicest sense of the word.

Alba grunted at me. "Eh. You look alright, Red. I'd date you."

I eyed her carefully. She made me wonder sometimes if she actually did prefer girls, but I'd never gone so far as to ask. I mean, after all, it was only the second week of witch college and I'd barely scraped the surface of trying to get to know *any* of these girls. And after the week we'd had, what with solving the Morgan Hartford murder, rescuing Jax from her abduction and saving the life of a town girl, we just hadn't had the time to get to know each other yet.

"Uh, thanks?" I said with a chuckle. "I guess we already

know Hugh would date me, I mean he *did* ask me out. That was the easy part. Now I actually have to be witty and cute and stuff. I'm not much of a witty, cute girl. I'm more of the hopelessly weird and gloomy type. He's probably not going to like me much."

"What's not to like?" asked Sweets, the fifth member of our Witch Squad, a moniker we'd been nicknamed by the rest of the student witches here at the Paranormal Institute for Witches during the first week of school. Sweets's real name was actually Mildred Porter, but she'd been nick-named Sweets, and it was no wonder. Not only was she the sweetest of the sweet, personality wise, she was also a baking matchmaker. She could match couples together by baking the potion into a sweet recipe. She also liked to eat her concoctions which was probably why she was more than a tad on the overweight side. Personally, I thought her figure added to her charm and she had quickly become one of my favorite people at the school for witches.

"Aww, you're a doll, Sweets," I said, giving her a thankful little smile. "It doesn't change the fact that I'm beyond nervous. What time is it?" I asked the room.

Jax looked at the alarm clock on her desk. "Seven o'clock. What time is Houston picking you up?"

"Seven-thirty sharp, remember?" I said. I wasn't sure how anyone could have forgotten that little detail. He'd asked me out in the quad in front of the whole school, including my group of friends. It had been absolutely humiliating to say the very least.

Jax laughed. "Oh yeah, and *wear something pretty, no sneakers*," she remembered.

"Yeah, he's lucky he told her that, otherwise she'd be wearing her Chuck's as we speak," Holly said, rolling her eyes. "You just look a thousand times better like this."

"I, personally, like to be comfortable," I told the girls. "Especially in college. Why do I need to look like – this – in college?"

"To snag a boyfriend," Holly said with a little shrug.

Jax and Sweets nodded. "Agreed," Jax said with a smile.

"I agree with Red," Alba said, leaning against my dorm room door. "Comfort is key in college. I could wear sweatpants and sweatshirts every day to class."

Holly raised an eyebrow. "You do wear sweatpants and sweatshirts every day to class."

"Hello? The elevation of Aspen Falls makes it colder here than it ever is at this time of year in New Jersey," said Alba. Alba was a New Jersey native. Her family owned a furniture moving business in the city which made her powers of telekinesis very handy to have.

Holly, with her blond hair and blue eyes, was a true California girl. Sweets was from Georgia and Jax claimed she was from all over, but it had been recently revealed that not only was she the daughter of Sorceress Stone, the headmistress of the Institute, but she also wasn't a witch. We hadn't had time since the big reveal to discuss it in more detail, but she had promised someday she'd give us the scoop.

I hailed from Dubbsburg, Illinois, a small town outside of Chicago. My mother, Linda, had recently dropped me off at the Paranormal Institute for Witches, which was located in Aspen Falls, Pennsylvania, a small college town nestled high in the Appalachian Mountains. It was a beautiful town with large stands of scarlet oak and hemlock trees. Even though I'd never been in Aspen Falls during any other seasons, fall was, by far, the best season to be here.

"Just because the days are cool now doesn't mean you

have to dress like a polar bear," Holly said with her hand on her hip.

"At least I *wear* clothes," Alba retorted.

"What's that supposed to mean?"

Alba shrugged and jerked her head towards Holly's low-cut blouse. "You know what that means. You don't wear your heart on your sleeve; you wear your breasts on your sleeve."

Sweets's eyes opened wide. "Alba! That wasn't very nice!"

Alba and Holly exchanged annoyed glances. "What? We all know that Holly's shirts leave little to the imagination."

"But you don't have to be rude about it," Sweets said with a little frown.

"Fine," Alba growled.

"Anyway, girls. I'm not trying to *snag a boyfriend*," I told them.

"Of course you're not. Just like these three idiots aren't," Alba said with her arms crossed and a frown on her face.

"Geez, who sank your battleship?" I asked her indignantly.

"Ugh, I'm going to my room," she retorted grumpily. She promptly turned on her heel and left my room with a slam of the door.

"What's with her?" I asked.

"I think she's upset because her family hasn't called her once since she's been here," Holly said with a little frown. "She's constantly checking her cell phone for messages and she never has any."

"My family hasn't called either," said Sweets, sticking out her lower lip and looking pouty. "That didn't bother me until just now. Why *hasn't* my family called me yet?"

"Because you're twenty years old and don't need

Mommy and Daddy checking in on you every fifteen minutes?" I suggested.

"You're nineteen and *your* mom checks in on you every fifteen minutes," she retorted.

"That's different. My mom's all alone back home. Oh, plus, I haven't had time to tell you what she told me earlier today."

"What did she tell you?" Jax asked as she jumped onto my bed and curled her legs up underneath her.

"Big news," I started then looked down at my watch seven o' five. "Okay, I have a few minutes. Brace yourselves."

"Oooh, this sounds juicy!" Sweets said with a big smile which dimpled her chubby cheeks.

"It sort of is. I really haven't had time to process it yet. I feel like I'm still in a state of shock," I began.

"Gosh, out with it already!" Holly said, scooting Jax over so she could sit down on the bed next to her.

"You want the long version or the short version?"

"Long!" they answered in unison.

"Okay," I began, taking a deep breath. "When my mom was young, like sixteen, she fell in love with this guy. He was hot and this really amazing wizard. But he was older and my granny didn't really like him for some reason. Which does *not* surprise me in the least, my granny doesn't really like anyone."

"Runs in the family, eh?" Holly quipped.

I glared at her. "Do you want to hear this story?"

She pressed her bright pink lips together and nodded, wide-eyed.

"So she did a spell which bound my mother and her hot wizard boyfriend from ever laying eyes on each other again."

"Aww, that's so sad," said Sweets. "I wonder if a match-making spell could trump a binding spell?"

"That's a good question! We'll have to ask my mom that in class on Monday," Jax said excitedly.

I eyed them both with frustration. "*Anyway*, so, yeah, my mother and her boyfriend had to break up and she was all sad and depressed and stuff and she didn't notice what was going on…" I took a breath.

"What didn't she notice was going on?" Holly asked, hanging on my every word.

"She didn't notice that she was *pregnant!*" I revealed dramatically.

"With you?" Jax asked. "The hot wizard guy was your father?"

I shook my head. I had no idea who my father was, but not because my granny had bound my mother or myself from contact with him, as he had left my mother of his own accord. "No, not with me. With a *son!*"

"A son?" Jax gasped.

"You have a brother?" Holly asked, her eyes opened wide in shock.

"Apparently," I said nodding.

"How did you have a brother your whole life and you never knew it?" Sweets questioned me.

I took a deep breath as my adrenaline took a slight surge. "Well, I wasn't done with the story. After my mother gave birth, she was really tired and needed to take a nap. My granny said she was going to take the baby to the nursery so that my mother could get some rest. My mother didn't really want her to, but granny insisted and when mom woke up and asked to see her son, she was told that her mother had given him up for adoption. The papers were all signed and it was too late!"

The girls' eyes and mouths opened wide. No one spoke for a few long moments while that news sunk in.

Sweets shook her head. "She couldn't just *give away* your mother's baby without her permission?"

Just relaying the story had caused my pulse to thump loudly in my ears and filled my eyes with unshed tears. I took a big swallow. "My mother wasn't eighteen. There was nothing she could do. And my granny refused to ever tell her what she had done with my brother."

Jax jumped up and threw her thin arms around my shoulders. "Oh, Mercy. That's such a horribly sad story."

Two fat, unwanted tears slid down my cheeks. I quickly wiped them away and silently hoped that no one had seen them. "Yeah," I choked out.

Holly jumped up and passed me a tissue. "Oh, now look, you're ruining your makeup!"

Drat, they'd seen the tears, I thought, as two more sets of arms encircled my shoulders. I rolled my eyes as the group squeezed me hard. I wasn't really into public displays of affection. Or affection at all for that matter. "Okay, okay. Thanks, girls, but that's good," I finally said when I had had all that I could take.

The girls all retreated back to their seats around my small dorm room. "I can't believe you've got a *brother* you've never met out there somewhere," Jax said in astonishment.

"Yeah, and why did your mother wait so long to tell you?" Sweets asked. "She waits your whole life and then she tells you *today*? Of all days? We finally got Jax back and solved Morgan's murder...you'd think she'd have given you a little time to decompress from all of that."

I nodded. "Yeah, I could have used a little more time to relax. That's really all I want for tonight, is some time to relax, but here's the thing," I began again. "She told me now because my brother found her. He came to see her."

"Stop it!" Holly exclaimed. "You're kidding me!"

"Not kidding. When she got back to Dubbsburg after dropping me off here at school, he was at her house waiting for her."

"That's crazy!" Jax said in bewilderment.

"Yeah, so he stayed with her for a while and then he decided he wanted to meet me, I guess. So he's on his way here."

"Wow, so how do you feel about all of this?" Sweets asked me.

"You know, no one asked me, no one was like, 'Hey, Mercy, you want to meet your long-lost brother?' He just decided to show up. It's absolutely ridiculous. I don't need a *brother*. I don't *want* a brother. I was perfectly content with it being just my mom and me and now this random guy shows up and I'm supposed to be all, 'Oh, you're my brother, and I love you so much,'" I said in a mocking voice.

"Wait. This guy is on his way here?" Holly asked, shooting up to stand on her feet. "When?"

I lifted both of my arms up and shrugged my shoulders. "I don't know. Mom wasn't sure when he'd get here. She said anytime. But sit back down," I said pointedly to Holly. "You're not dating my brother, so let's just get that out of the way. Brothers are off limits. Girl code."

Holly sat back down casually. "What? I didn't say I wanted to date him!" she admonished.

I shook my head with my eyes closed. "You want to date *everybody*."

"So you just wait around here for him to show up?" Sweets asked nervously.

"No! He's not a kid. He's an adult. I'm not going to wait

around for him. Besides, I have a date, remember?" I said. The words made me think to look at my watch again. "Oh my gosh, girls, I better go."

"All that and you've got to run now?" Jax asked with a little pout.

"We'll talk more after my date, okay?" I asked her and then shot her a little wink.

"Okay, promise?"

I nodded. "Promise."

I shut the door behind me and stood quietly in the hallway for a long moment taking a deep breath. The thought of having to meet Hugh and my brother's pending arrival made my stomach do somersaults. Instead of turning right to go down the staircase to the lobby, I took a left and knocked on Alba's door.

"What?" she grunted from inside.

"It's Mercy," I hollered. Alba was a grouchy soul, but I could trust her. She was honest and direct, and she meant well. Plus I appreciated her lack of enthusiasm for *everything*. Sometimes a girl just doesn't want to be perky and cheerful and Alba gets that more than any of the rest of the girls in the Witch Squad.

"What do you want?"

"Just let me in, alright," I hollered back.

She opened the door and stared at me. "Don't you have a date to get to?"

I shrugged. "He can wait a minute or two. Can I come in?"

Alba made a huffing sound but opened the door wider to let me in. Her dorm room was nothing like mine. Jax had decorated ours before I'd even checked into the dorm. She'd covered the cold tile floors with grey plush carpeting and she'd lined the stone walls with movie posters and put cute aqua and grey bedding on the top bunk. At first, it had disgusted me, but as our room became the meeting place for our little circle of friends, I'd reluctantly grown to appreciate the coziness of it.

Holly and Alba's room, on the other hand, was pretty sparsely decorated. No wall to wall carpeting or movie posters for them, but Holly had covered her bed with a pale pink bedspread and some cute little throw pillows. Alba's bed was covered with a navy blue quilt that looked like it had seen the insides of a washing machine about twenty too many times. They did, however, have a cozy saucer chair that I envied and I quickly made a beeline for the round comfy seat.

"Really? You're staying?" she asked, looking down at me in the chair.

"I just wanted to see what's going on with you. The girls said you're extra grumpy lately."

"Well they're extra annoying, what can I say?" she said caustically.

"Something's gotten under your skin, I can tell."

Alba threw herself down onto her bed and rolled onto her back. She dug her cell phone out of her pocket and held it up in the air in front of her face.

"Waiting for someone to text you?" I asked her.

She slammed the phone down on the bed next to her. "Why would I be waiting for someone to text me?"

I shrugged. "I don't know. When's the last time you heard from your family?"

Alba sat up and peered at me. "Just stay out of my business, Red."

I held up two hands in the air. "Fine, fine. Just wanted to help."

We sat together quietly. Neither with anything to say. Finally, I said softly. "I'm sort of nervous about this date."

"I don't understand why you're nervous. You've hung out with this guy before."

I shrugged as one finger found my hair and began to twirl a curl nervously. "I don't know. I suppose I kind of like him," I answered honestly.

"Nothing wrong with that," she muttered.

"Yeah, but I'm not really the type of girl that needs someone."

"Everyone needs someone," Alba said matter-of-factly. I thought I heard her breath hitch in her throat. I craned back to see if I could catch an emotion on her face, but she quickly covered up whatever I might have caught.

"You need someone?"

"I was talking about *you*, Red."

"You said *everyone* needs someone."

"Everyone but me I meant."

"You didn't say everyone but you."

"I'm saying it now," she growled. Then she looked at her watch. "Don't you have somewhere to be right now?"

"Kicking me out?" I asked her with a little laugh.

"More like forcing you to put your big girl panties on. I'm sure Hugh's waiting for you."

"Alright, I'll go. We can talk more about this later."

"Nothing to talk about Red. I'm fine."

CHAPTER 2

My high heels on the wide curving stone staircase made a flat clicking noise as I made my way to the Winston Hall lobby. I held onto the ornate baluster tightly as I walked, praying that I wouldn't twist an ankle and roll down to the first floor. I attempted to walk casually across the marble tiled floor to the other side of the lobby where my date had promised to meet me. I felt like Bambi on stilts in the heels, and I had to hold both hands out by my side to keep from falling as I carefully navigated the slick tile floor. *Stupid heels. Why did I let Holly talk me into wearing shoes with stilts on them?* I wondered.

As I exited the side doors of the lobby to the courtyard we shared with the Paranormal Institute for Wizards next door, I held my breath and silently begged the spirits not to let me fall before I made it to Hugh. He was already standing there, on the cobblestone next to my very favorite scarlet oak tree whose leaves were the most perfect shades of orangey-red. He had his back to me, but the cowboy hat and cowboy boots were a dead giveaway that it was him. He was the only cowboy wizard that I'd ever met before and most certainly the only cowboy wizard that attended the all men's school next door.

The click of my heels on the cobblestone and the sound of the door slamming behind me caused him to turn around. And there he was again. Houston Brooks. That strong chiseled jaw, those hazel eyes underneath that wide brimmed hat – he was such a good-looking man. His tall, lean, muscular body rocked forward from the heel of his boots and launched him towards me.

I immediately noticed the appreciation in his eyes when he saw me. I exhaled a sigh of relief and quietly thanked Holly for forcing me to look like I did. Being a girly girl didn't come naturally to me, and for this tiny moment in time I was thankful I had a friend who knew how to be a girly girl for me.

"Mercy me, don't you look prettier than a peach!" he said as I approached him.

I felt warmth fill my cheeks but tried to maintain my confidence. "Thank you. You look pretty handsome your-self, Houston."

"Hugh, really, only my mother calls me Houston and my Great Aunt Betty and I'd prefer not to think about those lovely ladies on a night such as tonight," he said with a mischievous smile and that adorable little Southern drawl I picked up on every time he spoke.

"All right, Hugh, where are we going tonight? You said to dress nicely. I assume this will do?" I asked, taking a step back so he could see me clearly. The gentle breeze rustled up long strands of my auburn hair and tossed it smoothly about my shoulders.

Hugh took his hat off of his head and held it to his heart. His sandy blond curls encircled the tips of his ears. "Oh, darlin', you could set a block of ice on fire in that dress. I'm a little bit worried one of these other yayhoos might swoop in and snatch you up if we don't get out of here soon. Shall we?" he asked and extended an elbow to me.

His funny little compliment caused an involuntary laugh to bubble out of my mouth, putting me slightly more at ease. "Yeah, let's go."

I took his arm and let him lead me through the lobby of the men's dorm. We passed by a tall man with a scar above his right eye. His hands were buried in the sleeves of his black robe.

"Sorcerer," Houston said, greeting him with a little nod as well.

"Houston," the man replied, looking down his thin nose at us as we passed by him.

When we were out of earshot, I whispered to Houston, "That's Grandmaster Flash."

"Excuse me?" he asked.

"That guy back there. I call him Grandmaster Flash."

"That's the Headmaster of the men's school," Hugh explained. "We just call him Sorcerer."

"I see. Well, I call him Grandmaster Flash and don't tell him I said this, but dude freaks me out!"

"Yeah, he's dark as the devil's ridin' boots," Hugh agreed.

"Okay?" I said confusedly.

"It's just an expression," Hugh explained.

"You seem to be full of those," I told him with a little laugh.

He squeezed my arm a little tighter as we exited Warner Hall and veered down the path to the men's parking lot on the other side of campus. Since being a student at the Institute, I hadn't ventured that far in the other direction. I enjoyed checking out the scenery on their side of the courtyard. It was a nice evening, a perfect seventy-seven-degree temperature with only a light breeze blowing. The fresh air scent filled my lungs, and for the first time in forever, I could actually say I felt like smiling for real. I surmised that was what happy felt like.

Hugh led us to a big black pickup with a bit of rust above the back driver's side tire. "She's not real pretty, but she's an amazing beast of a truck. I've had her for years." He opened the door and helped me up into the cab. When I was seated comfortably, he shut the door behind me and went around to get in on the other side.

After he slammed his door shut and sat next to me, I asked him bluntly, "How old are you anyway?" Manners weren't always my strong suit.

"Twenty-three. I know. I'm a bit old to be starting wizard school, but as my daddy always says, better late than pregnant, right?"

"Sure," I laughed, "what made you decide you wanted to go to school finally?"

Hugh pushed the keys into the ignition, and with a mighty rumble, the truck roared to life. "Well, I don't come from a paranormal family. My mother was a school teacher, and my daddy owns a ranch just outside of Odessa. Mom retired about three or four years ago, but Dad's still working on the ranch. I worked for him straight out of high school. The plan had been to go on to college after a year of working for him, but then I just wasn't feeling it. I started feeling like maybe I had a greater purpose in life."

Hugh maneuvered the big truck down the long Institute driveway and down the hill towards downtown Aspen Falls.

"What kind of greater purpose?"

He rolled his window down and leaned to the left casually with his left elbow out the window and his right arm on the steering wheel. "I really didn't know. That was the thing. I just knew college was a waste of money if I didn't know my purpose. So I kept working for Dad and then when I turned twenty, I discovered I had abilities that no one else in the house had."

"Like what? I've wondered what kind of things you can do."

Hugh turned to me and gave me a little wink. "I've wondered what kind of things you can do too, darlin'."

"Hugh!" I said with a laugh and swatted at his arm playfully.

"Settle down, settle down. I was talkin' 'bout your *gift*, just like you were talkin' 'bout mine."

I smiled and leaned back in my seat. "I'll show you mine if you show me yours."

"Don't tempt me, darlin'," he said with a wide smile.

I'd lobbed that one at him. I suppose I would have been shocked if he hadn't at least bunted. I rolled my eyes at him.

He laughed and sat up straight in his seat, putting both hands back on the wheel. "Fine. See that road sign up ahead?" he pointed up ahead.

I looked up and saw a green arrow pointing to the right. It read Aspen Falls Recreational Park 2.2 mi. "Yeah?"

"Keep watchin' it now," he said and nodded his head at the sign as we neared it.

Just like that the sign flipped over and pointed to the left. The words were upside down now.

"Houston Brooks! Fix that this instant!" I said with a big laugh.

"Yes, ma'am," he said as he nodded at the sign,

reversing it once again. His eyes crinkled in the corners when he smiled at me.

"Well, that's hardly worth going to wizard school for," I told him, unimpressed.

He reached over and squeezed my knee. "Your turn."

"Fine. Ummm. I always know when it's going to rain." I gave him a cheesy smile, flashing him all of my teeth while my eyes squinted shut.

"Attractive, Mercy Mae. Very attractive. My Uncle Earl always knows when it's going to rain too. He says he can feel it in his hip," Hugh said as the truck pulled into downtown Aspen Falls. The small kitschy shops with brightly covered awnings were mostly closed for the evening, but as we pulled onto Lemon Street, we found ourselves in the heart of the Aspen Falls nightlife.

"How does The Whiskey Grille sound for supper?" he asked, pulling the truck off to parallel park in front of a rustic-looking restaurant with two big whiskey barrels out front. Soft country music poured out of the big speakers underneath the corrugated tin roof awning. Wood fired smoke poured into the open windows and made my stomach churn excitedly.

"Oh, my gosh, that smells so good. The smell of a wood burning stove in the fall is my absolute favorite smell!" I said and hopped out of the truck before he had a chance to come around and open my door for me.

"Mine too," he said, catching up to me on the sidewalk. "Did I mention how great you look tonight? I mean, you always look great, but, wow…just wow," he said looking at my long legs.

"You said that, but thanks, Hugh," I grinned.

The inside was just as rustic as the outside. A split rail fence separated the bar area from the seating area, and the walls were covered with raw cut cedar boards and more corrugated tin. It was date night in Aspen Falls, and all of the couples in town must have come to The Whiskey Grille for supper. The place was packed. Despite the crowd gathered in front of the hostess table in the lobby, the waiter was surprisingly able to find us a table, and he seated us almost instantaneously.

After the waiter handed us our menus and promised to be back shortly, I looked at Hugh excitedly. "No wait, how awesome is that?"

"And front row parking, too – looks like *someone's* got skills," he said winking at me suspiciously.

My jaw dropped. "Hugh Brooks! Is this one of your tricks?" I demanded.

He peeked out at me above his menu. "Your move, darlin'," he smiled sweetly.

"Fine. I see and talk to ghosts," I said as I peered down at my menu nonchalantly.

"Nice," he said. "I can control the weather."

"Really? That's interesting, how did you learn to do that?"

"Well, I didn't really have to learn to do it; it just sorta came to me. It started out by me praying for rain with my family. And then it would rain. I always thought it was God answering my family's prayers. And then I prayed for rain a few times on my own, and it rained. Then one day I was supposed to take this girl from town out on a picnic, and it was raining! I just wished it would stop raining and it did. Then I began to notice a pattern. If I got really upset about something, it would thunderstorm. If I were down or depressed, it would be a rainy day. If I were in a good mood, the sun would be shining."

"You don't think it's the other way around. Maybe the weather was influencing your moods," I suggested.

Hugh smiled at me as he folded up his menu and sat it in front of him. "Sweetheart, I can control the weather. Did you not notice the perfect temperature outside?"

I nodded as I looked out the window next to our table.

"You're welcome," he said lightly. "I can control it now. I don't let my emotions control the weather anymore. I'd be out on the ranch, and I'd bust my hand on something, and I'd curse, and a streak of lightning would shoot across the sky. Damned near burnt my momma's chicken coop to the ground one day when I was out doing chores. It didn't take long before I realized I needed to get that under control. So I sort of taught myself how to breathe and control it. Now, the weather is at my disposal! At least the local weather anyway, I can't, like, make it rain in South Dakota or anything spectacular like that."

"Well, that's a pretty cool party trick to have," I said. "I definitely don't do anything that awesome. I can talk to animals, er, ani*mal*," I corrected.

"Can you? That would have come in handy on the ranch. Who have you talked to lately?"

"My mom. Well, my cat, Sneaks. Okay, I guess my mom *is* my cat Sneaks."

Hugh nearly spit out the water he was sipping. "Your mom is a cat?"

"No, my mom is a *witch*. She lives in Illinois. She did some kind of a spell and is now able to see and talk to me with the help of this stray black cat that likes to climb into my dorm room window. She calls it Skitches."

"Skitches? I thought you said the cat's name was Sneaks?"

I laughed. "She calls the spell Skitches, you know, Skype

for Witches – Skitches? Because we can see and talk to each other like you can on Skype…no computer necessary! Yeah, so I can talk to Sneaks, but I've never tried talking to any other animals. This is a new thing, though."

"Well, that's kinda handy."

The waiter came and took our order. After he left, I decided to share my biggest new news with Hugh. "I actually talked to my mom earlier. She told me a big secret. Wanna hear?"

"Sure, darlin'. I'd love to hear anything you've got to say!"

"I've got a brother that I've never met before. I didn't even know he existed until a couple of hours ago."

"You're kidding me?"

"No. Long story, but when my mom was a teenager she had a boyfriend that my grandmother didn't approve of. She got pregnant and my granny actually took the baby and gave it away for adoption without my mother's permission."

Hugh's jaw dropped. "That's got to be illegal or something!"

I shrugged and took a sip of my water. "She was only sixteen. Even if it was illegal, I'm sure my mother wouldn't have known how to get her baby back legally."

"That's so sad," said Hugh. He reached his tanned arms across the table and grabbed my hands off the table. "You've had a rough day then. Are you alright?"

"Yeah, I'm fine," I said quickly. I didn't really feel like admitting to Hugh that I was not looking forward to meeting this "brother."

"You sure? That's kind of a big deal. You weren't your mother's firstborn. She's probably been thinking about him all these years, and she never shared that with you? You could have nieces or nephews out there that you've never met before!"

I pouted out my bottom lip. "Thanks a lot, Hugh, none of that had occurred to me yet. I guess I do have a reason not to be okay."

"Are you going to meet this brother?" Hugh asked.

"Yeah, Mom said he's coming to find me," I admitted.

"He is? When?"

I shrugged and looked outside. "I don't know. Tomorrow or something? He's on his way to Aspen Falls to find me."

Hugh's head jerked back. "That's a bit odd, don't you think?"

"Odd? In what way?"

"A brother that you've never met is coming all the way to see you? Why wouldn't he call first? Or send a letter? Or just friend you on Facebook or something. Do you even know what he looks like? Or what his name is?"

"No, I have no idea what he looks like or what his name is. Mom said that when he was a baby, he looked just like his father and that's what caused my granny to take him away. She didn't want my mom seeing her ex every day when she looked at the baby. My grandmother bound my mother from ever seeing or talking to this guy again."

"Why would she do that?" he asked.

"I guess because he was older. And he was a wizard, a very powerful wizard. I don't know all the details. My mom was pretty cryptic. She told me to watch out for my brother, though. She called him special."

"Your mother called your brother *special*? Is that the word she used?"

I nodded as I thought back on the exact conversation we'd had. "Yeah, pretty sure she said special. Why?"

"Like special as in special needs?"

"Mmm, I didn't take it that way. I took it as in – precious to her."

"Maybe he's got special abilities or something," Hugh suggested. "Is he a wizard?"

"I have no idea. I would have to guess that he is. I mean his father was a wizard, and his mother is a witch. But then again my roommate's mother is a witch, and she's not a…" I stopped short of finishing my statement. That had come out accidentally.

"Your roommate's not a what?" he asked, quickly catching my blunder.

"Nothing, never mind," I said and looked up at the waiter bringing us our food.

Hugh looked up at him too. "Thank ya kindly," he said to the waiter as his eight-ounce steak and baked potato landed in front of him.

"Now what were you saying about your roommate?" Hugh asked, looking at me carefully.

I moved my plate around in front of me, adjusted my silverware and put my napkin in my lap carefully. "I shouldn't have said anything about Jax. It's a secret actually," I whispered across the table to him.

"Who am I going to tell?" he shrugged.

"I don't know, your roommate?" I suggested as I cut off a small piece of chicken.

"Why would I tell Juan? He doesn't even know Jax."

"It doesn't matter. What matters is that I promised Jax I wouldn't tell her secret, and I can't."

"I'll let you have a bite of my steak if you tell me," he offered with an adorably cute smile.

I laughed. "You promise you won't tell anyone?"

He crossed his fingers over his heart. "You can bet the

farm on it."

"Jax isn't a witch," I whispered. "Her mother is Sorceress Stone. That's why she's going to school with us, but she's not a witch. She has no powers." I omitted the fact that The Black Witch who lived in the castle on the hill was her aunt. I didn't think that all needed to be thrown out in the open this early in the relationship.

"Well, she has no powers, *yet*," he added, passing me a bite of his steak.

"Thanks," I said and took the bite. "Mmm, that's good. What do you mean – yet?"

"Jax is the tiny little thing, right?" he asked. "Dresses like a witch with the tights and pointy shoes."

"And the big black witch's hat, yeah, that's Jax," I said with embarrassment.

"She can't be very old."

"She's seventeen," I told him.

"Golly, only seventeen? She *is* young. Makes me feel a bit like a granddad. How old are you? I reckon I've never asked."

"You reckon?" I said with a little laugh.

"Are you makin' fun of my talk, Mercy Mae Habernackle?" he squinted at me from the side of his eyes.

I laughed again. "No, sir. Your drawl is pretty darned cute."

"Well thank ya kindly," he said in an extra drawn out drawl. "Now, how old?"

"I'm nineteen," I said honestly.

"I guessed as much. Now, back to your roommate. She's only seventeen years old. I didn't learn about my powers until I'd turned twenty. Makes sense to think that she just hasn't come into her own yet."

"Interesting. I hope you're right," I said. I was sure Jax

hoped the same thing. That someday she'd get her powers and she'd be just like the rest of the women in her family. For now, she felt she had to overcompensate by dressing up as much like the clichéd witch as possible to make people not notice that she wasn't *actually* a witch.

Despite the fact that I wasn't sure what we'd talk about on a date, as I hadn't ever actually been on a real date before, or had a real boyfriend before for that matter, we seemed to find plenty of topics for conversation. When dinner was over, and Hugh suggested we just take a little drive before we go back to our dorm rooms, I was happy to agree.

He pulled his truck back onto Lemon Street, and we drove to the Aspen Falls Park where we parked and sat and listened to music, switching the stations back and forth between country channels and the rock stations I preferred. Conversation flowed like water and before I knew it minutes turned into hours and as the easy chatter finally began to wind down; I could feel a physical tension building between us. I suddenly wondered if Hugh was contemplating kissing me. My heart began to pound in my ears, and I felt a shiver run down the length of my spine. I visibly shuddered.

"Are you cold?" Hugh asked. He immediately rolled up his window as I wrapped my arms around myself.

"Mmm," I shivered. "A little." I'd been getting the shivers a lot lately. I got them the morning that Morgan Hartford was murdered and I had them the night that Jax went missing. I was pretty sure I'd even gotten them the night of the big bonfire by the Black Witch's house. Shivers generally meant something big was imminent, but I didn't want to tell Hugh that. I had a feeling that I knew what was imminent.

He reached into the back of his truck and pulled out a navy blue and grey Houston Texans zip up hoodie. "Here, put this on," he suggested as my jaw began to quiver slightly.

I leaned forward as he scooted over to wrap the sweater around my shoulders. I let him leave his arms around me for an extended moment. I looked up into his hazel eyes and smiled lightly. "Thanks."

He smiled back and smoothed away a stray hair, stashing it sweetly behind my ear. "You're welcome. You've got the most beautiful green eyes that I've ever seen," he said quietly.

Despite my chills, I felt heat creep into my cheeks. Then his forehead leaned towards mine. His face was so close that I could feel the heat of his breath on my lips. And then the sound of my phone ringing in my lap broke the electric current between us. He sat up straighter, and we both looked down at my phone. The hypnotic moment was broken.

"I'm sorry," I whispered. I looked at the number ringing through. It didn't pull up a name in my contacts, and I didn't recognize the number. "I-I don't know who it is," I stuttered nervously. "I don't have to get it."

He shook his head and smiled at me. "It's okay, go ahead, get it."

I nodded and swiped the little green phone symbol. "Hello?"

"Mercy? Mercy Habernackle?" I heard a deep male's voice through the other end of the phone.

Goosebumps pebbled my arms as I responded. "Yes, who is this?"

"It's Reign. Reign Alexander. I'm your brother."

CHAPTER 3

M y jaw dropped, I looked up at Hugh instantly.

"Who is it?" he whispered.

I held a finger to my lips to shush him.

"Mercy? Are you there?" Reign asked.

"Yeah, I'm here. I hear you're coming to visit me this week?" I began cautiously. I didn't know what else to say. I'd never had a brother come find me before. I guess it wasn't something you could plan for.

"I've run into a little problem, actually." His deep voice through the phone seemed to make the shivers on my arms worse.

"What kind of problem? Car problems?" I asked, not sure what I would be able to do if his car had broken down in Ohio or something.

"No. Not exactly…"

"Where are you?" I asked.

"I'm at Jimmy's Bed & Brew," he sighed audibly through the phone.

"Where's that?" I asked.

"Downtown," he said.

"Downtown where?"

"Downtown Aspen Falls."

My chin jutted forward as my brain began to piece everything together. "You're in Aspen Falls? You're in town?"

"Yeah. I got a room above this tavern. There was a sign on the way into town."

My mind began to race. Should I offer to go over there? Should I invite him to come to my dorm? Should someone be around when we meet for the first time or should it be a private event? I didn't know how to respond. "Okay. And you've got a problem?"

"Yeah, a big problem. Is there any way you could possibly come over here?"

"To Jimmy's?"

"Yeah."

"When?"

"Umm, right now if possible?" I detected a note of concern in his voice.

I looked over at Hugh, who was trying to keep up with what was going on. "Hold on," I said and then muzzled the phone with my hand.

"My brother is in town already. Something happened I think. He needs me to come there."

"Where's he staying?"

"Hang on," I said to Hugh and then put the phone to my ear again. "Where is Jimmy's Bed and Brew?" I asked Reign.

"I don't know the address. I just followed the signs. It's downtown Aspen Falls. Look for the flashing lights. Look, I really gotta go, but the sooner you can get down here, the better."

"Okay," I said and hung up the phone.

"Where is he?" Hugh asked.

"He didn't know the address. It's a tavern called Jimmy's Bed and Brew, and it's somewhere downtown. He said to follow the lights."

"What lights?" Hugh asked, looking around. It was pitch black out in the park. The street lamps illuminated the sidewalk around the park, but the parking lot was completely black, shadowed from the moon by a row of tall maple trees.

"I have no idea. Come on, let's drive around and look for it. Do you mind?"

Hugh shook his head like he didn't mind, but his face was no longer that of a moony-eyed cowboy, now the flirty little twinkle in his eye had gone and was replaced with a somber protective look. "Not at all. Let's go."

He pulled his truck out of the parking lot and we headed back towards Lemon Street and there, just up the street from where we'd had supper a couple of hours before was a barrage of flashing police lights. "What in the world?" I asked as we pulled into an empty parking spot a block away from the huge scene out front of the bar.

Hugh and I jumped out of his truck at the same time. Nearly forgetting I was wearing heels, I almost twisted my ankle landing on the concrete sidewalk. In seconds Hugh was at my side. He held onto my elbow and pulled me up. When I was steady on my feet, I felt his fingers intertwine with mine and together the two of us made our way to Jimmy's. Yellow police tape had cordoned off sections of the block and a tall policeman was guarding the entrance. We tried to push past him, but he halted us.

"No one passes the police tape," he said.

"But my brother is in there," I argued.

"I'm sorry, but no one in or out until Detective Whitman gets here and says otherwise."

"I'm here, Brewer," said a voice from the alleyway around the corner. A tall dark-haired man with a mustache and an 80's style khaki sports coat followed behind the voice. Detective Mark Whitman reminded me of Magnum PI without the Hawaiian shirts. I only knew who Magnum PI was because my mom had a huge crush on Tom Selleck while I was growing up.

"Detective Whitman!" I exclaimed.

"Mercy? What are you doing down here at this time of night? You turning into an ambulance chaser or something?" he asked.

Hugh looked at me in confusion. I shrugged and looked up at Detective Whitman.

"Ambulance chaser? What are you talking about? There's no ambulance here."

"It's on its way. If you don't know what I'm talking about, then why are you here?"

"My brother is in there. He just called me and said I needed to get down here right away."

"Your brother? Who's your brother?" he asked, confused.

"Reign Alexander," I said. The sound of my brother's name coming out of my mouth seemed foreign to me. Reign Alexander. It was like I wasn't speaking English.

"What is he doing inside?"

"I have no idea. He just called and asked me to come down. I – I was on a date," I explained. Hugh squeezed my hand for support.

"Why is there an ambulance on its way, Detective?" Hugh asked.

The number of locals who had heard about an incident

at the bar or who had seen the lights and were curious was mounting. People were scattered about outside the caution tape. Detective Whitman eyed them all before motioning for us to follow him past Officer Brewer and into Jimmy's. "Let's talk about it inside. I was probably going to have to call someone at The Institute to consult anyway."

The smell of stale beer and cheap cologne inside the tavern made my stomach turn almost instantly. The bar was crawling with police officials and only a handful of patrons. That's when it occurred to me that of the handful of patrons, I couldn't pick my brother out in a lineup, and silently I hoped that I wouldn't have to. I had no idea what was going on but watched as a police officer approached Detective Whitman the minute we stepped in the door.

"Detective, she's up here, follow me," he said.

"Who's up there?" I asked. "What's going on around here?"

"There's no easy way to say this. A woman died here tonight. We suspect foul play," he said bluntly. "She's this way, follow me."

Hugh squeezed my hand again then reached out to stop Detective Whitman from progressing forward. "Detective, I don't think Mercy needs to see a dead body."

The detective looked at me questionably.

I squeezed Hugh's hand back. "It's okay, Hugh, I've seen a dead body before, I can handle it."

"You sure?"

"Yeah, let's go."

We followed Detective Whitman to the top of the stairs where the Officer led us to room #203. Inside, there was a woman sprawled out on the bed. Her middle section was covered with a bed sheet, but she was clearly naked underneath the sheet. An officer was interviewing a man in a pair of boxer shorts who was standing next to the bed. The man was tall with broad shoulders and had washboard abs and olive colored skin. He had a serious case of five o'clock shadow. Nervously, he ran a hand through his thick black wavy hair and then planted it on his hip.

The officer that had led us up the stairs pointed at the nearly naked man. "Detective, this is the man that found her like this."

Detective Whitman nodded and then stepped forward to shake the man's hand. "I'm Detective Whitman. You are?"

"Detective." He gave Detective Whitman a polite nod as he shook his hand. "I'm Reign Alexander."

My eyes nearly shot out of my head. That was my brother? *Holy shmoly! Now I know what happened to all the good genes in the family! Mom gave them to him before I was born!*

"Look, I didn't do this," he said immediately. "I've told all these guys a hundred times. I woke up and she was dead. I called 911 immediately. I didn't do anything to her."

"Right, well, considering you were the last person to see Miss…" Detective Whitman looked down at the clipboard he was holding. "Bradshaw, alive, I'm sure you can understand why you'd be questioned."

The man nodded.

Detective Whitman looked back at Hugh and me. "Well, Mercy, I suppose you'd like to talk to your brother?"

Reign's eye's nearly popped when he heard my name. "Mercy?"

Detective Whitman looked at Reign and me curiously. "You didn't recognize your sister?"

"It's a long story. We've actually never met before," I said lightly. There were too many people in the room and it disheartened me that I had to meet my brother here, under these circumstances.

Reign shifted about uncomfortably. I could tell he didn't like the circumstances we were meeting under either.

"How is it possible that you have never met your own brother before?" Detective Whitman asked me suspiciously.

Hugh stepped forward. "I can give you the lowdown, Detective. If you can let Mercy and her brother have a minute alone?"

Reign's gaze shifted down to the floor while mine shifted to the detective.

He rubbed the back of his neck and then nodded. "Yeah, I guess that would be fine, but just a minute and not in here, this is a crime scene."

"Can I have my clothes now?" Reign asked the detective quietly.

Detective Whitman nodded. "Yeah, go ahead."

Reign looked at me intensely. "Do you mind waiting a minute?"

"No, go get dressed," I said. Meeting my brother for the first time was awkward enough, throw in a dead body and him in his underwear and we had a downright bizarre meeting.

Reign grabbed a pile of clothes off the floor and strutted past me to the second floor shared bathroom.

"I'll explain things to the detective, is that alright?" Hugh asked me quietly.

"Yeah, I'd appreciate that," I nodded.

"Are you going to be alright? This is quite a bit to take in?"

I nodded, but I didn't know if I meant it. The fact that my brother had been found in the same room as a dead woman had shaken me. My mother was going to flip out. I

43

really didn't know what I was going to tell her. "Yeah, I'll be okay. I'm glad you're here with me, though."

"Me too," said Hugh as he squeezed my hand one more time. The bathroom door down the hall opened with a creak and Reign stepped out. He had donned a pair of Army boots, black jeans, and a v-neck t-shirt.

Tentatively I stepped into the hallway, giving Reign a tight-lipped smile.

With his clothes on he looked a lot more confident and he seemed to stand up straighter. "So, you're my sister. That feels weird saying it. Sister," he began with a crooked smile.

"Yeah, and you're my brother. That definitely feels weird to say, too. I've always been an only child."

"Me too," he said.

I didn't know whether or not I was supposed to hug him or shake his hand or just stand there and be awkward, so I opted for the latter. I had never been much of a hugger and shaking my brother's hand seemed like an odd thing to do. I had so many things I wanted to know and wanted to ask him, but this wasn't the time nor the place.

"So, what's going on with all of this?" I finally managed to croak out.

"Yeah, *this*. I have no idea. I got into town, checked in at the bar, had a few drinks with some of the people downstairs and next thing I know, I'm waking up next to a dead chick." He rubbed his head as if he were in a daze.

"You didn't know her?" I asked, stunned.

He shrugged nonchalantly. "Eh, I mean, I'd met her downstairs. Okay, *maybe* I flirted with her, but I certainly don't remember bringing her back to my room."

"Did you *sleep* with her?"

"Well, obviously, we slept together, but I don't know if we *slept* together, if that's what you mean."

"How did she die?"

"I have no idea, honestly. I woke up with a splitting headache and there was a woman in the bed next to me. I knew it was the woman from the bar, and I'll admit, I knew she had a boyfriend. I *guessed* we had done something he wouldn't exactly approve of, and I didn't want her in my room anymore. I figured he'd come looking for her and I didn't want my room to be the place he found her."

"Where's the boyfriend?" I asked him.

He shrugged and looked around. "No clue. Like I said, I have no idea how this happened."

"How do you *not* know what happened tonight?" He wasn't making any sense.

"I guess I had too much to drink," he admitted. The way he wouldn't make eye contact with me made me feel like he was either lying or embarrassed. I really hoped for the latter.

"Apparently." I could hardly look at him either. The whole situation was just too bizarre and I was extremely disappointed in finding out that this supposed *brother* was such a mess.

"Look, I'm really sorry that this is the way we have to meet. I would have never wanted to meet you under these conditions, but I swear, I didn't do this."

"Okay. Well, it's the detective you need to convince, not me," I said and held up my hands in front of me.

"No, I need to convince you. I don't want you thinking your brother is a murderer. I'm not. I didn't do this, Mercy." His dark onyx eyes pleaded with me silently.

"Okay," I said. I didn't feel like having this argument with my brother here in front of all these police officers. "So. You had some drinks. Flirted with some guy's girlfriend and woke up in bed with her and then what?"

"I shook her, trying to get her to wake up, but she didn't move. So I turned on the light next to the bed and when I saw her, I could tell something wasn't right. She looked sort of pale and she didn't look like she was breathing. I checked for a pulse and when I didn't find one, I called the police."

I let out a heavy sigh. "Wow. I can't believe this is happening," I said stunned. Of all nights for this to happen. I'd just helped to solve the Hartford girl's murder and now this?

"I'm really sorry, Mercy. You look dressed up. I suppose I ruined your evening?"

I shrugged. "Just my first date with a guy, no big deal."

"Oh man, I'm really sorry. I didn't mean to get involved in any of this."

"Do you know who the woman is?" I asked him.

"I know her name is Harper," he began. "She said she's from Aspen Falls. She was coming home to see her parents. Apparently, she hadn't seen them in years."

"What else do you know about her?" I heard come from the doorway. I turned around to see Hugh and Detective Whitman walking towards us.

Reign shook his head as he tried to recall everything he knew about Harper Bradshaw. "Nothing really. She was with her boyfriend. Dude's name was Vaughn something. She was a pretty big flirt. If I got her back to my room, it didn't take much convincing. I mean, she was all over me for a while there. Her boyfriend was getting pretty hot. He's the guy you need to be questioning, not me."

"We've got him downstairs already. My men are on it." Detective Whitman assured us.

Suddenly we heard a commotion coming from downstairs. "Where is she? Where's Harper?"

CHAPTER 4

I peered over the wooden railing to see a distinguished looking white-haired man in his late sixties hollering at an officer in the middle of the bar. "Sir, you're going to have to calm down," said the officer.

A woman with a helmet of meticulously groomed golden hair in a navy and white pantsuit was standing next to him. Her thin hands shook slightly while she stood closely by his side. "Henry, don't yell at the officer," she chided him.

"Louise, something has happened to our daughter, and I demand to know what it is!" he hollered pointedly at the officer.

Detective Whitman took that as his cue to head downstairs. He turned back to look at Reign with a steely-eyed glare. "Don't go anywhere."

Reign rolled his eyes and paced back into the doorway of his room to lean against the door frame.

"I'm going to see what her parents have to say. Come with me?" I asked Hugh in a whisper.

Reign and Hugh exchanged suspicious glances as Hugh and I followed the detective down to the first floor.

"I'm Sergeant Henry Bradshaw. This is my wife, Louise. Harper is our daughter. Why won't anyone tell us what's going on with her?" the man asked the officer incredulously. "Someone called us and told us that we needed to get down here right away, something happened to Harper."

"Sergeant Bradshaw, I'm Detective Whitman, we met at a VA benefit last fall." Detective Whitman extended his hand to Harper's father.

Sergeant Bradshaw peered at him carefully. "Yes, Detective Whitman, I remember you. Good job on that Hartford case, by the way. There was a write up in the paper this morning," he said shaking Detective Whitman's hand. "Can you please tell me what's going on with my daughter?"

Detective Whitman looked uncomfortable. He would have to be the one to break the bad news to Harper's father. My heart tugged for this mother and father who had obviously not been told what to expect when they got down here.

"Yes, how about we step over here to talk?"

He turned around and motioned towards his wife. "Louise, Detective Whitman wants to speak to us." Then he turned back to Detective Whitman. "Thank you."

The three of them walked past me towards the back of the bar where a forensics team was already combing through the things behind the bar.

"This is quite the hub-bub," said Mrs. Bradshaw to Detective Whitman loud enough for me and Hugh to overhear. "What has Harper gotten herself into now? I didn't even know she was in town, and she's already causing a scene."

Detective Whitman cleared his throat and shifted his

weight. "Mrs. Bradshaw, Sergeant Bradshaw. There's really no easy way to say this…" he trailed off. "Harper's dead."

Sergeant Bradshaw's face went ashen. "No," he choked out as he grabbed his wife's hand.

Louise Bradshaw sucked in a breath as a perfectly manicured hand covered her open mouth. "*Our* Harper? Surely you've got the wrong Harper. That's what this is. A case of mistaken identity. Like I said, our Harper isn't even in town. She lives in Connecticut. She hasn't been home in years."

Sergeant Bradshaw's eyes filled with tears. "Where is she? I need to see the girl."

"I'll take you to her. She's upstairs. You can follow me," said the detective.

Sergeant Bradshaw nodded and patted his wife's hand lovingly. "My wife shouldn't see this. She's got bad nerves," he said. "Louise, you stay here. I'll go find out if it's really Harper."

Detective Whitman looked over at me. "Mercy, would you mind keeping Mrs. Bradshaw company until the Sergeant and I come back."

I swallowed the lump in my throat hard. I'd watched Sorceress Stone, the headmistress of the Paranormal Institute for Witches deal with the grieving family in the Hartford murder. She was so smooth. Her very presence seemed to calm them, or perhaps she had only bewitched them. Some witches had that effect on others. I nodded.

"I'll come with you," Hugh whispered before squeezing my hand for support.

The detective and Harper's father went upstairs, leaving Hugh and me to comfort Mrs. Bradshaw. The poor woman's hands shook like a leaf. I didn't know what to do or what to say, so I just did what came naturally to me. I reached out and touched her hand gently. She looked up at me. Her blue-grey eyes were glassy. I was sure she feared the worst and hoped for the best. That it wouldn't be her daughter. That it would be someone else's Harper.

"I'm so sorry, Mrs. Bradshaw," I said as gently as I could.

She shook her head as a tear broke loose and slid down her cheek. "It's not our Harper, I'm sure. Our Harper hasn't been home in years." Her strong words didn't match the fear evident in her eyes.

I just nodded silently. Unsure of what else I could say. I didn't know Harper, and I didn't know Mrs. Bradshaw. "Do you remember the last time you saw her?" I asked, just trying to fill the empty space between us.

She sat her purse on the counter. It was emblazoned with the letters LV on the golden buckle. Silently, she opened it and pulled out a tissue then dabbed at the corners of her eyes. "It's been years. I couldn't even tell you the last time we saw Harper. She's a wild one, you know. Both our girls are actually. She does her own thing. I don't know why she'd be in Aspen Falls, especially without calling first. It's just not like her. There's simply no way this girl can be our Harper."

"You've got two daughters?" I asked.

She wiped her nose with her tissue as she nodded. "Elena. She's younger than Harper. She lives in town, but sometimes I wish she'd have gone with Harper. The two of them have always gotten into so much mischief. Aspen Falls just can't handle that type of behavior. It's a small town you know. People talk. The rumor mill has spun for years about the Bradshaw girls."

"Maybe Harper told Elena that she was coming home. She may have assumed that Elena would have told the two of you?" I asked uneasily. I really hated getting in the middle of the apparent family drama, but it looked like there was going to be a murder investigation and I figured it would be important to know who knew Harper was in town. I couldn't very well let my brother take the rap for the girl's death if he swore that he had nothing to do with it. My mother would never let me hear the end of it if Reign was arrested for murder on his first night in town and I did nothing to stop it.

Louise Bradshaw shook her head. "I don't think so, dear. Elena was over to the house last night. She needed to borrow money and spoke to Henry. I'm sure if she'd told Henry that Harper was in town he would have told me."

Heavy steps on the wooden stairs caused us all to look up. Detective Whitman was leading Sergeant Bradshaw back downstairs. The elder man gripped the stair railing as he solemnly made his way back downstairs. His face conveyed shock and horror all at once. Louise went to him at the bottom of the stairs.

"Henry, tell me it wasn't Harper up there," she insisted.

Sergeant Bradshaw opened his arms for his wife and engulfed her in them. "It was Harper, Louise. Our Harper is gone." His words were barely audible, just a slight whisper as if he were scared to say them aloud and make them real.

Louise's eyes erupted with tears, and the two of them began their grieving together. Detective Whitman came around the corner at the bottom of the stairs. "Mercy, can I see you for a moment?" he asked me and then pulled me out of the earshot of the grieving couple.

"Have you perhaps, had any feelings or have you sensed anything thus far?" he asked me point blankly.

I shook my head as I looked around. "Not yet. But I really haven't been looking for anything, to be honest. This is quite the extraordinary night. I met my brother for the first time tonight and then to have all this happen concurrently, it's a lot to take in."

"Yeah, I'm sure it is. Well, if you do, get some kind of a read on the situation, I trust you now. You know you can come to me, after everything with the Hartford case, I know that we need to trust each other. Promise?"

I gave the detective a half smile. That was a good thing to hear. Trust wasn't something I had before coming to Aspen Falls. "Yeah, okay. I promise. As long as you keep me in the loop with everything with my brother. You think this was a murder, don't you, Detective?"

"I've got no choice but to treat this as a murder. Young women in their twenties don't just up and die for no reason like that. We'll have an autopsy done and go from there. For now, I'm going to have to do my interviews. Unfortunately, Mercy, your brother was the last person to see Harper Bradshaw alive. He's my main suspect. No one knows him – you don't even know him, from what Hugh told me. It's his first night in town, and now a girl is dead. It's pretty suspicious; you've got to admit that."

Heat filled my face. "It's Harper's first night in town too. And her boyfriend's. Right? This looks like a jealous rage murder situation to me. I think you need to focus this investigation on her boyfriend." While I hoped that this was something that Reign couldn't do, I had to agree that I didn't know him. I didn't know if he was a good guy or a bad guy. He wasn't raised by my mother or anyone in my family. He could very well be evil. I had no way of knowing. What I did know was that I was going to have to explain all of this to my mother and she wasn't going to like it, not one little bit.

"Yes, and her boyfriend's. I'm on my way to go question him now."

"Maybe I should come with you while you question him. I might be able to help."

Detective Whitman raised a hand. "Oh no. I appreciate you helping where you can, but I think that would be overstepping. In addition, your brother is involved, and that would be a conflict of interest. Regardless of the fact that the two of you don't know each other. Just keep me informed if you learn anything new from a paranormal standpoint." Detective Whitman walked around me, towards the back room where I was sure they were keeping the boyfriend and the bartender.

I followed him and put a hand on his arm to stop him. "Wait a minute, Detective. So I'm just supposed to tell you everything I know, but you don't have to tell me anything you know? I don't think that sounds like a very fair arrangement. Why should I help you then? I thought you wanted me to trust you and vice versa?"

"Look, Mercy, I will trust whatever you tell me that your senses are telling you. You've got to trust me. My senses are telling me that your brother isn't a great guy. He looks like trouble. I'd be careful and don't just blindly trust everything he says," said the detective before leaving me behind.

I felt Hugh's hand on my shoulder. "He's right, Mercy. You don't know anything about Reign. He could be nothing but bad news. He had a dead woman in his bed. He stole some guy's girlfriend. He was so drunk he doesn't remember what happened. Things aren't looking good for your brother. I'm really sorry, but I don't want you to believe whatever he tells you without question."

"I need to talk to my brother," I said quietly. The room felt like it was spinning and all I knew was that I wanted to get off the ride. But until I'd talked to Reign, it probably wasn't going to happen.

Hugh and I started towards the stairs. The Bradshaw's had moved to a table and chairs where they sobbed with each other. Upstairs Reign was patiently waiting. He'd thrown on a black leather jacket. The combination of the black jacket, Army boots, and his thick black disheveled mane really contributed to the "rebel without a cause" vibe he was throwing off. Maybe Detective Whitman was right. Maybe I needed to be cautious around Reign.

"Can I talk to you?" I asked him.

"Yeah, of course, let's go to the end of the hallway, there's a couch we can sit on down there," he suggested and then shot Hugh a dirty look. "Who's this cowboy?"

"Oh, Reign, this is Hugh, Hugh, this is Reign," I introduced awkwardly.

Hugh extended a hand to my brother. Reign ignored it and looked at Hugh pointedly. "I'd like to speak to my sister *alone*, if you don't mind."

Hugh took offense and puffed up his chest. "I do mind as a matter of fact."

I squeezed Hugh's arm. "I'll be alright," I told him quietly. "Wait for me downstairs?"

He gave Reign a warning glance before nodding at me. "Okay, holler if ya need me."

"Okay, thanks," I said and walked to the other end of the hallway with Reign close behind.

A set of tan sofas and a pair of end tables were arranged on top of an area rug at the end of the hallway. "Have a seat," Reign said, motioning towards one of the couches. Once I had taken a seat, he settled himself on the one opposite me. He leaned forward with his elbows on his knees.

"I'm really sorry that this is how we have to meet," he said nervously.

"I am too," I agreed.

"I know I said this already, but I want you to know that I would never, never hurt anyone. Especially a woman. I know I didn't kill that girl," he asserted. "It was probably a pretty dumb thing to do to sleep with her, especially since she was obviously here with a boyfriend, but she was coming on to me, and I had had a lot to drink. It's just been a long couple of weeks, and I had a long drive. I just needed to cut loose and relax. I had no idea this would happen."

"Okay," I said quietly. My senses weren't telling me anything. They weren't giving me a read and telling me how I should feel about my own brother. The whole thing felt surreal. "Let's not talk about that. You're my brother. How about we talk about that?"

A little smile perked up Reign's face. "Yeah, I have a sister. That's some pretty big stuff. Our mom is pretty awesome," he began.

I nodded and tried to smile, but I felt my heart tug instead. "Yeah, Linda's great. I miss her; I really wish she were here right now. I don't know how to get you out of this, Reign." I admitted and suddenly found tears rolling down my cheeks. Where had those come from? I didn't even realize that I had tears to cry.

"Oh, shoot," he began and left his sofa to sit next to me. He put a strong arm around my shoulder. "Mercy, I'm so sorry this is happening. I'm sure it was enough to learn you had a brother. Don't cry."

Before I knew what was happening, Hugh was pulling Reign off of me. "Don't touch her," he hollered at my brother.

"Get your hands off of me, cowboy!"

"Hugh! It's okay. He was comforting me," I protested.

Hugh's nostrils flared. His fists were balled and at the ready by his side. "Mercy, I think it's time I took you home."

"Yeah, you probably need to get some sleep," Reign agreed, looking equally as upset and ready to throw down as Hugh. "Tomorrow will look better and we'll have a lot of this figured out. Not much we can do tonight."

"Well, what will you do tonight?" I asked Reign nervously.

"He'll be coming with me," said Detective Whitman from the stairs. "I'm taking Reign downtown."

CHAPTER 5

It was dark and chilly when we pulled into the wizard's parking lot in the wee hours of the morning. I was thankful that Hugh had given me his sweater to wear or else I'd be freezing in the tiny little dress I had on. The ride home had been quiet. I could tell Hugh was stewing on the fact that he didn't necessarily care for my brother and I was stewing on the fact that I was going to have to tell my mom what had happened. It was too soon to sort out my own feelings for Reign, but I was more worried about what this whole mess would do to my mother.

Hugh walked me back to Winston Hall, and when I tried to tell him that was far enough, he said he wanted to walk me all the way to my dorm room door. Despite our date getting hijacked by a murder investigation and my brother showing up, it was still a date after all.

"I'm sorry things got so messed up," I said to him at the door as I shifted nervously on my bare feet. I'd long since taken the high heels off, and I carried them slung over my shoulder with one hand.

He smiled at me as I unlocked my door. "It's not your fault. I just want you to know that despite everything, I really had a good time getting to know you tonight."

"Yeah, I had a good time getting to know you too, I'm really glad that you were there with me when everything went down. I'm not sure I could have done all of that alone."

One of Hugh's arms lifted to lean on the door frame, and he took off his hat. Without a word, he leaned in to kiss me goodnight, but before he could, the door behind me flew open. Jax appeared in the doorway wild-eyed. "Mercy? What are you doing out so late?" she asked me. "I've been worried about you!"

Hugh made a low guttural sound and rolled backwards against the wall. It was the second kiss that had been interrupted that evening.

"Oh, I'm sorry, Jax. Our date got sidetracked, I'll tell you all about it in the morning."

Jax looked Hugh up and down, as if it had been his fault for keeping me out so late. "Goodnight, Houston," she said pointedly.

Hugh put his hat back on his head and tipped his head at the two of us. "G'night ladies. Sweet dreams. I'll talk to you tomorrow, Mercy."

I OVERSLEPT THE NEXT MORNING, AND WHEN I FINALLY DID wake up, Jax had already left for breakfast. I hastily threw on a pair of jeans and my high-top Converse sneakers and my favorite Pretty Reckless t-shirt. I looked in the mirror to see makeup from the night before smudged all over my face. It took only seconds to steal one of Jax's makeup removing wipes and clean up the mess, exposing a tiny display of freckles across the bridge of my nose. I finger combed my long red hair and swept it all onto my left shoulder, hastily braided it, and secured it with a ponytail holder. I blindly searched the room for my glasses, then threw on a sweatshirt and was just about to leave when I heard a noise at the window.

A black cat had just landed gracefully on the windowsill. I sighed, I had hoped to be able to make it out of the room before Sneaks came looking for me.

"How was your date?" I heard my mother's voice come out of the black cat's mouth.

"Good morning, Mother," I said reluctantly, as I zipped up my hoodie.

"Good morning, Mercy. How was your date?" she repeated.

"Snoopy much this morning?"

"I'm sorry, but I waited up for you last night, and you never came home. I sure hope you and Houston didn't go doing anything stupid. It was only your first date. I hope you didn't, you know, have *sex* on your first date."

"Mother!" I hollered.

"What? Please don't tell me that that's why you were out so late?" Sneaks squeezed her eyes shut and then peered out of one eye carefully. "And if that *is* what you were doing, I sure hope that you were safe."

"Mother!" I covered my face with my hands.

"I know we've had this talk before, Mercy, but it only takes one time, you know."

"Ugh! Mother! It's none of your business, but no, that's not why we were out so late. Something happened last night. I didn't want to have to tell you this right away in the morning, but I guess you're here…" I began.

Sneaks leapt off the windowsill and onto the desk where she sat down and curled her tail around her body. "Oh dear, I'm afraid to ask. What happened?"

I chewed on my bottom lip nervously. How do you tell your mother something like this? "Where do I start?" I asked.

"Start at the beginning. How was the date?"

"You are so snoopy," I retorted before sighing. I knew Mom wasn't going to leave it alone. "The date was good. We had supper downtown, then we went to a park, and we talked and listened to music. While we were talking, I got a phone call. It was Reign."

"Reign called you?"

"Yeah. He's in town."

"Already? Wow, he made good time. Did you get to meet him?"

"Yeah, I met him." My stomach flipped uneasily, as I pulled up my desk chair to sit face to face with Sneaks.

"*And*...what did you think?" she asked excitedly.

"Mom...something happened. Reign got himself into some trouble."

"Trouble?" her voice changed immediately. "What kind of trouble? What happened?"

"I'm not exactly sure, to be honest. I don't really know who to believe. Detective Whitman and Hugh think I should be careful with believing Reign."

"Detective Whitman? There's a detective involved in something related to your brother. Oh no. Did he do something? What happened?"

"There's no real easy way to say this, Mom, so I'm just going to come right out and say it."

"Yeah! Say it, Mercy, you're freaking me out here."

"Detective Whitman thinks Reign murdered a girl. He was found in bed with a dead girl."

"What? Reign murdered a girl?"

"I don't know if he murdered her or not, but he slept with her. And when he woke up she was dead. So the police are kind of leaning towards Reign as their prime suspect."

"Mercy…"

"Mom, do you know much about Reign? Detective Whitman and Hugh both think he's not a great guy."

"I don't know a lot about him, but he's *my son*. My child could never kill another person, Mercy."

"I know, Mom, that's kind of how I feel. But I don't know this guy at all. He looks sort of like a bad boy."

"Looks can be deceiving, Mercy. Look at your friend Jax. She was overcompensating for not being a witch by dressing like a witch. Reign could just want to look tougher than he is. He was given up for adoption after all. He may have some abandonment issues to deal with."

"So, I don't know what to do, Mom. I don't know how to help Reign."

"Where is he now?" she asked.

"At the police station. He and the other guys that were there last night are all being interviewed by the cops."

"Okay. I should come out there. Reign needs me. You need me," she asserted frantically. I could practically hear her packing her bags as we spoke.

"Mother! No! You don't need to drive clear back over here. We'll figure it out. I'll help him. The girls and I will figure it out. Okay? Listen, I've got to get to breakfast, I'm starving. And I've got class. I'll talk to you later."

"Okay, love you, Mercy. Be safe. Two murders in a week. I'm starting to wonder how safe Aspen Falls really is!"

I SCURRIED DOWNSTAIRS TO GRAB SOMETHING TO EAT BEFORE they closed the cafeteria, but was disappointed to find that they had just stopped serving breakfast, so I swung into Paranormally Delicious, the coffee shop in the lobby of our dorm and grabbed a double caramel macchiato and a puff pastry from the glass case. I took it to the courtyard and was happy to see that the girls were still there, though they were just finishing up their breakfast.

I slid down between Alba and Sweets with a huff.

"Thank goodness you guys are still here. I have so much to tell you about the night I had!" I began.

Sweets eyed my pastry carefully. "Is that an apple turnover?"

"Jax told us you didn't come in until the wee hours of the morning, looks like the dress worked wonders, huh?" suggested Holly, winking at me.

I shot Jax an annoyed glare, causing her to investigate the last few bites of her omelet silently.

"Or is it cream cheese?" Sweets asked, still investigating my breakfast. "It kind of looks like cream cheese, mmm, the cream cheese ones are sooo good."

Cinder and Libby, twin witches who were in their second year of school at the Institute, were seated at the table as well. "Hot date with the cowboy, huh?" Cinder asked as she finished off her cup of coffee.

"I hear he's quite the charmer," Libby added.

Cinder echoed her sister, "Quite the charmer!"

"Girls! Quit!" I admonished. "I have so much to tell you! Things on the date went south last night."

"Oooh, things went south? Do tell!" Holly exclaimed excitedly.

I palmed my forehead. "Holly! Get your mind out of the gutter!"

"Oh my gosh, Holly," Jax agreed, rolling her eyes.

"What? You weren't thinking that's what she meant?" she swung her eyes towards Alba pointedly.

"Why are you looking at me? Why would my mind go to the gutter?" Alba looked offended.

"Would it be possible for you guys to zip it, for like, two minutes? So I can tell you what happened? There was another murder last night, ya know."

A collective gasp went up around the table.

"What?"

"Again?"

"Another one?"

"Who was it?"

"Where?"

"How did you hear?"

The questions went on and on. I held up a hand to silence everyone. "I'll tell you everything I know. It was a woman in her twenties. Her name was Harper Bradshaw. She's from Aspen Falls originally, but she lived in Connecticut. She came back to town with her boyfriend and was staying at Jimmy's Bed and Brew downtown and this other guy, this stranger, I guess, sort of stole her away from her boyfriend and next thing he knew this new guy woke up in bed with her and she was dead."

"Wow, so the stranger killed her?" Holly asked, nodding.

"He claims he didn't. And I kind of believe him. He says to look at the boyfriend; he was jealous."

"Like you should just believe the stranger? I mean, of course, he's gonna say that he didn't do it. Who would just say, *oh, yeah, I did it*? That's ridiculous," Jax ranted.

I gnawed on my lower lip nervously. "Okay, well, there's more to the story…" I began. I didn't know how to tell the rest of the girls that the mysterious stranger was none other than my illegitimate half-brother.

"Ooh, it sounds juicy, do tell!" said Holly excitedly, leaning towards me with her elbow on the table.

"I don't know about juicy, but it's how I got involved. The stranger, this new guy in town, he's well, he's my brother."

"You're brother?" Alba asked, astonished. "I thought you were an only child."

"Oh, you missed that earlier," Jax said. "Mercy's mom had a kid when she was sixteen, and her grandmother gave him up for adoption. He's coming to find her. Wait. He *found* you?"

I shifted uncomfortably in my seat. "Yeah. His name is Reign. And, girls, I'm worried. What if my brother killed that woman?"

"You think your brother killed her?" Libby asked, astonished.

"I really don't know what to think. Hugh and Detective Whitman told me to watch out for Reign, that he's shady. I want to believe him when he tells me that he didn't do it, but I don't know what to think."

"Who else could have done it?" Alba asked.

"Well, Detective Whitman said they are questioning Reign, the boyfriend, and the bartender. I suppose there could have been more people in the bar last night, but I don't know."

Libby leaned forward conspiringly. "I'll bet it was the Black Witch."

I rolled my eyes as I took a sip of my macchiato. "Why in the world would you think the Black Witch killed Harper

Bradshaw? She probably doesn't even *know* Harper Bradshaw."

"Because she's, well, you know, super creepy and stuff."

"Last week you thought the Black Witch killed Morgan Hartford and she had nothing to do with it," I pointed out.

"So, she still could have killed Harper Bradshaw. Just because she didn't kill Morgan doesn't mean anything."

I reached under the table and squeezed Jax's hand secretly. Libby and Cinder didn't know the truth, that Jax was really Sorceress Stone's daughter and the Black Witch's niece. I was sure Libby's accusation didn't make her feel very good. Jax squeezed back but wouldn't look up and make eye contact with anyone at the table.

"I'm sure the killer isn't the Black Witch, you can't just go around accusing her of everything, just because she's 'ya know, creepy.'"

Libby shrugged and muttered, "Fine."

"Did any of your senses go off when you were there?" Jax asked, finally looking up from her plate.

I shook my head. "No, it was such an emotional event that they didn't. Not only was I just meeting my brother for the first time, but there was the murder, and Detective Whitman asked me to talk to Harper's mother while the father identified the body. It was horrible. Her parents were a wreck. To have to tell someone that their daughter is dead is horrible."

"Did you look for the girl's ghost?" Alba asked me.

"Honestly, I didn't even think about looking. I was so preoccupied with my brother being the accused and all. I'm so worried. We've got to figure out if Reign was involved. For my mother's sake. She's a mess already. I just talked to her this morning."

"Sounds like the Witch Squad has some investigating to do," Sweets said enthusiastically.

"Yeah, it does sound like that." I looked down at the Batman watch on my wrist. "But we're going to be late for class. We probably should go. We can do some investigating later."

CHAPTER 6

Classes seemed to drag on longer than usual. My toe wouldn't stop tapping, and I probably checked my watch two dozen times during my last period Potions class. I knew that Sweets was right. It was time for the Witch Squad to do some serious investigating. I couldn't wait to get out of class and find Reign and do some digging with the girls. I couldn't let my brother go down for a murder that he promised me he didn't commit.

The minute class was out I headed for the courtyard. Alba, Sweets, Jax, and Holly were all there waiting.

"Okay. It's time to get serious. We need to figure out what to do about my brother," I began as I approached the foursome in the quad.

Jax saluted me. "Aye aye, Captain. Just tell us where to start!"

"Well, I think we need to start by going over to Jimmy's Bed & Brew," I suggested.

Alba nodded. "Agreed. Step one is going back to the scene of the crime. Stone would agree, I'm sure."

Sweets looked anxiously between each of us. "Wait,

67

we're not telling Stone are we? I mean, after last time and all. I just figured we'd…"

"We're not telling Stone," Alba barked, her voice heavy with annoyance.

"Oh, well, you said…"

"I just said Stone would agree. I didn't say we were going to involve her in this. That would be ludicrous. Stone's just red tape. We don't need any more red tape than we will already have," Alba explained to her impatiently. Sweets already seemed to be on the short end of Alba's nerves.

"Step two is to check out that hottie," Holly quipped, nodding her head towards the tall, dark and handsome man that had just exited Winston Hall.

My face flushed bright red as the man coming towards us ducked out of the shadow of the scarlet oak tree, and I realized it was none other than Reign.

"Oh, my gosh, Holly! Stop! That's my brother," I said in disgust.

"*That*'s your *brother*?" she asked, dumbfounded.

"Over here, Reign," I hollered at him and waved him over.

The sun shone brightly in his eyes, he put one hand up to shield them and tilted his head slightly to the side. A slow smile spread across his face as he approached.

"Mercy, there you are. The woman at the desk in there said you were probably at lunch right now," he said.

"Yeah, we just got out of class. We were actually just discussing your case," I began. "I guess I should introduce you to the girls. They're going to be helping us prove your innocence. Reign, this is Jax, my roommate," I said and pointed to Jax.

Her blue eyes sparkled brightly as she shook his hand. "Wow, it's so nice to meet you, Reign."

I caught the tiny wink he shot her in conjunction with a sly smile. "Hey, Jax, love the hat," he said and tapped the rim of her black witch's hat.

Her face lit up even more. "You do? Thanks!"

"And this is Holly," I said, pointing towards at Holly.

Reign's eyes scanned Holly up and down appreciatively while a lascivious smile spread across his face. "Hey, girl."

Holly had managed to ratchet her boobs up yet another notch in her scoop-neck sweater before being introduced, and she stood in front of him smiling like a Cheshire cat. "Hey, Reign," she purred seductively.

I had to swallow hard a couple of times not to lose my lunch. I should have guessed that the girls would crush on my brother. Not that I could blame them. He was a pretty good-looking guy, but the minute I'd heard the word *brother*, all engines shut down. Now my friends lusting after my brother made me feel weird.

"This is Sweets," I said. "Sweets, this is my brother, Reign."

Sweets immediately got tongue tied. "Um, yeah, um…hi."

"Sweets, is that your real name?" he asked.

"Um, no, but I, um, all my friends call me, uh – Sweets," she stuttered.

Reign shot her an encouraging smile. "Cool, well, it's nice to meet you, Sweets," he took her hand and kissed the top of it. She stared at him, mesmerized. When he released her hand she took it back and giggled excitedly.

"And this is Alba. She and Holly are roommates," I told him.

Alba took her time sizing up Reign. Debating whether or not she considered him to be the shady character that Hugh and Detective Whitman had labeled him to be. She was clearly unimpressed. "Sup," she said to him with a little head nod.

He chuckled. "Sup, Alba. So you girls have this case in the bag, or what?"

"Hardly," I said with wide eyes. "We just got out of class. We are going to run down to Jimmy's and do a little digging. I assume you're done at the police station?"

He nodded and raised one eyebrow. "Yeah, that was a ball of laughs."

"They let you go, though. That was a good sign," I said.

"All they have is me in bed with her. They've got nothing else right now. They don't even know how she died yet."

"So, who do you think did it?" Holly asked Reign.

Reign shifted his weight as he gave Holly a big smile. "My money's on the boyfriend. Last thing I remember before waking up, he wanted to throw a few punches my way. We took it outside. He threw one punch. I stepped out of the way and countered with a blow to his gut. That's all it took. He heaved himself up off the ground and stormed off. I went back inside, Harper was alone, and I offered her a place to sleep for the night," he said innocently.

Holly's eyes were big as she absorbed every word he was saying. "Well, that was sure sweet of you, to you know, offer her a place to stay, since her boyfriend was being such a jerk."

"That's exactly what I told the gumshoe down at the police station," Reign asserted.

"Listen, girls. I really haven't had a chance to get to know my brother. Could we maybe go down to Jimmy's a little later? I'd like to spend a little one-on-one time with Reign before we go, is that alright?"

Sweets nodded understandingly. "Of course it is. You two take as much time as you need. We can go down to Jimmy's whenever you want."

"Thanks, Sweets. Jax, you don't mind me commandeering the room for a little while do you?"

Jax shook her head and rubbed my arm. "You just take all the time you need. Get to know your brother. We'll all go sleuthing later."

"Thanks, girls. Reign, do you mind if it's just the two of us for awhile?"

"Not at all, that's why I came to Aspen Falls. To get to know my lil sis."

I smiled nervously. Reign didn't feel like the big brother I needed all my life. I only hoped that once I got to know him that would all change.

"Yeah, so I grew up in a small town in Nebraska," Reign began once we'd seated ourselves comfortably back in my dorm room.

"That's pretty interesting. Tell me about your parents, or, I mean the people who raised you all this time," I suggested.

"Well, I was adopted by a nice couple. My adopted mom was a lunch lady at the school, and my adopted father worked at the bank. I didn't have any siblings, just me and Mom and Dad. It was a great life. I had a ton of friends and played on the high school football team."

I was surprised Reign was a football player. He looked

too rebellious to be a star quarterback or something else as innocuous as that. "What did you do after high school?"

"I moved to the city to go to college. But I had to put off college and work for the first year to be able to afford to go. You know how that goes. One year becomes two years and two years becomes four years, and then well, you realize you probably won't ever go by that point."

"When did you find out that you were adopted?" I asked him.

"I was twelve. I found my birth certificate in a box of mementos my mother had stored under her bed, and it had our mother's name on it as my biological mother," he told me. "I knew I'd have to go find her someday, but I wanted to wait until I was an adult."

Something about Reign's story was making me incredibly wary of him. My sensors were going off like crazy. I was sure that he wasn't being completely honest with me, but I couldn't put my finger on what exactly he wasn't being honest about. "You're twenty-four, you've been an adult for six years, why come find Mom and I now?" I asked suspiciously.

"I hadn't wanted to search out my mother because I was always afraid I'd hurt my adopted mother. Then she died about three years ago, and it took me awhile – I was grieving. And … I don't know; the time just finally felt right. I was in between jobs, and I just decided now was the time."

"I'm sorry about your adopted mother," I said quietly.

He looked down at his hands in his lap. "Yeah. Now, enough about me. Tell me all about *you*," he insisted and leaned Jax's desk chair backwards so that he was rocking on only two of its two metal feet.

I shrugged as I stretched out on my side across my bed, leaning on my elbow. "Not much to tell. I grew up with a single witch mom. I got in a bit of trouble in high school, and then I graduated. I was out for a year, and then I started getting in bigger trouble so *people*, mostly the law, you know, thought it might be a good idea for me to get some 'specialized help.' Mom shipped me off to witch college. And here I am."

"Witch college, that's really interesting," he began. "So, you're, like *a witch*."

I nodded. I had just assumed that was something that he already knew. "You knew that, right?"

"Oh, yeah, yeah, of course," he assured me.

"And you're…" I began.

"Paranormal?" he finished.

I gave him a half smirk. "Yeah."

"Yeah, I suppose you could call me paranormal," he said. His onyx eyes twinkled darkly as his mouth curled up into a grin.

"Do you know anything about your real father?" I asked him. I was totally curious who that was, who my mother could have possibly fallen in love with that my granny didn't approve of.

He shrugged. "I don't know much. I know I look like him," he said. "At least I did when he was younger. Our mom told me that."

"So he was handsome too?" I said with a little chuckle.

He chuckled back. "Maybe."

"Do you know who he is?" I asked. I was dying to Google him and see what I could find out about the man my mother had loved before she met my father.

"Do we have to talk about this now?" he asked. He shifted about uncomfortably in his seat.

"I guess not," I said quietly. I didn't know my father either. I hated to make Reign uncomfortable by talking about his biological father. I assumed he didn't know who his dad was either. The awkward silence that followed made me change the topic of discussion. "So what did you think of Linda?"

"Linda's awesome. She's really really awesome. I'm only upset that I didn't get to meet her earlier in my life."

"Yeah, that's a real bummer. I'm really sorry our granny took you away from her. Gran's nosy, but she isn't a bad woman."

Reign grimaced. I could feel the tense energy radiating off of him. "It is what it is. There's nothing we can do about it now."

"Yeah." My heart hung heavily in my chest. I loved my grandmother, but I hated what she had done to our family. I hated the fact that I could have had a big brother growing up and I never got to know him.

The two of us sat together for several long moments of awkward silence.

"So now what?" I asked him nervously. I didn't know what kind of a relationship we would have now and I wasn't the most demonstrative of people. Was I, like, supposed to hug him or something? That would be too weird.

"What do you mean?"

I splayed my hands out in front of me and widened my eyes. "I don't know. What kind of a relationship do we have now? We're not kids, we can't just go out and play together now, and everything will be normal. This is strange. I don't know how to be."

Reign stood up and walked over to the side of the bed. I sat up and allowed him to sit down next to me. "Just be you, Mercy. You seem like a pretty cool chick. I'm proud to have you as a sister."

My heart swelled up at his words. Secretly, I'd always dreamed of having a big brother. And to find out that I had one and he was proud to have me for a sister made me feel good. "You are?"

"Yeah! Of course, I am. And I feel horrible about this whole dumb situation I got myself into. I should have never gotten involved with that woman when I knew she had a boyfriend. Women and I have a love-hate relationship," he said, rolling his eyes as he sighed. "I love them, and they love to hate me."

"So you're saying you're a big flirt?"

He laughed hard. "They flirt with me too. It's a two-way street, ya know."

"But you initiate the flirting?"

He laughed and wiped the corners of his mouth with his thumb. "Something like that. Anyway. I really appreciate that you and your friends are going to help me. Have you talked to Linda about all of this yet?"

"Yeah, I told her this morning. She's totally freaking out. I knew she would be."

"Oh, geez," he leaned forward, putting his elbows on his knees he let his head fall into his cupped hands. "This is all so screwed up. I feel horrible."

"Don't worry, the girls and I will figure it all out. Do you want to go with us when we go back to Jimmy's?"

Reign stood up and walked towards the door. "Absolutely. I need to go back there anyway. All of my stuff is still there. When I got out of the police station, I got in my car and came straight here."

"Are you going to stay there tonight?"

He shook his head and shot me a crazy look. "Are you kidding me? There was a *dead* girl in my bed last night.

That's a little morbid, don't you think? I believe I'll pass on that. Are there other places to stay in town?"

"We can ask around. We aren't allowed to have men overnight in our rooms, or I'd just let you stay here. I'm sure there is another bed & breakfast in town."

"Okay, we'll figure it out. Let's go. I'm anxious to get myself off the hook."

CHAPTER 7

Jimmy's Bed & Brew looked far different in the daylight hours than it did in the wee hours of the morning. In the dark and with the presence of the entire Aspen Falls police force, it felt like a seedy ramshackle little dive. In the daytime hours, with light streaming in from two open windows, it just looked like a quaint little hometown café.

The girls and I filed into the bar, one by one. Reign had driven himself and was right behind us as we entered the bar. A gangly fellow with long wavy brown hair was working behind the counter.

"That's Jimmy," Reign whispered in my ear as we all approached the bar.

"You're back," Jimmy grunted at Reign. "You just need to get your stuff and go."

Reign held up his hands in defeat. "Yeah, yeah, man. I'm going. I didn't do it, ya know."

"Cops think ya did," Jimmy snarled back.

"Of course they do. Convict the last guy to see her alive? That makes their jobs much easier, now doesn't it?"

"Look, I got no interest in you, that girl or her boyfriend, or the cops. I just don't want my bar to be associated with a murder. It's not going to be good for business. So just get your stuff and hit the road."

"Yeah, I told you, I'm going," Reign shot back. "Come on, ladies, up here."

"I'll be right up," I said to my brother.

He nodded and led the girls up to his room. When they were out of earshot, I looked at Jimmy. He had one side of his hair tucked behind an ear, but the other side hung in front of his face like a shield. "So. What can you tell me about last night?" I asked him bluntly.

He snorted at me. "What's it to you, Red?"

"Just trying to get to the bottom of all of this. Sort out the facts."

Jimmy slung a towel over his shoulder and put both hands on his bar. "Listen. I told everything I know to the cops. Spent the entire night over there getting grilled. I'd just like to get my place cleaned up. Look at it; it's a mess. All those cops tracking in and out all night, making messes all over the place."

I looked around, aside from dirty floors, it didn't look that messy. "I see. Well. Just tell me this. Did you see Reign leave with Harper?"

"Leave?"

"Did you see him take her to his room?" I asked.

Jimmy shrugged and began wiping off his bar top. "It was a busy night. People coming and going. Hard to keep track of who went where and when."

"So you *didn't* see them leave together?" I asked.

"Maybe I did, maybe I didn't. What's it to you?"

"Like I said, I'm just trying to get to the bottom of all of this. You realize you're probably a suspect too?"

Jimmy stopped cleaning and glanced up at me. "How do you figure that? Because I was here? That's a load of B.S. if I ever heard it."

"Well, Reign's a suspect, and all he did was be in the wrong place at the wrong time."

"And take that girl to bed with him. Don't forget that. Of course, he killed that girl. Doesn't take a rocket scientist to figure that out. She was alive when they left, and dead when they found her, that's all I know."

"So you *did* see them leave together?"

"Listen. They were all pretty toasted last night. Her, him, and the boyfriend. I saw him flirting with her. I saw the boyfriend getting jealous. I saw him and the boyfriend go outside to settle the score and only one came back in. Your friend and the girl hung out for a little while and next thing I know, everyone's gone."

"And so Reign and the boyfriend went out to settle the score and yet you don't think it was the boyfriend that did this? You think it was Reign?"

"Look, I really don't know. And I really don't care. All I know is that it wasn't me."

"Did you know either Harper or her boyfriend?" I asked.

"I met them both last night."

I shook my head as I leaned against the bar. "I mean before last night. Did you know either one of them?"

"They were from out of town, how would I know them?"

"I hear Harper came from an established family in town. Henry and Louise Bradshaw."

He avoided my gaze as he went back to cleaning his counter. "I'd never met the broad before in my life. Now, listen. I've got a lot of work to do, why don't you go help your boyfriend get his stuff out of my place."

I laughed out loud while I jogged up the stairs. "He's not my boyfriend. He's my brother!"

Upstairs Reign had just finished shoving the rest of his stuff into his backpack. Holly was lying on her stomach on his bed with her boobs mashed against the comforter, nearly causing a wardrobe malfunction. Sweets, who couldn't control a single thought in her head around my brother, sat next to Holly on the bed giggling like a mad woman. Between them and Jax, who continually left the Institute in her ridiculous witchy ensemble and Alba who was a reincarnation of Oscar the Grouch, I was absolutely mortified. I rolled my eyes as I entered. Sometimes my friends were just so embarrassing.

Frustrated, I groaned at the girls. "Holly, you realize there was a dead girl lying right there about eight hours ago."

Her eyes widened, and she shot out of bed like a cheating wife in the middle of the day. "What? No! I hadn't even thought…I…ewwww," she squealed.

Sweets jumped off the bed too. "Omigosh," she said, and when Reign looked at her with one raised eyebrow, she giggled again.

I palmed my forehead, mashing it into my brain. It had been a long night and a long day, and I had no idea how we were going to get Reign out of the situation he was in. Alba and Jax, seated at the little round table in front of his bedroom window, looked bored. "Did the two of you even look for clues?" I asked them. I had expected little from Holly and Sweets in the way of sleuthing, but I was counting on Jax and Alba to keep the show rolling while Reign packed.

Jax leaned on the table. "We looked. What's to find?"

Alba nodded in agreement. "Yeah, ditto. We looked around. I don't see anything."

"Ugh," I groaned. "How are we supposed to solve this case? The bartender thinks Reign did it. Did you guys check the clos—et?" I asked, opening the closet. I was stunned to find a blond girl curled up on the floor of Reign's closet. Her face swiveled up, frightened, the second the door opened, and the bright light hit her.

"What's this?" I asked Alba pointedly and motioned towards the girl.

Alba shot out of her chair and looked in the closet. "What's what?"

I peered at the girl again before it dawned on me. "Harper?"

Her eyes opened wide as she heard her name. She turned to look at the rest of the people in the room who had all gathered in front of the closet. "You – you can see me?" she asked nervously.

"Mmhmm," I murmured nodding.

"You see Harper?" Jax asked excitedly.

"Yup."

"How can you see me?" Harper asked, holding her arms out on either side of her and looking at them. "No one could see me last night when the police were here. I'm – dead, you know," she whispered the word dead as if it were a secret.

I gave her a tight little smile. "Yeah, I know. I see dead people," I said plainly. "You can come on out of the closet." I took a step back, accidentally stepping on Sweet's foot who was crowded around behind me.

"Ouch!" Sweets hollered.

I waved my arms back and forth at everyone. "Guys,

give her some space, go sit back down," I ordered. Reign looked at me nervously. I couldn't tell if he was freaked out by me being able to see Harper's ghost or if he was freaked out because I was able to see Harper's ghost and she might reveal something he didn't want to be revealed.

"You can see ghosts?" he asked.

"Yup. Come on out, Harper."

Harper reached back and pushed herself off of the floor. I would have offered her a hand up, but I hadn't learned how to touch ghosts yet. It was a skill that I had wished I'd had during the last murder investigation. Morgan Hartford had been a very scared seventeen-year-old, and I had wished I'd been able to comfort her, even just a little.

Standing there in her tight red dress, with her eyes cast downward, she looked like a sad, wet puppy and understandably devastated.

"Are you alright?" I asked her.

Without making eye contact she shook her head from side to side, mashing her lips shut like a stubborn little girl who refused to eat her broccoli. I looked around the room. All eyes were on her, even though no one else could see her they were staring into the empty closet. To her, I was sure it felt like they were staring at her. I could see how that would be intimidating.

"Guys, can Harper and I have a minute alone?" I asked the group.

"Of course," Jax chirped as she bounded off her seat. "Let's go everyone."

Alba grudgingly got up off of her chair and led Holly, Jax, and Sweets out the door with Reign following them. "We'll wait downstairs for you," he said quietly.

When everyone had gone, I shut the door behind them and sat down on the bed. "I'm sorry, Harper. I didn't introduce myself. I'm Mercy, and those are my friends. We are all here for you," I told her gently. "We came to try and solve the mystery of your death."

That made her peer up at me. "You are? I don't even know you. Why would you be here to do that?"

"Because. You died under suspicious circumstances. We need to know if someone hurt you. Do you remember what happened last night?"

Harper rubbed her head as if she had a lingering headache from the night before. "I was here with Vaughny," she began.

"Who's Vaughny?" I asked her.

"Oh, he's my boyfriend. Or he – *was* my boyfriend. I guess he's not anymore," she sniffed, and suddenly she was crying dry tears. "Why can't I cry real tears?" she cried. Her absence of tears seemed to cause her to sob harder yet. She pounded her balled fists into the sides of her legs.

I tried not to make light of Harper's situation, but her disappointment in not being able to shed tears was a tad on the funny side, but I held it in. "Because you're a ghost, Harper."

She sniffed harder and wiped her nose with the back of her hand. "I am, huh?"

"Yeah, you are."

"Can I walk through walls?" she asked me with a tiny bit of a smile.

I gave her an encouraging smile back. "Some ghosts can," I told her. "Have you tried yet?"

She shook her head. "No. I've been too scared to leave this room. The police were here forever. They've only been gone for a few hours. And I didn't want to leave my body, but then they took it, and I didn't know what to do then. I've just been hiding in the closet all night."

"I was here last night, and I didn't see you. You must have been hiding in the closet then."

"Maybe. I didn't see you either. Why were you here last night?"

"My brother called me to come down here."

"Oh, why did he call you to come down here?" she asked.

"That's not important. What's important is what happened to you. What do you remember?"

"Well, like I said, I was here with Vaughny last night. We drove in from Connecticut to see my parents. But it was late, so we decided to get a room here. Then we went downstairs to have a few drinks. And this guy came in, and he was really hot, and he started flirting with me and then Vaughn got all mad, and he threatened the guy. They went outside and the next thing I know, I'm in this room, and I'm super sleepy, and then everything just goes black. Needless to say, I never woke up."

"So, you have no idea how you died?" I asked her.

She sucked in a distraught breath as she visibly reconciled the fact that she was dead. "No," she managed to squeak out.

"Do you think Vaughn would hurt you?" I asked her gently.

I could tell her eyes wanted to well up with tears again, but they just wouldn't. After making an ugly cry face for a few seconds she stomped her foot down on the hardwood floor, but it didn't so much as make a creak. "UGH!! Why can't I cry? It's like having to yawn, but not being able to! It's so frustrating!"

I sighed, slumping forward on the bed. "I'm sorry, Harper. I really want to help."

"Helping won't bring me back to life again, though. You can't do that, right?" she asked me.

I chuckled lightly. "Haha, if only that was a power that I had."

"Tell me the truth, Mercy. Why can you see me?"

I bit my lip nervously. "You really don't want to know," I assured her.

She hastily sat down next to me on the bed. "No, I *do* want to know. I'm dead, and we're talking to each other. Nothing would shock me at this point."

"Okay, fine. I'm a witch." I said it plainly without any fanfare. I hoped that she wouldn't turn and run. I needed Harper for this investigation.

Harper blinked several times in quick succession. "Okay. I can handle that. See, I'm not even scared of you," she announced proudly.

My head snapped back. "Why would you be scared of me? I'm not like an evil witch or anything. I was just born with supernatural powers. Technically, that means I'm a witch. My mother is a witch. My granny's a witch. My brother's a…" I stopped myself. What was this? I was already including my brother in my diatribe to ghosts?

"Your brother's a what?"

"Nothing," I snapped, more angrily than I had intended.

"Sorry," she whispered back. I could hear it in her voice, she wanted to cry again. Gosh, crybaby ghosts were so difficult.

"No, I'm sorry," I relented. "I shouldn't have snapped at you. It's been a tough couple of weeks. We need to get down to business, Harper. I need to figure out who killed you. You never said. Is it possible that Vaughn did this to you?"

She shook her head firmly. "I don't believe Vaughn would do this to me."

"But you were flirting with Reign. Maybe Vaughn got jealous, and maybe he would do this to you if he was jealous enough," I suggested.

"I guess we can't rule it out, but Vaughn loved me. It freaks me out to think I could have been living with a killer!"

"What about Reign? Is it possible that he did this to you?" I asked as my stomach performed cartwheels.

Harper bit at her fingernails as if she were really doing so. "It's possible. I really didn't know him well. We just flirted around all night. And then Vaughn wanted to lay him out, but apparently, he laid one on Vaughn. I didn't go outside for that. They made me stay in."

"So you really have no idea who it could have been?" I sighed.

"No. I really don't."

"So, who knew you were in Aspen Falls yesterday?"

She paused thoughtfully and tried to dredge through old memories. "Gosh, remembering anything feels like I'm pulling a heavy block out of a river. It's really hard to do. You know, like when you're having a dream and someone is chasing you, and you want to run, but you can't because your feet feel like they are anchored down by weights and you can barely move? That's what it feels like to have to remember specific details."

"Yeah, I've heard ghosts describe that similarly before," I assured her.

"Yeah, so, I'm really not sure who I told that I was coming. Oh! Wait! I told my sister, Elena. I just remembered telling her that I was coming home because she told me that we would go hang out."

"Are you close to your sister?"

She scrunched up one side of her face as she thought. "I wouldn't say *close*. We got along, but we weren't like besties or anything. I've been gone for a long time. I wanted her to move out to Connecticut with me, but she always turned me down. We used to be really close when we were teenagers."

I hated to do this, but I had to ask her. "Do you think she would have anything to do with this?"

Harper looked astounded that I would even dare to ask. "Oh, heavens no! Elena wouldn't have it in her to hurt me. We were always on the same side. Even when we didn't get along, we were a team."

"What do you mean on the same side?"

"You know, against our parents. No matter what our parents threw at us, we always knew we had to stick together. What was good for one of us was good for both of us, you've got a brother, I'm sure you know?"

I felt a tinge of regret surge through my body. I didn't know what it felt like to grow up with a sibling. "I didn't grow up with my brother, so I really don't."

She looked down at the floor. "Oh, I'm sorry."

"It's okay."

There was a knock at the door.

"Come in," I hollered.

Jax peeked her head, hat and all, inside the room. "Hey, I hate to rush you, Mercy, but the bartender is getting really annoyed with us and Reign's sort of getting mad at him. I'm afraid there's going to be a scuffle if we don't get Reign out of here."

"Oh, geez," I said and rushed to my feet. I looked back at Harper. "You should come with me, in case you

87

remember something I'd like to be able to know right where to find you."

She smiled sweetly but shook her head. "I appreciate the invitation, but I'm honestly scared to go anywhere. I'm a ghost. I'm not real. I don't know that I'm ready to leave this room yet."

I gave her a sympathetic smile and nodded. "Some ghosts like to move around, and some don't. You'll be fine here. I promise to come back and visit you when I have more information. Okay?"

"Bring Elena with you when you come next time?"

Her request surprised me. "Oh, I can try."

"Good. Thanks, Mercy. Good luck."

I gave her a reassuring smile before following Jax downstairs where Reign and Jimmy were embroiled in a heated exchange.

"I told you to pack up this crazy train and move it down the line," Jimmy hollered at him.

"And I told you, let's take those threats outside and settle this like men," Reign hollered back.

"Whoa, whoa, whoa," I asserted as I came running down the stairs. "There will be no settling threats outside, Reign. The two of you need to relax." I pointed specifically at Reign, the one I had any chance in controlling. When I caught his eyes in my glare, he visibly cooled off a few degrees. Not many, but enough for me to feel comfortable in pointing towards the front door. Reign growled at Jimmy, but spun on the heels of his Army boots and left.

"There, now, we're leaving. Alright. Relax," I said to Jimmy.

"Took you long enough," Jimmy snapped back.

The girls and I followed Reign outside where we found

him pacing back and forth on the edge of the curb. He ground a fist into his hand as he walked.

Jax held a hand up next to her mouth. "Someone's upset," she said as an aside, pointing towards Reign.

"Yeah, we've got to get him out of here," I told the girls. "But I still want to go talk to Detective Whitman and see what new information he's got. How about Alba and I run down to the police station and you three take Reign back to the dorms. We can't take him to the police station with that chip on his shoulder."

Holly's eyes widened excitedly. "Yeah, *whatever* you need, Mercy. You know we're here for you."

"Yeah," Jax agreed. "No problem. We'll take good care of your brother."

I turned and looked at Sweets. "Alba and I would need to drive your car, and you will all have to ride with Reign."

Jax, Holly, and Sweets looked across the street at the shiny black sports car that Reign had ridden here in.

Sweets nodded emphatically, as she handed me the keys. "Yeah, absolutely, Mercy. Like Holly said, whatever you need."

I rolled my eyes at my friends. "Gee, I hate to put the three of you out," I snarked.

Alba puffed out the breath she'd been holding.

"No problem at all," Holly said. She obviously hadn't caught my blatant sarcasm. "Reign, come on, we're catching a ride with you!"

Sweets raised a hand as Alba and I walked away with her keys, "Shotgun!"

CHAPTER 8

"Ugh, I thought we'd never get rid of them all. I'm sorry, Red, but your brother has got some serious anger problems," Alba said as I got behind the wheel of Sweets's car.

"Oh, *Reign* has an anger problem," I snorted at Alba.

She ignored my retort and looked out the passenger window. "Tell me the truth. Do you think he did this?"

Suddenly my palms felt clammy, and the back of my neck felt sweaty. "I don't know," I lamented.

"You think he could have, though?"

"Do I have a choice? He was found in bed with her. And the list of suspects is so low. It's pretty much either the boyfriend or my brother. I mean, I doubt the bartender did it – why would he? And no one else knew she was in town. So Reign's got a fifty-fifty chance of being guilty."

Alba squinted into the sun as we turned into the police station parking lot. "We're going to need to find the boyfriend."

"Yeah, I agree. He's one of our key witnesses." I put the car in park and Alba and I sat looking at each other.

"So before we go in, I need to know what Harper told you in there."

"Honestly she didn't know much. She didn't finger anyone. She told me exactly what Reign told me. Reign and Harper flirted. Vaughn got upset. He and Reign took it outside. They had a little scuffle, Reign got a punch in, and Vaughn vanished. Reign came inside, offered to take Harper back to his room and that's what they did. She doesn't remember anything after that, and neither does Reign. Next thing she knew, she was waking up as a ghost."

Alba leaned her head back against the headrest. "Wow, that's harsh."

"Yeah, it is," I agreed. We sat together silently for a few minutes, lost in our thoughts. "So what's the plan in there?"

"We've got to question Detective Whitman," Alba stated plainly.

"Duh, I mean do we tell him that I saw Harper?"

"Not much to tell."

"Okay, then let's see what he shares with us. If he isn't forthcoming with us, then we'll use Harper as leverage."

Alba grinned at me. "I like how you think, Red."

The two of us exited the car and entered the police station. Officer Vargas stopped us at the front desk. His bushy eyebrows looked like two furry black cats sitting atop an open window. I'd recognize the man anywhere thanks to those eyebrows.

"Is Detective Whitman here?" I asked him.

He peered out from underneath his furry black cats at Alba and I. "Aren't the two of you the ones that provided misinformation in the Morgan Hartford murder investigation?"

I winced. "Yeah, well, maybe at first."

"But we fixed it, in the end," Alba added.

"Sure you did." He leaned back in his chair, unconvinced.

"Yeah, as a matter of fact, we did," I said cocking my head to the side.

"What do you need with Detective Whitman today?" he asked with a sigh. I could tell we hadn't impressed him.

"We need to talk to him," Alba muttered.

"He's busy."

I crossed my arms in front of me. "He's not busy."

Officer Vargas grimaced. "Maybe he is, and maybe he isn't. You'll need an appointment."

I rolled my eyes and pulled my cell phone out of my back pocket. Quickly I dialed and pressed the phone to my ear.

"Detective Whitman," I heard a deep male voice say.

"Hello, Detective, this is Mercy Habernackle," I said.

"Mercy, I'm glad you called. I need to talk to you. Can you possibly come down to the station?"

I smirked into the phone. "I'm down here right now, but Officer Vargas is hassling me and my friends."

"Oh, I'll be out in a second," he said, and the line went dead.

I snapped my phone shut and held the phone up to the bulletproof window separating Officer Vargas and Alba and I. "Looks like I've got an appointment," I said smugly.

"Vargas! Let Ms. Habernackle and her friend in please," we heard coming from an office in the back.

Officer Vargas pulled himself upright in his chair and pushed a button under his desk. A buzzer sounded and we pushed our way through the door. "He's back there," he grunted at us.

I shot Officer Vargas a sweet as pie smile. "Thanks, sweetheart," I cooed at him as we brushed past his desk.

"In here," Detective Whitman hollered.

We followed the voice and found his desk back behind the copy machine. His office had the pungent aroma of strong coffee and stale cigarettes.

"Ugh, are you a smoker?" I asked, holding my breath as I walked into his office.

Alba waved her hands in front of her to shoo the awful smell out the door.

"I'm trying to quit, why?" he said gruffly, as he finger-pecked the keyboard in front of him, looking up and down between the paper file in front of him and the computer screen.

"Because your office reeks," Alba said harshly.

Detective Whitman looked up at us finally. "Well I'm sorry, the maid's on vacation."

"It's called Febreeze. You should try it," Alba retorted.

Detective Whitman's response made me suddenly curious about his personal life. "Are you married?" I asked him bluntly.

"I'm sorry, did I miss National Rag on a Detective day on the calendar?" he said, crossing his arms and leaning backwards in his chair.

I shrugged as I sat down on one of the two chairs in front of his desk. "We aren't ragging on you. I just asked if you're married."

"No," he barked. "Divorced."

"Ah, she didn't like your smoking, huh?" Alba said knowingly.

Detective Whitman narrowed his eyes as he leaned forward in his chair. "How did you know that?"

Alba lifted her eyebrows as she shrugged her shoulders. "I'm a witch."

I had to laugh. While Alba did have the ability to read someone's mind on occasion, it came and went, it wasn't much of a stretch to guess that his ex-wife didn't like her house *or* her husband smelling like a dirty old ashtray.

"Okay, yeah, so back to the fact that you're witches. What do you have for me on the Harper Bradshaw case?" he asked. His gruff manner suggested we'd annoyed him with our questioning.

Alba waved a finger at him. "Oh no, you first."

He looked at both of us. I could practically see the wheels turning in his mind. Share with us or don't share with us. Finally, he threw his hands up in the air. "Fine. The initial toxicology report is back. She was poisoned. Now you."

I looked at Alba uneasily. I wasn't sure if I should share. She gave me a tiny nod. "We found Harper's ghost."

He leaned forward in his chair excitedly. "Re-eeeally."

"Yes. Now your turn," Alba said smarmily.

Detective Whitman looked down at the file on his desk, and then he looked up at me. I could tell he had news I didn't want to hear. My belly began to churn anxiously. "Reign's got a record."

"Ugh," I said, exhaling the breath that I didn't even know that I'd been holding. I let my head fall into my hands as I slumped down into my chair.

Alba touched my arm and gave it a little squeeze. "What kind of a record?" Alba asked the officer for me.

"I can't disclose his record. But he's got quite the past. Murder wouldn't be too out of character at this point." Detective Whitman looked at me sadly. "I'm sorry, Mercy."

Hot tears stung at the backs of my eyes. I closed my eyes

until the feeling began to recede. How in the world would I tell my mother that Reign had a criminal record and that murder wouldn't be out of character for him? What if we were trying to prove Reign's innocence and he *wasn't innocent?* The thought made my mouth go dry.

"I need a drink; do you have any water?" I asked him.

Alba stood up. "We passed a water cooler when we came in. I'll go get you a drink."

"Thanks," I whispered as my mind continued to reel.

After she'd gone, Detective Whitman leaned across the desk. "I'm sorry, Mercy. Reign's record doesn't prove that he did this, but I don't want you getting hurt. You need to be careful around him. He's got some violent charges on his record."

The word *violent* hung like a dark rain cloud over my head. I forced myself to nod. "Okay," I whispered.

"Did Harper know who killed her?" he asked me.

I shook my head. "No, she only told me what we already knew. Vaughn and Reign fought over her. Reign offered her a place to spend the night, and she went with him. She said she doesn't remember anything else until she woke up as a ghost."

"Did she tell anyone that she was going to be in town?" he asked.

"She said she remembers telling her sister Elena that she was going to be in town."

Detective Whitman nodded. "I've got an interview set up with Elena later today."

Alba returned with a small paper cone filled with water. She handed it to me, and I swallowed it down in one big gulp. "Thanks," I said to her with a tight little smile. "How are Harper's parents doing?"

"Not good. They have a lot of regrets. I guess their relationship hasn't been the best these past few years. And now that she's gone and it's too late they are really upset. Which is to be expected."

"I'll talk to Harper about that, maybe she can offer some solace to her family in regards to their relationship."

"I'm sure they'd like that," he said quietly. He rearranged the files on his desk. A picture of a man was paper clipped to one of the files.

"Who is that?" I asked and pointed to the picture.

"That's Vaughn Carlisle, Harper's boyfriend."

"You've got a file on him too. Does he have a record?" I asked.

Detective Whitman gave me a nod of approval. "Good question. He *does* have a record. Again, I'm not going to share his record either, but let's just say he and Reign are still in the running for best bad guy in town."

I glanced down at my watch. It was getting late. "Okay, well, we have to get back to the dorms. We have a lot to do. Thanks for the information."

I PACED MY DORM ROOM UNEASILY, WEARING A PATH IN THE plush grey carpeting. Holly, Alba, and Sweets had gone back to their rooms after we shared with them that Harper had been poisoned. Jax and Reign remained. I knew Sneaks would be back at any moment and I'd have to tell my mother what Detective Whitman had told me about Reign. How would I do that with him standing right there?

As I paced, I noticed the sun was reflecting off of an object on the windowsill in front of Jax's desk. "What's this?" I asked Jax, lifting the object which turned out to be a small shot glass that said Jimmy's on it.

Jax lunged off of the top bunk in a panic to snatch the glass from my hand. "Oh, that, I – uh," she stammered.

Her reaction coupled with the name Jimmy's on it made me stomp a foot at her. "JaclynRose Stone! Did you steal this from Jimmy's?"

Reign raised his eyebrows and snorted. "JaclynRose Stone? Seriously, sis?"

Sis? Since when was I, *sis*? I ignored Reign's response, and Jax ignored my question.

"Jax! Did you steal this from Jimmy's?" I asked her again.

She stashed the glass on the top shelf of her closet. "It was a memento."

"A memento? Of a murder?" I asked her in disbelief. "Who does that?"

"No, not a memento of a murder," she said shyly. "Perhaps I neglected to tell you that I might be a *bit* of a klepto-maniac."

Reign laughed again. "How are you a *bit* of a klepto?"

Jax smiled shyly at him. "Fine, I'm not a *bit* of a klepto, I *am* a klepto. I've been to the doctors. It has something to do with my OCD," she confided.

When I wouldn't toss a smile her way, she crumbled. "Whaaat? I can't control it. Sometimes when I'm in a stressful situation, I take something. I'm sorry! I can't help it!"

"Ugh," I grunted. My friends were just so weird! My life was just so weird. It made me wish, once again, that I'd never been born with the gift of being a witch. If I hadn't been born a witch I'd be normal right now, and I would never have gotten in trouble back in Dubbsburg, and I'd be home right now with my mom. Or I'd have a boyfriend, and we'd be hanging out together like a normal couple.

That made me think of Hugh. Hugh was the first person in a long time that actually made me feel normal. I suddenly wished I was with him. I pulled my phone out of my pocket and shot him a quick message. "Hey, Hugh, want to hang out later?"

"Who are you texting?" Reign asked, looking over my shoulder.

I pulled my arms away from him and shoved my phone back in my pocket. "None of your beeswax, *brother*."

"Oh!" he sang. "You're texting the cowboy. What do you see in that jerk anyway?"

"Hugh's not a jerk," I told him angrily. The walls suddenly felt like they were closing in on me and I couldn't breathe. "Who shut the windows?" I asked in a panic.

Reign looked at me like I was crazy. "I did. It looked like it was going to rain."

I sprinted over to them and slid them open with a grunt. The brisk fall air poured in, and I sucked in a deep cleansing breath. That felt so much better.

"We leave the windows open. For Sneaks," Jax confided in Reign.

"Who is Sneaks?" Reign asked.

"My cat," I told him quickly. I didn't need him knowing about Mom's charming little party trick. I'd save that for another day when I wasn't feeling so uneasy about my brother.

"Listen, Reign. I'm getting really tired. I need a nap. Have you found a place to stay yet?" I asked him.

He pulled his smartphone out of his back pocket. "Yes, I just made online reservations at a bed and breakfast across from the police station."

"Nice, Detective Whitman will love that," I assured him grouchily.

"Someone definitely needs a nap," he said to Jax as he pointed at me.

"Quit!" I hollered.

"I'll go so you can unwind. She's all yours, JaclynRose," Reign hollered as he left the room.

Jax shot me an evil look. "It's Jax!"

CHAPTER 9

S even o'clock couldn't come fast enough. Dressed in a pair of skinny jeans, my high-tops and what I considered to be my "nice sweater" – a rust colored duster over my 'Keep Calm and Witch On' t-shirt – I skipped out the door and down the stairs to meet Hugh. Someone had left the front doors and the doors to the quad open, and a perfect fall breeze was zipping through Winston Hall's lobby.

I had managed to take a nap, and between that and the idea of getting to see Hugh again, I felt lighter than I had all day. I let one finger sneak out of the extra-long sleeves where I had my hands buried and used it to push my glasses up the bridge of my nose. Then I tucked a strand of red hair that had escaped my braid behind my ear.

Hugh was in the courtyard waiting. I had the urge to run towards him and plant myself snuggly in his arms. I could use those big cowboy muscles wrapped around me right about now. It had been a tough day and a tough couple of weeks. My problem was that I had a hard time convincing myself to do such a thing. Public displays of affection came easily to girls like Holly and Jax, but to me, hugging Hugh would have shown vulnerability and I wasn't very good at doing that.

Instead, I saddled up to him and bumped his hip with mine. "Hey," I said with a shy smile.

"Hey, yourself," he drawled back. Gosh, I'd missed that drawl. Something about it comforted me. "I'm awful glad you texted. I wanted to hang out with you again, but I know you been busy as a one-legged man at an ass-kicking convention."

I chuckled. "All out of ass-kicking's tonight," I said honestly. "I just need a night to relax a little."

"So, what would you like to do, Miss Mercy Mae? You want to go into town and have some supper?" he asked. "I'm hungry as a poor man grocery shoppin' on payday."

"Yeah, I'm pretty hungry too," I said rubbing my stomach. Hugh threw one of his thick arms around my shoulder, and together we ambled towards his pickup in the men's parking lot. "Tonight, let's not go somewhere all 'date fancy,' let's just go somewhere we can relax and be ourselves like a café or diner or something," I suggested.

Hugh squeezed my shoulder a little closer to him. "That sounds like my idea of the perfect night."

Downtown Aspen Falls was quite the thriving kitschy community. The big waterfall in the middle of the town square was the epicenter of all the activity. With cute little boutiques, shops, bakeries, restaurants, and bars radiating out from it, it was easy to find a simple little diner to hunker down in.

We chose a booth in the back where no one really seemed to notice us except the frumpy waitress, but even she seemed eager to forget we were there. There was a window across from us that faced the alley and let in just enough light to remind us that it was still daytime outside.

We both ordered a burger, basket of fries, and a soda then we settled into the booth, getting comfortable with our backs against the wall and our legs and feet up on the fake leather seats. Hugh had hung his cowboy hat up on the coat hook on the side of the table, giving me a really good look at him.

"I like the way your hair curls up around your ears when you take your hat off," I told him with a little smile.

"When I was younger I used to hate the curls. I always had my mom cut them off." He smiled, flashing his perfectly straight teeth.

I yawned and leaned my head back against the wood paneling on the walls. "It feels so good just to sit here and relax."

I could feel his eyes on me, but I didn't move. "You're awfully pretty when you're relaxed."

I could feel heat rising up into my cheeks. "You're awfully sweet when you want to be," I laughed.

"I'm not trying to be sweet, Mercy Mae, I'm being honest."

I turned my head to look at him. His hazel eyes were trained on me causing me to fidget in my seat. "How was your day?" I asked him awkwardly, changing the conversation.

He took the hint that he was making me uncomfortable and leaned his head back against the wall. "It was long. I worried about you mostly."

"You did?" I asked him in surprise.

"Mmhmm," he murmured with his eyes closed.

"Why were you worried about me?" I asked. Besides my

mother, I'd really never had anyone worry about me. It was a new feeling.

He shrugged. "Oh, just because of everything happening with your brother." He sat up in the booth and put his feet back down on the floor. "How was your day?"

I sat up too, curling my legs up underneath me in the booth as I faced him. "Oh, it was a day. I found Harper's ghost," I revealed carefully.

"Ahh, the ghost appeared, that's gotta be mighty helpful."

I wrinkled my nose. "Eh, she didn't know much. She was poisoned. Detective Whitman told me that. She really didn't know what hit her."

"What else did Detective Whitman know?" Hugh asked.

I pulled my legs up underneath me tighter and leaned forward onto my elbows. "Ugh," I groaned.

Hugh tilted his head sideways. "What happened?"

"He just doesn't have much nice to say about Reign."

"Like what?"

"He's got a record."

Hugh nodded. "I guessed as much. What kind of record?"

I didn't want to say it, but I knew I had to be honest. "A violent one."

Hugh's eyes opened wide as he gave me a single nod. "Yup. I never felt right about that kid."

"Kid," I nearly snorted soda out my nose. "He's older than you by a year."

That did nothing to impress Hugh. "Listen, a guy like that ain't worth the price of the shoes he's wearing."

My head snapped back. "Hugh! That's my brother."

Hugh hung his head. "I'm sorry, darlin', but he's shady as an oak tree. He's got secrets. I can read a guy like that.

He's trouble. And I don't want you gettin' caught up in his trouble."

My stomach began to churn. Why did this have to be happening? Why was my stupid brother ruining a date with Hugh again?

"Can we talk about something else?" I lamented.

Hugh reached across the table to take my hands in his. "I'm sorry, Mercy Mae, what would you like to talk about?"

"I don't know. Movies?" I muttered.

Hugh chuckled. "I haven't watched a movie in probably well over a year."

Suddenly, from the window, I caught a glimpse of a man in the alley behind the restaurant. The discovery gave me renewed life and I sat up straight in my chair. "That's Vaughn Carlisle!" I told Hugh.

"Who's Vaughn Carlisle?"

"He's the boyfriend. Harper's boyfriend. Detective Whitman says he's got a record too."

Hugh spun around in his seat to follow my gaze. "I don't see anyone in the alley."

"Well, he's not there now, but he was. I saw him. I know it was him. Detective Whitman had a picture of him on his desk. Maybe we should go see what he's up to – skulking around in a back alleyway. That's pretty suspicious."

"He was skulking? How exactly does one skulk?" Hugh asked me with a mischievous smile.

"I don't know, you know, he sneaks around in alleyways and acts all suspicious. Like Vaughn was just doing. Come on. We should go check it out."

Hugh gestured towards the empty table. "But we haven't even had supper yet! And I'm starving!"

"We'll come back!" I promised as I scooted out of the booth.

Hugh hung his head, but scooted out too and stood next to me, grabbing his cowboy hat. "You owe me one, darlin'."

"Fine, I owe you another one," I smiled.

He chucked me under the chin as his hazel eyes met mine squarely. "You remember that, now."

I gave him a happy little smile and he threw his arm over my shoulder. "We'll be right back," he hollered at our waitress as we breezed out the door.

"Now what do we do?" I asked him.

"Oh, I have to have the plan for this stakeout?"

"Well, you're a cowboy, don't you know what to do?"

With his hands on his hips, he shook his head and raised his eyebrows at me. "I'm a cowboy. I ride horses and tend cattle. I don't sneak around in alleyways after criminal types."

I sighed. "Fine, follow me." I led us around the building on the sidewalk until we got to the back alley. I flattened myself against the brick wall and then carefully poked my head around the corner. The alley was empty. "All clear," I whispered to Hugh.

"Okay, Stephanie Plum," Hugh whispered back.

My head snapped around to catch him winking at me. "Stephanie Pl...? I thought you said you didn't watch movies," I snapped and playfully swatted his arms.

"I might have a thing for Katherine Heigl," he shrugged as I swatted at him again. He laughed but followed me around the corner as I led us into the alleyway.

The alley was empty. Together we searched every nook and cranny and parked car between the businesses. There were several back doors though and it was entirely possible that Vaughn had gone into one of them. "Do we wait for him to come out or do we not?" I gnawed on my lips as I looked in both directions.

"We give up. Come on, darlin'. I'm starving. Let's go eat. It might not have even been him anyway."

Suddenly a door slammed somewhere in the alley. I shoved Hugh backwards into a shallow doorway and stuffed the two of us into it. His hat toppled off his head and he caught it with the tip of his boot and held it to his side. With our bodies smashed together so tightly, I could feel Hugh's heart pounding against my cheek. It was the closest physical contact we'd ever had, which made me a bit uneasy. I looked up and our eyes met. For a split second, I thought he was going to lean down and kiss me, but then we heard a voice break the silence.

"No, I won't be back for a few days," said the man and then silence followed.

"Cut me a break, my girlfriend just died," he said again. It was pretty obvious we were hearing one side of a phone conversation.

"I don't know, maybe next Tuesday."

I looked up at Hugh and pointed towards the voice. I really wanted to peek out and make sure it was Vaughn. He shook his head at me as if to say 'No, don't do it.'

"With her sister."

My eyes opened wide and my head cocked to the side.

"They are pretty upset....yeah, I know....okay....yup, I'll call you when I leave town....later."

I heard feet shuffling away from us, so I held my breath and poked my head out of the doorway just a fragment. A stocky man was walking towards one of the doorways we'd passed in the alley. He opened the door and went inside, slamming it shut behind him.

I lurched out of the doorway with enthusiasm. "That was him!" I whisper yelled at Hugh. I threw a fist into the air. "Yes!"

Hugh chuckled. "So it was him? What does that mean?"

"He's staying with Harper's sister, Elena," I said.

"He didn't say that?" Hugh questioned.

"Fine, his exact words were, *'with her sister.'* What else would he be doing *with her sister*?"

Hugh took off his hat and rubbed the top of his head and then put his hat back on. "Okay, it *could* have been what he meant, but you don't know for sure."

"I will!" I hollered and picked up my phone.

Hugh looked at me curiously. "What are you doing?"

"Googling Elena Bradshaw's address."

"Why?"

"There are apartments up there," I said and pointed to the top of the building that Vaughn had just disappeared inside.

I did a quick Google search and found exactly what I was looking for. "Elena Bradshaw lives at 420 W. Orange Street, Apt. 2B."

"Geez, you found *that* on Google?" Hugh asked with surprise.

I laughed. "You can find *anything* on Google."

"Maybe you should Google that brother of yours," Hugh suggested, only half joking.

I gave it only a second of thought. "Maybe sometime I will, but right now, we need to find out what our address is."

Hugh nodded and the two of us walked back towards the sidewalk. The building Vaughn went in was on the opposite side of the alley the restaurant was on, so we walked around to the front of that building. The apartments were over Quick Copy, a small copy and office supply store. The street sign on the corner of the block read Orange St.

"Ha!" I said excitedly and pointed to the sign. "Orange!"

Hugh walked up to the front of the office supply store. "420. You called it, darlin'!"

"Eee," I squealed. "Now I need to interview Elena!"

Hugh and I linked arms and headed back towards the diner. "What will interviewing Elena tell you?"

"I don't know, but isn't it interesting that Vaughn is staying with Elena?"

Hugh shook his head. "You've lost me. No, it's really not that interesting. He was her sister's boyfriend. Why is it interesting to you?"

I shrugged. "If my sister was just killed, I don't know that I'd be inviting her possible killer boyfriend into my apartment to stay with me. That makes me wonder if perhaps they have their own relationship and if *perhaps* they were in on this together."

Hugh gave me a half grin as we re-entered the diner. "I think you're reaching, Mercy Mae."

"Maybe, but I've got to do what I've got to do to get my brother in the clear."

"What you've got to do is Google that brother of yours. Put those detective skills of yours to good use."

I patted his chest lightly and smiled at him. "Don't worry, Hugh, I'll do my research and I'll *prove to you* that my brother's not as bad as everyone thinks he is."

I've got to…for my mother's sake!

CHAPTER 10

Dinner had done little to relax me, but it had given me new hope that I could prove someone else had committed Harper's murder. Hugh used his powers to draw us a beautiful sunset for the ride home. Orangey pinks lit up the horizon while he said goodbye to me at the quad doors to Winston Hall. Since Jax had interrupted us at my dorm room the night before, we'd decided to say good-night away from that distraction.

"I had another really great time," Hugh said, pausing to stare into my eyes. "Your eyes look so bright tonight."

"I've got renewed hope that I'll be able to save my brother!" I told him.

He looked disappointed. "Oh, shucks, I thought maybe it was me that put that twinkle in your eye."

My pulse thrummed a steady beat in my ears as I smiled at him. I wanted to reach out and pull his adorable face to mine and plant a big kiss on those pale pink lips of his, but I just couldn't make myself do it. It wasn't that I was shy. I wasn't a shy person, exactly. I didn't know what was wrong with me.

"You do put a twinkle in my eye, Hugh," I said simply.

"And you put one in mine," he whispered as his head lowered to mine.

"You're back!" Sweets hollered excitedly, as she came through the quad doors with an ice cream cone in her hand.

Jax and Holly came stumbling behind her. "Hi, Hughey," Jax exclaimed cheerfully. "You want some ice cream? They're having an ice cream social in the lobby tonight!"

Hugh groaned as he pulled his head back. We were interrupted once again. "Next time I'm kissing you in the truck on the way home!" he whispered in my ear.

I smiled broadly at him but felt a faint sense of relief. Kissing and all of that jazz was just foreign to me and I was thankful to be able to put that on the back burner for now. "Want some ice cream?" I asked him.

"They have sprinkles and hot fudge chocolate!" Sweets said encouragingly to Hugh.

Hugh laughed. "No thank you, ladies," he dipped his head at us. "I best be gittin' back to my room. I've got a bit of work I need to get done."

"Bye, Hugh," Holly said with a wave.

"See ya, Hughey," Jax called.

Sweets's mouth was too full of ice cream to say good-bye, so she waved instead.

"G'night, Mercy Mae, sweet dreams," he said as he turned around and walked away.

"Good night, Hugh," I called after him. "Thanks for dinner."

"Oooh, date number two," Holly cooed at me as I followed them to the marble tables in the courtyard.

"It wasn't really a date," I explained. "I just needed to get some fresh air. I was stressed out."

Jax took a big lick of her ice cream cone. "Sounds like a date to me," she remarked without taking her eyes off of her ice cream.

Sweets nodded as she smacked her lips. "Mmmhmm. If he bought you dinner, that's definitely a date."

I looked around. "Where's Alba?"

Holly groaned and rolled her eyes. "Ugh, she's in our room. She's upset about something, but she won't tell me what it is."

"Maybe it's just her personality, maybe she's not really upset about anything in particular," Jax suggested. Then she whispered, "I don't know if you guys have noticed, but she's just kind of a grouchy person."

I laughed. "Thanks for pointing that out, Captain Obvious."

Jax scrunched her nose up at me. "Sorry, I didn't know if everyone realized that."

"Yeah, she's just been extra grouchy lately. Something's up. She just won't tell me," Holly whined. "You should talk to her, Mercy. She *likes* you."

I chuckled. "Alba doesn't *like* me. She just tolerates me. You three get on her nerves."

Jax sucked in her breath and put a hand over her heart. "How do *I* get on her nerves?"

She was offended. I felt bad and knew I needed to count to ten and take a few deep breaths before I opened my mouth again. Sometimes my mouth seemed to get me into trouble. I closed my eyes and took a deep breath, slowly releasing it. When I was done, I looked up at the girls. "Sorry, girls, you don't get on her nerves, you're right, she's just a grouchy person. It's not you; it's her. I'm sorry I said that."

Jax threw an arm over my shoulder and squeezed. "Thanks, Mercy."

"I need more hot fudge," said Holly standing up. "Mercy, you want me to get you some ice cream?"

"Umm, sure. Thanks."

"What kind do you want?" she asked.

"I don't know, surprise me," I said with a smile.

Holly took her cup of ice cream and went back inside.

Jax took that as her opportunity to pounce on Sweets and me. "Sweets, I need a favor. But you *cannot* tell Holly. Neither can you, Mercy, promise?"

Sweets widened her eyes and swung them towards me as she licked her ice cream. "I don't want to keep secrets from Holly. She's one of my best friends."

"Well, I'm your other best friend and you can't tell her. Okay?"

I could tell by Sweets's expression it was killing her to not know what the big secret was and knowing might trump keeping a secret from Holly.

"Fine," she grumbled. "What?"

"Mercy?" Jax asked me.

"Why would I tell Holly anything?"

"Okay, eee," Jax squealed. "Sweets, I need you to do a matchmaking spell on me!"

I looked at Jax in surprise. "You're only seventeen. Why would you want to have Sweets do a matchmaking spell on you right now? You haven't even finished witch school yet!"

Sweets nodded vigorously. "Yeah, that doesn't seem like a very good idea. You're so young. I usually do spells on like women at least in their mid to late twenties or older!"

Jax didn't care. She clasped her hands together and slid

closer to Sweets on the bench. "Oh, puh-leeeeese, Sweets. I'm in love!"

This was the first that I was hearing of Jax being in love. Something seemed fishy. She'd never mentioned a boyfriend before today. "Who are you in love with Jax?"

"Yeah, you've never told me you were in love before," Sweets agreed as she began to nibble around the edges of her cone.

Jax trained her eyes on me nervously. "I'm in love with Reign!"

Sweets blanched. "Reign?" she asked. I could hear disappointment thick in her voice. I was sure she was just as disappointed in Jax as I was.

"Jax!" I scolded. "Reign is twenty-four-years-old. You're only seventeen. That's crazy talk."

"Nooo," she begged. "I love him!"

"You don't love him," I argued, dismissing her with a wave of my hand.

She crossed her arms angrily across her chest. "Yes, I do! He's so dreamy and he's charming and he's funny. He's perfect!"

"And he's under investigation for murdering a girl!" I added. I hated to do it. I didn't want Reign to be guilty, but I also wanted my roommate to be smarter than that.

"He didn't do it! Mercy, you know that. You know your brother didn't kill that girl," she argued.

"I hope that he didn't do it, but we don't know that yet."

Jax turned her attention back to Sweets. "Please, Sweets. You've just got to do this for me. Please say you'll do a matchmaking spell on Reign and me. Pretty please?"

Sweets winced and wouldn't make eye contact with Jax. "I don't know, Jax."

"I'll be forever grateful!" Jax begged. "Oh no, Holly's

coming back. Please, Sweets," she whispered. "Just say yes."

Sweets and I looked up. Holly was just coming through the courtyard doors. "Fine," Sweets growled grudgingly.

Jax leapt off of her seat and threw her tiny little arms around Sweets's neck. "Oh, thank you thank you thank you! I'm going to go plan out my outfit for our first date!"

Jax rushed past Holly. "Eeee," she squealed at her.

"What's she so excited about?" Holly asked us as she handed me a banana split and a spoon.

Sweets rolled her eyes with obvious annoyance. "Oh, nothing. She just thinks she's 'in love.'"

"Jax is in love? With whom?" Holly asked.

"With herself," I insisted and shot Sweets an angry look.

Holly shrugged but then her face lit up. "Listen, I'm glad I've got the two of you to myself for a moment anyway. I need a really big favor from the two of you."

Oh no.

"Mercy, I was wondering if you could set up your brother and me."

"No," I said expressionlessly.

"Stop," she said with a little laugh as she playfully slapped my hand. "And maybe, Sweets, you could do one of your matchmaking spells on Reign and me," Holly continued as if I hadn't just said no.

"Sure," Sweets said without a second thought.

"Really?"

"Yeah, sure. No problem," Sweets said and went back to finishing her ice cream.

"Sweets, you're the best!" Holly gushed and then fired me an evil glare. "I'm going to go make plans for our first date. Thanks, Sweets! I knew I could count on you."

Holly took off, taking her sundae with her. I slid my

banana split aside and leaned over the table, so Sweets and I were closer together. "What gives? Why would you promise both of them that you'd do spells on them? My brother can't marry both of them and honestly, I don't want him to marry either!"

Sweets's chocolate-covered lips curled into a mischievous grin. "I don't know," she said with a shrug.

"You do too know. What's going on?"

"Fine, but you've got to promise not to tell Jax or Holly!"

I pulled an imaginary zipper across my lips.

"I have a *huge* crush on your brother too. I'm not going to match them with him! That'd be insane. And I can't do a spell on myself, that doesn't work." She giggled incessantly.

"What is going on around here? Are you all mad? My brother is good looking, sure, but why are you all losing your marbles over him? He's the prime suspect in a murder investigation. And he's *my brother*. Isn't there some kind of rule against dating your friends' brothers?" I asked. It was appalling to me how swiftly my friends had decided to treat my brother like a piece of meat!

Sweets stopped laughing and nodded up and down with a serious expression on her face. "Uh-huh. You mean like girl code?"

"Yeah, like girl code!"

"Uh-huh, yeah, girl code doesn't apply here. The girls and I talked about it."

"You talked about whether or not girl code applies to my friends dating Reign?"

She nodded emphatically. "Yes."

"Why not?!"

She fidgeted in her seat a bit. "Well, here's the thing. You didn't grow up with Reign. So technically, he wasn't your brother until like two days ago."

"No. No. No," I said, shaking my head in disagreement. "He's been my brother since I was born. I just didn't *know* about him."

She squinted her eyes and turned her head sideways. "Well, Jax, Holly, and I already ruled on the situation," she said as if that were that. "Sorry."

"That's not how girl code works! You can't make up new rules."

"Mmm, yeah, we decided we can."

"Ugh!" I groaned. "Well, then I call witch code!"

"You can't call witch code."

"Why doesn't it apply?"

Sweets shrugged. "Because witch code isn't a real thing."

"That's so not fair!"

"Okay, well, I better get back to my room. I've got a lot of homework to do. Bye, Mercy."

Alone in the quad, I let my head fall to the table. Why were my friends so nuts? Were all witches this crazy? "Ugh!" I groaned again.

"Mercy?"

I looked up. Libby and Cinder were standing beside me, each holding a book.

"Are you alright?" Libby asked me gently.

I nodded. "Yeah, thanks. I'm just frustrated."

"Okay," Libby said with a smile. "Hey, we've been meaning to talk to you."

Cinder glanced nervously at her sister. "We met your brother today. He's really cute."

Libby's eyes opened wide as she nodded in agreement with what her sister had just said. "Really cute."

"We were wondering if maybe you could set us up with him or something?"

I looked from one to the other. "Ugh!" I hollered at them and then took off, leaving my banana split on the table.

∾

JAX AND HOLLY WERE IN MY ROOM WHEN I GOT BACK. ALL I wanted to do was find Sneaks and talk to my mom. It had been far too long since I'd talked to her last and I had so much to tell her.

"Have you seen Sneaks?" I asked Jax dejectedly.

"No. It's been a while," Jax said.

I grunted and shut the door. I couldn't hang out with Jax, Holly, or Sweets right now. They were just riding my last nerve. I paced down the hallway to Alba's room and knocked on the door.

She opened it and gave me a once over before grunting at me, "What do you want, Red?"

"The kids are getting on my nerves," I complained.

I must have said the magic words. She opened the door wider and allowed me in.

"What are you doing in here?" I asked her, sniffing around. It smelled like lemon and garlic.

"Working on a project for potions class," she grumbled.

"Well, it smells good, whatever it is."

"So what are they doing that's annoying you, besides everything?"

I threw myself down into a saucer chair in the middle of the room. "They all want my brother. I get that he's nice looking and all, but is that all they want in a guy?"

"Your brother doesn't have other good attributes?" Alba

asked absentmindedly, as she flipped through the pages of her spell book.

That was a good question. I hadn't even considered what my brother's good attributes were. I'm sure he had them. But I'd been so obsessed with the murder that I really hadn't had time to think about what was *good* about Reign. I had only been worrying about what was *bad* about him.

"I honestly have no idea. I haven't gotten to know him. And that's the other thing. Sweets is claiming that they said the girl code that says your friends can't date your brother doesn't apply to me because I don't even know him yet. They say technically, he wasn't my brother until two days ago, and that means girl code doesn't apply."

Alba chortled. "That's three brains not equaling a whole one for ya," she said grimacing.

I leaned back in the chair and rubbed my face. "I'm just so stressed out! Why does there have to be this much drama?"

Alba looked around. "You live in a dorm full of female witches. It's like the drama capital of the world."

"You don't have drama."

She shrugged. "Yeah, so?" she said flatly.

I peered at her more closely. "Wait. Why *don't you* have drama? Are you in love with my brother too?"

"I'm so *not* in love with your brother that I don't even know if I *like* your brother," she muttered.

My spine stiffened and the tiny hairs on my arms prickled. "What's wrong with my brother?"

"Red, I'm going to start lumping you in with the half-wits if you don't plug your hole."

"Why are you so cranky lately?" I asked her bluntly.

"I'm not cranky," she countered.

"Is it hormones?"

She shot me an annoyed glare. "Red," she said warningly.

"Fine. Be cranky. We can be cranky together."

We sat together quietly for a few minutes. I twiddled my fingers as my mind jumped around. First I wondered if the reason that Alba didn't like my brother was because perhaps she didn't like boys at all. I wanted to ask her, I mean it wouldn't have bothered me if she didn't like boys, but I thought it would at least be nice to know. Maybe that was the big mystery of Alba that we were all missing.

I picked at the tiny cat hairs on my sweater. It occurred to me that I hadn't seen Sneaks since earlier in the morning. Of course, when I didn't want my mother nosing around, Sneaks was constantly underfoot. And when I actually *needed* my mother she was nowhere to be found. Go figure.

"Have you seen Sneaks today?" I finally asked Alba.

"No, I haven't."

Suddenly an idea came to me. "Alba do you have any idea how my mother commandeered Sneaks?"

Alba looked up at me. "Like how she did the enchantment spell?"

"Yeah, I mean if I wanted to be able to enchant an animal or something. Do you know how to do it?"

"No, but I could do some research on it tomorrow."

"Could you? I mean, would you mind? I'd do it myself, but I've got so much going on right now," I lamented.

Alba nodded. "That's why I'm here, to learn new stuff. I can ask Stone tomorrow. I'm sure she knows the spell or at least where I can find the spell."

"Perfect," I told her excitedly. "That makes me feel better. Thanks, Alba!"

CHAPTER 11

I woke up early the next morning absolutely *sure* that Sneaks would be on my windowsill or curled up at the foot of my bed waiting for me to open my eyes. To my frustration, she wasn't. The only bright spot was a simple text that I had on my phone from Hugh.

"G'mornin', sunshine." I could hear his country twang in my head and it made me smile. I shot off a hasty reply, took a deep breath and jumped out of bed to shower and dress for the day.

When I came back, Jax was waiting to go to breakfast with me. The squad was all there. Alba and Holly on one side of the table and Sweets on the other side. Jax and I sat down next to Sweets.

"Good morning," Jax chirped brightly to the table.

"Hey," said Holly as she looked up at us. "What's on the schedule today?"

"Class and then I think we should go interview Elena after lunch," I suggested as I took a bite of my breakfast sandwich.

"Who is Elena again?" Sweets asked.

Jax looked at Sweets before digging into her breakfast. "Harper's sister."

"Why are we going to go interview Elena?"

Sweets's question made me remember that I hadn't filled the girls in on the new information that Hugh and I had discovered after supper last night. "Hugh and I saw Vaughn last night. He was in this alley, and we followed him. Turns out he's *staying* with Elena right now."

"He's, like, staying at her house?" Holly seemed confused.

"Yeah, like, sleeping there. Isn't that sort of strange?" I asked the table.

"But are they sleeping *together*?" Holly asked.

"I have no idea, but isn't that the assumption?"

Holly's head jerked back. "That's where my mind goes."

"That's always where your mind goes," Alba grumbled.

"*Anyway.* The point is, if they *are* sleeping together, that would go to motive. And maybe they were in on it together. I want to see her today, and then I think we should go past Jimmy's again and talk to Harper."

"We could bring Reign along," Jax suggested quietly, trying not to call too much attention to the fact that she had suggested it.

I sighed. I didn't want my brother and my friends inter-mingling. Something about it just really poked a hole in my boat. "Reign's not coming," I said firmly.

"But…" Holly whined.

I shook my head. "He's not coming. We need to focus, and we can't focus if Reign is tagging along."

Holly, Jax, and Sweets hung their heads.

I took the last bite of my sandwich and stood up. "Okay, I'm going to go get a macchiato and then head to class. We'll meet up after lunch."

THE FIVE OF US CLIMBED THE NARROW BACK STAIRCASE OF THE Quick Copy single file. I knocked on the only door at the top of the stairs, and together we all waited with baited breath. A blonde that looked almost exactly like Harper answered the door.

"Elena?" I asked.

She scanned the five of us curiously. Thankfully, I had made Jax leave her stupid witch hat in Sweets's car. "May I help you?" she asked.

"My name is Mercy Habernackle. My friends and I are – I mean, were, friends of Harper's. We came to pay our respects," I fudged. "May we come in?" I asked her.

She shuffled from foot to foot, and I wondered if perhaps Vaughn was there and that was why she looked so nervous. "Umm, yeah, sure. Come in," she said and opened the door to allow the five of us to pass by her.

"Have a seat," she said and gestured towards the mustard-colored sofa and love seat underneath the picture window that overlooked Orange Street. Her apartment was small but cozy and warm. It smelled of pumpkin spiced candles and burnt pizza.

"Thank you," I said with a smile. "Oh, this is Jax, Alba, Sweets, and Holly."

"Hi," she said with a nervous titter. "How did you girls know my sister?"

The rest of the girls looked at me. "Umm, that's kind of a long story," I said nervously. "She hasn't been to Aspen Falls in a really long time."

Elena's eyes appeared glassy as she gnawed on her lip. "Yeah," she whispered through a choked breath. "I've really missed her and now…," she stopped talking, as a pair of fat tears slid down her cheeks. She reached forward and grabbed a tissue from the coffee table.

"I'm really sorry about your sister," Jax said quietly.

"Thank you," Elena whispered. The pain that she was in seemed to radiate off of her, and the suspicions that I had before coming to meet her seemed suddenly silly. Why would Elena be involved with her sister's boyfriend? A sister she obviously loved very much and was devastated that she was gone. My heart tugged inside of my chest. The pain to lose a loved one was so intense. I hoped I never had to deal with that.

"Have you heard anything more on the investigation?" I asked her.

She shook her head as she dabbed at the corners of her eyes. "No. Just that she was poisoned, but I'm sure that made the paper today, so everyone knows that."

I took a deep breath. I didn't know how to handle the situation, so I just decided to take the direct approach. "Can I be honest with you, Elena? It might be kind of hard to understand."

That made her interested in what I had to say. She looked up at me with interest. "Please do."

"Okay, well, the girls and I, well, we're…" I began, searching for the right way to say what I wanted to say.

"Witches?" she asked me bluntly.

I looked at the girls with wide eyes. "Yeah, how did you…?"

"Detective Whitman told my family that he had consulted with someone from the Paranormal Institute and they were helping with the investigation and that someone had actually seen my sister's ghost. I assume that was you five?"

We all nodded.

She pointed towards Jax and gave us a half grin, "Her outfit kind of made me assume it was you."

"Yeah, so we just wanted to come ask you a few questions."

Elena nodded and sniffed back her tears. I could tell she was trying to turn the page from grieving sister to justice seeking sister. She sat up straight and crossed her legs, prepared to get down to work. "Sure, I'll help however I can. I want my sister's killer to pay for what they did to her and our family."

"I think the police think it was either her boyfriend or the guy she was found in bed with when she died. Do you have an opinion on either one of them?"

Elena cleared her throat and uncrossed her legs, leaning forward in her seat. "Well, I obviously never met the man she was found in bed with. From what I understand that was a one-night stand type of situation. As far as her boyfriend goes, I've never met him either, so I wouldn't know if he's the type of person that could do something like this. I wouldn't think he was, though, not the way that Harper talked about him."

Alba tipped her head sideways and gave Elena a surprised look. "You've never met your sister's boyfriend?"

Elena crossed her legs again and shifted in her seat. "No, I – uh, I mean, Harper hadn't been home in years, and her boyfriend was from Connecticut. She was bringing him home for the first time to meet the family."

Holly sprang forward with a question. "Were you surprised that your sister would have cheated on her boyfriend the night she died?"

Elena cleared her throat again. "Not really. Harper and I talked a lot on the phone. She was very clear that while she and Vaughn were a thing, they had an open relationship."

That was the first I'd heard of this. "Meaning they could see other people?"

Elena nodded but refused to make eye contact with me. "Mmhmm."

"So, did Harper have *other* relationships outside of her relationship with Vaughn?" I asked in surprise.

"Yeah, they were more just physical relationships. Vaughn was the only one she considered her boyfriend, per se. But yes, she took advantage of the fact that they agreed they could be intimate with people outside of their relationship."

Alba cleared her throat. "Do you think Vaughn was in any relationships outside of theirs?"

Elena shrugged. "Like I said, I never met the guy, so I don't have any idea."

"Your sister never told you?" Holly asked.

Jax shot forward in her seat. "I'm sorry to interrupt, but may I use your restroom?"

Elena touched her neck nervously and then stood up. "Umm, sure, I'll show you where it is."

Jax stood up too and shot Elena one of her dazzling smiles. "It's fine, just point me in the right direction, I'm sure I can't get too lost."

"Oh, it's just the first door on the right down that hallway," she said and pointed to the hallway off the kitchen.

"Thanks," said Jax as she disappeared down the hallway.

Elena watched her until she disappeared into the first door on the right as instructed. Once Jax was safely stowed away inside the bathroom, Elena visibly relaxed. By now I was sure that Vaughn was hiding somewhere in the apartment.

"I'm sorry, what were we saying?" Elena asked the rest of us.

"I asked if your sister ever told you that Vaughn was seeing other women besides her. You'd think that would bother her," Holly pointed out.

"Oh, you know, Harper never really mentioned if he was," she said. "And I don't think she could get too bothered by it, it was their agreement and she was doing what she wanted to do, so it would only be right if he got to do what *he* wanted to do."

I nodded at her emphatically as if I were buying everything she was selling, even though my bullshit meter had hit the red zone the minute she said she'd never met Vaughn before. "Right, yeah, of course," I said to appease her. "Do you think Harper had any ex-lovers that could have done this to her?"

Elena's eyes swung upwards towards the ceiling as if she were giving that question some serious thought. "I really don't think so. The last time Harper was in Aspen Falls was high school. She had boyfriends in high school, but that was so long ago, and I don't remember any of them ending on bad terms or her ever speaking of anyone like that."

"Did you know that Harper was coming to Aspen Falls and bringing Vaughn with her?" Alba asked her.

Elena cleared her throat again and fidgeted in her seat. I could tell she was debating on whether or not to tell us the truth or not. Detective Whitman had told her that we were in contact with her sister's ghost, would she believe that enough to tell the truth – that she *knew* Harper was coming home? "Umm, yeah, Harper told me she was coming home," she finally admitted after a long pause.

"And who did you tell? That Harper was coming home, that is," Alba asked.

Elena's eyes widened. "Oh, Harper didn't want me to tell anyone that she was coming home. She said she wanted to surprise our parents."

"And you heeded her wishes?" I asked, seeking clarification.

"Uh-huh," Elena nodded.

Just then Jax emerged from the bathroom. Elena's gaze rested intently on her until she was seated next to the rest of us.

I looked at the girls. "Do we have any more questions for Elena?" I asked them.

They all kind of shook their heads.

"Oh! I almost forgot one of the main reasons I wanted to come and see you. Harper has asked for us to bring you to her," I shared. "She doesn't want to leave the Bed & Brew, so I told her I would try and bring you to her. That is, if you're up to it?"

Elena looked understandably hesitant at the idea of seeing her dead sister's ghost.

"Of course we understand if that's too much for you," Sweets interjected.

Elena took another long moment to consider the request and then sucked up a deep breath. "I can do it," she said unconvincingly.

"Harper will appreciate it," I said, trying to give her more of a positive reason to go to Jimmy's Bed & Brew.

"Yeah," she said exhaling a deep breath. "Are you going over there now?"

I stood up, "Yeah, I think we're all done here. The girls and I will head over there if you just want to meet us there?"

She gave us a tight-lipped smile. "Okay, yeah, I've got a few things to finish up here and then I'll just throw on a sweater and my shoes and be over there in say, a half an hour?"

I nodded at her and gave her an agreeable smile.

The girls all stood up, and we headed towards the door. "Thanks, Elena. I know you just made your sister very happy."

CHAPTER 12

"Hurry up, girls! We've got to get to Jimmy's quick. I want a minute to speak to Harper before Elena gets there." I jogged across the street to where we'd parked the car.

Sweets sighed as she caught a whiff of something delicious from a bakery nearby. "Oh, I smell apple pie!" she gushed.

I rushed back to her and linked my arm with hers, dragging her towards the car. "No time for pie right now, Sweets. We've got work to do."

Sweets stopped in the middle of the street. "But my blood sugar is low," she complained.

"We just had lunch," I argued.

"I'm hypoglycemic," she retorted.

"No you're not," Alba shot back.

Sweets shrugged and kicked a pebble on the road. "I might be. You don't know."

"Ugh," I groaned. "Sweets, we need to get to the tavern before Elena gets there."

"There's always time for pie," she groaned.

Jax gave me a sweet smile. "Oh, come on, Mercy Bear, there's always time for pie."

"Don't call me that."

"Why not? That's what your mom calls you," Jax pointed out with a shrug.

"That's different. She's my mother."

"So?"

"Fine, I'll start calling you JaclynRose, that's what your mother calls you," I said with a little laugh.

Jax deflated. "Fine," she spat out. "But there's still time for pie. Let Sweets have her pie."

"Ugh, make it snappy," I growled at Sweets.

Jax, Holly, and Sweets all made a dash to the bakery around the corner.

"I can't believe it. They're *all* getting pie!" I rolled my eyes and leaned back against the trunk of Sweets's car.

Alba slunk backwards, too. "We have time. Elena can wait downstairs while you go talk to Harper. I'll keep her busy."

That relaxed the tension in my shoulders slightly. "Okay, thanks. You find anything out about that spell I asked you about."

"I did, I asked Stone about it. She let me borrow an animal control spell book that has that spell in it. I haven't had time to look it over though. We can do the spell tonight; she said we can practice in the lab at school if we want."

"Perfect," I told her.

"You realize we'll need an animal for you to control. Do you have an animal you're going to use?"

That thought hadn't occurred to me yet. "Mmm, no. I guess I don't. Maybe we should stop at a pet shop?"

She nodded.

"I saw a pet shop around the corner from the Quick Copy. Let's go see what we can find."

We walked back across the street and around the corner. Two doors down from the Quick Copy was a small pet shop. A bell jingled when we opened the front door, and immediately a puppy sprang out of nowhere and attacked my ankle.

"Hey, little guy," I gushed at the beautiful chestnut-colored puppy that was rolling about by my feet. He was no bigger than a teddy bear, and his curly hair was just as silky smooth as one. He begged to be petted.

"He's quite the little looker," Alba said with a smile. That was how adorable this puppy was. Alba actually cracked a smile. Miracles can happen.

"Yeah, he is," I grinned. The puppy playfully nipped at my hand as I scratched his undercarriage.

"He's a Cavapoo," said a female's voice from the back of the shop.

Alba and I followed the voice to see the pet shop attendant walking towards us.

"We just got him in this week," she said. "He's a mix between a Cavalier King Charles Spaniel and a Poodle. Great little guy, so loving and sweet."

"Does he have a name?" I asked.

"He came in with the name Chesney. But he's young enough you could probably change it."

"Ohhhh, Chesney!" I cooed. "It's so fitting! Who would ever change that?"

"He's cute, but you can't seriously want to get a dog, can you?" Alba asked me. "I thought maybe we'd get a hamster or a goldfish or something."

"Why would I want to control a goldfish?"

Just then Holly, Sweets, and Jax passed by the window

of the pet store. I popped my head outside. "We're in here," I called.

The girls came running in with their Styrofoam containers of pie, and when they saw Chesney at our feet, they went wild.

"Oh, I want a puppy," Holly cooed.

"We're not getting a puppy," Alba growled.

"Can *we* get a puppy?" Jax begged me.

"You're not getting a puppy," Alba barked again.

"He *is* pretty cute…"

Alba sighed. "I thought we were in a hurry."

Sweets sneezed as she scratched the top of Chesney's head. "I think I'm allergic."

"It's probably just the pet shop," Holly said.

"He'd live in our room anyway," Jax pointed out. "But you could visit him. Please, Mercy, can we get him?"

I leaned my head sideways. I could feel myself relenting. He was too cute to pass up. "But we aren't allowed to have pets in the dorm."

Jax waved a hand in front of her face. "Oh, psh, I have connections," she said with a laugh.

"If you're sure?"

"Oh, I am, I am! Plus, we won't exactly have to tell anyone about him. Wait. What's his name? Do we get to name him?"

"He already has a name," said Alba.

"Ohhh," Jax pouted.

"His name is Chesney," the lady told Jax.

"Oh, Chesney! That's so cute!" said Jax, scooping him up. He nuzzled her cheek and then licked her face. She giggled like a five-year-old. "I love you, Chesney."

"I guess it's settled, we'll take the dog," I told the sales lady, pulling my mom's credit card out of my back pocket.

We spent fifteen minutes on adoption papers and picking out a few toys and some food for the puppy and then left with him in my arms.

"I can't believe you bought a dog," Alba groaned as we walked back to the car with Chesney cuddling my neck.

"You like him, I know you do," I pointed out with a big grin.

"So, that doesn't mean anything. Dogs are a lot of work."

I shrugged and rubbed my face against Chesney's soft fur. "We're in college. It's not like we're working sixty hours a week or something. One of us is always around."

"We better hustle, Elena is probably already over at the bar," said Alba.

We all hustled to the car and exactly three minutes later we were standing in the middle of Jimmy's Bed & Brew with Chesney in tow. Elena was, in fact, waiting for us at the bar when we got there.

"There you are," Elena said as she turned around with a glass of ice water in her hands. "I thought you were coming straight over."

I held up Chesney. "Sorry, we got distracted."

I nudged Holly in the ribs as we got closer to the bar.

"Hi, Jimmy," she purred excitedly.

Jimmy scanned the five of us. He recognized us immediately. "What are you doing back here?"

"We came to see you!" Holly exclaimed. "I brought you a piece of pie. I hope you don't mind!"

Jimmy looked at the pie and then at Holly. She was wearing a sweater that cinched just under her breasts, causing them to plunge forward more than usual. One of these days those breasts were going to hurt someone.

Jimmy's mouth curled up into a small grin as she seated herself at the bar right in front of him.

"I'd eat a piece of your pie," he told her. "I just hope you didn't bring that troublemaking murderer back with you."

That caused Elena's gaze to shoot up towards me. "What troublemaking murderer?"

"Reign Alexander, the guy Harper was fooling around with, we were interviewing him earlier," I told her. I didn't think it was necessary to tell her that Reign was my brother. That might make her clam up and right now, we needed her talking.

"Oh," she said. Then she stood up and walked over to me and whispered in my ear. "I'm ready to go see Harper now."

"Okay, just give me a minute with her first. I'll come and get you when she's ready to see you."

Elena nodded and sat back down at the bar with Sweets, Holly, and Jax who were already seated and working on devouring their pie. Alba gave me a little nod as she leaned against the counter at the end of the bar.

While Holly had Jimmy properly distracted, I made a mad dash with Chesney for the stairs. Quietly we made our way to the second floor and back to the room that I knew Harper would be waiting for me.

"Harper," I whispered loudly, as I entered the room and shut the door behind me. "Harper!"

I heard a small noise come from the closet. I opened the door and found Harper seated on the floor of the closet again, hugging her legs. "Harper! Why are you in the closet again?"

She stood up and gave me a sad face. "It's dark in the closet. I just want it to be dark. I'm so sad that I'm dead. I don't want it to be bright and sunshiny all day."

My heart sank for her. It would be such a horrible thing to be dead and still running around as a ghost. "I brought you two surprises," I practically sang to her, trying to lure her out of the closet.

That did the trick. Harper lunged forward out of the closet and into the room.

"Oh! A puppy! You brought me a puppy?" she asked as a brilliant smile covered her face. "What am I supposed to do with a puppy, Mercy? I'm dead!"

I laughed. "I just brought you the puppy to see. I'm not going to leave him here. Isn't he cute?"

"He made me smile, that's for sure," she agreed. Then she looked down at her hands. "I wish I could pet him. I can't touch anything."

"Have you tried?" I asked her. "Some ghosts can, you know."

"I've tried touching things in the room. It doesn't work."

"Well, I brought you a better surprise anyway," I told her.

"You did? What?"

"Guess?"

"Did you convince Elena to come and see me?" she asked excitedly.

"Yes! I did! She's downstairs right now," I told her.

"Well, bring her up!"

I scratched my scalp as I debated how to break the bad news to her. "I wanted to talk to you first. Here's the thing, Harper. I have a suspicion, and I thought maybe you could kind of hint around with Elena and find out if it's true."

"What do you mean?"

"Elena told us that she's never met Vaughn. Is that true?"

Harper put a hand on her hip. "No, she met Vaughn.

Elena came out to see me once in Connecticut. That was about two years ago. She met him then for sure."

"Why would she lie to us about that?" I asked Harper.

"I have no idea. Maybe she just forgot she'd met him. It was a while ago."

"Elena also mentioned that you and Vaughn have an open – well an open relationship," I finally just spat out.

Harper's jaw dropped open. "Sort of. I mean how did she…? I never told Elena that!"

"You never told Elena that you and Vaughn had an open relationship? Then how did she know that?" I asked Harper.

Harper shook her head. "I have no idea! I can't believe she told you that I told her that!"

"But did you?"

"Did I what?"

"Have an open relationship with Vaughn?"

Harper's pale face blushed pink. "Sort of. It was complicated."

"Were you allowed to sleep with other men?"

"Sometimes."

"Was he allowed to sleep with other women?"

"Do we have to talk about this?" she asked, I could tell this line of questioning was making her uncomfortable.

"We don't have to, but I'm trying to understand why Elena would have lied to us," I pointed out.

"Yeah," she said softly.

"Should I bring her up here? You can tell me what I should ask her."

"Okay, I'm ready," Harper said nodding her head as she sat down gently on the bed.

I nodded and sat Chesney on the floor. "I'll be right back," I said to the two of them.

Carefully I peeked my head out the door and then tiptoed down the stairs. Holly was rattling on and on to Jimmy about how hot Tom Cruise was in the movie Cocktail. "Can you pour drinks like that?" I heard her ask as I cautiously made my way down the stairs.

When I was almost to the bottom, I peeked my head around the opening to the first floor and caught Alba's eye. I nodded at her and she, in turn, poked Elena in the back. Holly, knowing what the plan was, worked at getting Jimmy's attention to follow her as she moved around the other side of the bar. "Oooh, what kind of drink is this, it looks yummy," she cooed as she picked up a bottle from behind the bar. Jimmy swung around to take it out of her hands while Elena hightailed it up the stairs unnoticed.

"Hurry, in here," I whispered from Harper's room.

Elena slunk into the room, and I shut the door behind her. "Where's Harper?" she asked immediately.

"She's in here," I told her. "You just won't be able to see her, but I can communicate between the two of you."

"That's kind of awkward," she told me.

"Tell her not as awkward as that night she accidentally tripped over the sprinkler head and broke her ankle when we were on vacation in Florida," Harper said to me.

"Ha!" I said with a little laugh.

"What's so funny?"

"Harper said to tell you that it's not as awkward as that night you accidentally tripped over the sprinkler head and broke your ankle on vacation in Florida."

Elena's eyes nearly bugged out of her head. She clapped a hand over her mouth.

"I told you, Harper's here," I said with a little laugh. Being an intermediary between ghosts and people they used to know could be fun sometimes.

"Wow! Hi, Harper," Elena said shyly.

"Tell her I said, hey sister-sister," Harper sang with a smile.

"She says 'hey sister-sister,'" I passed on the greeting.

Elena smiled behind wet eyes. "That was from a show we used to watch. She used to call me sister-sister. Wow. I can't believe she's here. Tell her I miss her so much."

"She can hear you," I whispered to her. "You just can't hear her."

"I miss you, Harper, and I love you so much, and I'm so sad that you're gone," Elena told the dead air around her.

I pointed at the bed. "She's sitting on the bed." I scooped up Chesney, and the two of us sat down at the little table and chairs underneath the window.

"Tell her I love her and miss her too."

I repeated her sentiment to her sister.

"Ugh, this is so hard," Elena said as the tears began to cascade down her cheeks.

"I know," I agreed.

Harper looked equally pained as she sat on the bed, but I knew she wasn't able to cry no matter how much she wanted to. "Ask her why she told you that she'd never met Vaughn before."

"Harper wants to know why you told the girls and me that you'd never met Vaughn before."

Elena looked down at the wooden floorboards and shrugged. "I don't know. It just came out that way."

"Ask her how she knew about the open relationship thing," Harper instructed.

"Harper asked how you knew about the open relationship she had with Vaughn. She said she never told you that," I told Elena.

Elena took a deep breath as color flooded her cheeks. "I'm sure she told me."

Harper shook her head insistently. "Nope, I know I didn't. I thought she'd tell me I needed to leave Vaughn. I knew my family wouldn't like that."

"She's insistent she didn't tell you. Maybe Vaughn told you?" I suggested lightly.

Elena didn't speak.

"Harper wants to know why Vaughn is staying at your apartment right now," I said. Harper's head snapped back to stare at me open mouthed. I hadn't gotten around to telling her that, but I needed to know the answer.

"Vaughn is staying with my sister?" Harper asked, stunned.

I didn't respond to her. I wanted to take in Elena's reaction. She shifted nervously from foot to foot. "She knows Vaughn is staying with me?"

I nodded.

"How does she know that? Has she been to my apartment?" Elena's face was crimson red.

"Yeah, she has," I lied.

Harper trained her eyes on her sister.

"Oh my gosh," Elena cried, her hands covered her face and she backed up against the wall and slid to the floor. "She saw us together, didn't she?"

Harper's jaw dropped. "Are they sleeping together?"

"Harper said she knows you're sleeping together," I half whispered to Elena.

Elena's shoulders began to shake with her sobs. "Oh my God, I'm so sorry, Harper," she bawled. "I didn't mean for it to happen, but it happened."

Harper stood up and went to the window. She couldn't look at her sister anymore.

"It was Vaughn! He made a pass at me the weekend that I stayed over at your house two years ago. And he pursued me!"

"Ask her if they've met over the last two years," Harper whispered to me.

I swung my eyes sadly towards Elena. I hated seeing what was happening between the sisters, but I knew this was getting us closer to solving Harper's murder. "Harper wants to know if you and Vaughn had any meetings over the last two years."

Elena's eyes were wild and distraught now. "Yes. But it was Vaughn. He wouldn't let up."

"Where?" Harper asked.

"She wants to know where."

"We went to Vegas a couple of times," Elena admitted.

"How many times?" I asked.

"I don't know, maybe two or three?" she suggested.

"You mean three or five?" I corrected.

Elena shrugged. "Okay, it was a lot. We met a lot. And it wasn't just Vegas. I flew out to Connecticut twice, and he met me out here once. I don't know how many times we met."

Harper spun around. "Vaughn came to Aspen Falls?"

"Vaughn came to Aspen Falls?" I repeated.

Elena's face crumpled. "Yeah, once. He didn't meet anyone. We stayed hidden away in my apartment the whole weekend."

"Ask her if she did this to me, Mercy. Ask her!" Harper yelled.

Sadly, I looked at Elena.

"What does she want to know?" Elena asked, despondently.

"She wants to know if you did this to her."

"No!" Elena yelled at the air. "I swear, Harper. I loved you."

"Then Vaughn did this," I answered back.

"No, he couldn't have. There's no way. He would never hurt either one of us," Elena cried.

"But you don't know that. It all makes sense. Vaughn saw an opportunity to pin the murder on Reign, and he took it so he could be with you," I pointed out.

Elena shook her head and buried her face in her hands. "No!"

As her shoulders shook, I turned to Harper. She was visibly shaken. I hated what had been done to the relationship between Harper and Elena, but I felt like the truth had to be revealed.

"Make her go," Harper whispered. "I can't look at her anymore."

CHAPTER 13

The girls and I left Elena, crying at the bar, for Jimmy to deal with as we took Chesney and made a beeline for the door. On the way to the police station, I told the girls of the newest revelations. Tensions in the car were high.

"So you're sure Vaughn killed Harper?" Sweets asked as she tore around the corner at full speed.

"I'm sure," I bounced my head as if to punctuate my declaration. "Now we've established motive. We already had opportunity."

"What about means?" Holly asked.

"She was poisoned. How hard is to get your hands on poison?" I threw that question out to everyone in the car. I had no idea. I'd never tried to poison anyone before.

Jax and Holly shrugged.

"Mmm, speaking purely from a potion maker stand-point, you can order just about any obscure ingredient on the web these days," Sweets offered as her tires squealed into a parking spot at the station.

"So you're saying he would have had to order something off the internet to kill her?" I asked. "Sounds like premeditated murder to boot!"

"No, I'm just saying that he *could have* ordered poison off of the web. I don't know what she was poisoned with; maybe it could be purchased locally."

"I'm not sure they have that back on the toxicology report or not, we can ask Detective Whitman," I said. "Come on, let's go."

"Are you bringing Chesney with you?" Alba looked down her nose at Chesney disdainfully.

"Yes, I'm bringing Chesney with me. He's a baby. We can't leave a baby in the car!" I barked at her.

"Geez, I was just asking," Alba growled back.

We breezed inside. The twin cats were still perched high atop Officer Vargas's eyes. "Hello, Officer Vargas," I sang as the wind blew the door shut behind us.

He rolled his eyes. "Not you girls again. Don't you ever go to class?"

"Of course we do, silly," Jax said with a grin as Chesney licked her chin.

Alba eyed Officer Vargas. "We need to speak to Detective Whitman again, please. It's very important. We have new information in the Bradshaw murder."

"Fine," said the officer. He picked up his phone and dialed a number. "Those *girls* are here to see you again." He said, girls, as if it were a dirty word. "Okay." He hung up the phone. "You can come back."

"Thank you," I nodded as he pushed the buzzer to unlock the door. "No need to walk us back, we know the way!" The five of us marched through the central offices back to Detective Whitman's office where we filled his office to capacity.

"So the Witch Squad is back," he said, leaning back in his chair.

I narrowed my eyes at him. "How did you know the girls at school call us that?"

"Who do you think told me?" he asked with a chortle.

"Stone?" I asked.

"Of course."

"Do you and Stone have a thing together or something?" I asked him, gauging Jax's reaction out of my periphery.

"A thing?"

"Yeah, like a *romantic* thing," I asked, gesturing with my hands.

Detective Whitman leaned forward in his chair and flipped through the day planner on his desk. "I'm sorry, I don't have any appointments scheduled today to discuss my personal life."

"Touché," I said.

"Tell him," Holly whispered. "I want to get home. I have things to do!"

"Yeah, tell him," Jax agreed.

"Tell me what?" Detective Whitman asked suspiciously.

"We have some new pieces of information that we think will solve this case."

"Oh really. I think I'll have to be the judge of that." He leaned back in his chair and steepled his fingers.

"Did you know that Vaughn Carlisle and Elena Bradshaw were having an affair behind Harper's back?" I asked.

The detective's eyebrows shot up. "No, I didn't know that. How did you discover this and are you *sure*."

"Yes, we're one-hundred percent sure. I happened to see Vaughn last night in the alley behind Elena's apartment. So, today the girls and I paid her a visit. She lied to us about knowing Vaughn. She said she'd never met him before."

Detective Whitman nodded. "That's exactly what she told me too."

"Well, that's not true. We went and visited Harper's ghost, and she said that Elena spent a weekend with her and Vaughn in Connecticut about two years ago. So I confronted Elena about it. With Harper in the room, she was forced to admit that she did indeed know Vaughn. I continued questioning her until she admitted that she and Vaughn had been having an affair ever since that weekend two years ago."

"Interesting," he said.

"I asked Elena if she killed Harper and she claims that she didn't, but she also lied to us about knowing Vaughn. So I asked her if Vaughn killed Harper and she claims that she doesn't know. She doesn't *think* he did, though. So there you go, Detective. You've got motive and opportunity nailed down. Is the toxicology report back in yet?"

"Not the complete report, that takes a little time. But preliminary reports are showing arsenic poisoning. It's looking like you're making a solid case against Vaughn and Elena. Where is Elena now?"

"We just left her. She was down at Jimmy's. I'm sure Vaughn is in her apartment."

"Oh!" Jax hollered excitedly. "I just about forgot! When I went to the bathroom in her apartment I found this!" she pulled a men's deodorant stick out of her back pocket. "I assume it's Vaughn's unless Elena likes smelling like a man!"

"Jax! You stole that?" I asked her.

"What? I thought we might need evidence that Vaughn

was in her apartment!" She reached out and handed it to Detective Whitman.

He took the stick and set it down on his desk. "Um. Thanks?"

"You're welcome," Jax said proudly. "Now you can test it for like DNA or something!"

"Okay, so, now that we've cracked the case for you is my brother off the hook for this murder?" I asked him pointedly.

"Without solid evidence that Vaughn or Elena actually were the ones that poisoned Harper, we aren't completely out of the woods yet, but it does look like we have more of a case now against them. I'll have officers go out and bring them in. You can tell Reign that I'll ease up on him a little bit."

"Good!" I exclaimed.

Jax jumped up in the air. "Yay!"

"Woohoo!" Holly cheered.

Sweets clapped her hands excitedly. "Awesome!"

"Whoopie," mocked Alba in a flat tone.

Jax hustled out of the office and waved at everyone to follow her. "Come on, girls. We need to go break the good news to Reign!"

"Yeah, let's go," Holly agreed following Jax out.

I shot Detective Whitman a thankful smile. "Thanks, Detective. Keep me informed once you get the case locked down for sure against Vaughn."

"Will do, thanks for all your help, ladies," he said as we left the room.

"Bye, Detective Whitman," Jax called back. "I'll tell my mom you said hi!"

∾

Reign answered the door shirtless. His thick black hair was tousled, and his cheeks were red from the apparent nap we'd just woken him up from. "Hey, ladies," he said as the five of us piled into the room he was renting.

Holly, Jax, and Sweets each had a hug for him as they passed him by and in turn, he gave them each a kiss on the cheek. Alba just glared at him as she passed by with her hands firmly entrenched in the pockets of the hooded sweatshirt she was wearing.

I was the last to enter. "Napping?" I asked him as I sailed into the room with Chesney slung over one shoulder.

"Whoa, who's this guy?" he asked, reaching out to touch Chesney's paw.

"This is Chesney. He's mine."

"You got a dog?"

"He's a puppy," I corrected him.

"You realize a puppy is a dog, right?"

I shrugged. "We've got news for you." I eyed the girls as we stood about his bedroom in a circle. I wondered who was going to break it to him first.

"We know that Vaughn killed Harper!" Jax exclaimed excitedly, as she threw her skinny little arms around Reign's neck. Reign's arm instinctively encircled her middle, practically enraging Holly.

"What?" Reign asked in disbelief.

Not to be outdone, Holly stepped forward. "Her sister, Elena, was having an affair with Vaughn and that's why he killed her. We just told Detective Whitman! They're going to arrest them both. You're pretty much off the hook. Isn't that exciting?" As Jax let go of Reign's neck, Holly launched herself at him, catching him off guard, they tumbled backwards onto his bed, and she landed squarely on top of his bare chest.

"Oh, hey there," she said with a giggle as her breasts tumbled forward, practically knocking him out.

"Hey there, yourself," Reign said, giving her a little pat on her ample bottom.

"Okay, okay," I grumbled and pulled Holly off of my brother. "Enough of that. Detective Whitman says you're *probably* off the hook. He agrees that this was likely a whole affair gone wrong thing."

"That's so great. I'm so relieved! Thanks, sis, I really owe you," said Reign as he threw his arms around my shoulders and squeezed Chesney and me tightly. I stood there woodenly on the receiving end of affection from a brother I'd only just met two days prior. I realized I still didn't know this guy. We were related by blood, and I didn't even know him. It made me sad. Stiffly, I flopped an arm onto his back and patted it as if he had a disease I didn't want to catch.

"She's really not much of a hugger," Jax whispered to him.

He smiled at me, flashing his straight white teeth. *Dammit, why did he get all the good genes*? I wondered.

"Yeah, I'm not much of a hugger either," he admitted. "But I owed her one for all the sleuthing she's done. Hell, I owe you all a hug for everything you've done for me."

Jax was the first in line to accept a hug from Reign. He lifted her clean off of her feet, squeezed her tight and spun her around twice. Jax giggled the whole time.

He pecked Sweets on the cheek and then enveloped her in a bear hug, causing her face to flush crimson red. I knew she'd be giggling the whole way home.

When Reign got within five inches of Holly, she planted a smack on his lips before he could hug her, causing him to flush red and Jax and Sweets to fume silently. He tried to hug Alba but with a hand out in front of her, she stiff-armed him. "No hugging zone," she growled, pointing at herself with her other hand.

Reign winked at her. "Got it." Then he let out a heavy sigh. "Now things can get back to normal. You have no idea how relieved I am. You know, Mercy, there's some stuff I've been meaning to talk to you about. Maybe now that we've got all this murder stuff behind us, I can tell you."

I shook my head and waved a hand in the air. "Oh no. I've had enough, *'Mercy, I need to tell you something'* to last a year. How about we get Vaughn and Elena behind bars and let a week or even two slide by before we introduce any more drama into my life. Okay?"

Something dark flashed behind Reign's onyx eyes making me fearful of what it was he had to say. I needed to be in a better place before any life changing revelations were made. And I needed to talk to my mom and fill her in on all the details. I was sure she'd be back in our dorm room when we returned.

"We should go, ladies. Reign, let's have dinner together soon, and we'll do all of the brother-sister stuff. Like wrestle or make fun of each other or whatever it is that brothers and sisters do. Alright?"

Reign nodded. "Most definitely. I have no plans to leave Aspen Falls for a while. I came to get to know my sister, and I have nowhere else I'd rather be right now."

Holly, Jax, and Sweets shed a sigh of relief.

I pulled Alba aside as we left Reign's room. "We have *got* to work on that spell."

"Tonight," she promised.

AFTER SUPPER THAT NIGHT, ALBA, CHESNEY, AND I FOUND ourselves tucked away in the school potions lab with the spell book that Sorceress Stone had loaned to Alba.

"This spell has *got* to work," I told Alba as I nibbled on my lower lip.

"It will, we've got everything we need here."

I looked at Chesney nervously. "It's not going to *hurt* him is it? Because if it is, I just couldn't…"

Alba shook her head. "No, I asked Stone, she said it doesn't. She said animals used in these kinds of spells only feel like they are in a fog or haze. We're essentially putting a veil over his eyes. It won't hurt at all, and it's only temporary of course, so when you aren't conjuring, he will just be a normal dog."

"Good," I said as I scratched the top of Chesney's head. "He's such a cute little guy."

Alba rolled her eyes but then relented and scratched Chesney's head too. "Yeah, I guess he is. Okay, here's the list of what we need. Ginger root," she called out.

I scanned the length of the spice cabinet behind us. "Got it!"

"Dash of empherisious leaf," she added.

"What letter does that start with?"

"E."

"Got it," I said and slammed a little bottle down on the lab counter.

"Half a teaspoon of hogstooth extract."

"Hogstooth extract, got it!" I sat the liquid down next to the other two jars.

"And two spider eyes," she said.

"Eww, well that's gross. Tell me I don't have to drink this!"

"No, it cooks down into a paste. We'll encircle both of your eyes with the potion, and you'll have a chant."

"And then I'll be able to use Chesney like mom uses Sneaks?"

Alba nodded. "That's the goal."

I opened the little containers and carefully put each item into a small cauldron of boiling water, and we watched as the bubbling water enveloped the ingredients. "Okay, now what?" I asked.

She shrugged, peering down at her spell book. "Now we wait. The water needs to boil the eyes down, and that ginger root takes a little while to absorb the rest of the ingredients."

"So what do you want to do while we wait?" I asked her, scratching behind Chesney's ears.

"Sit quietly and relax?" she suggested.

"Or we could talk," I countered. "I know something's been bothering you, Alba. Care to share?"

She looked at me with annoyance. "What do you think?"

I sat Chesney on the counter and jumped up to sit beside him, letting my legs dangle off the edge of the counter. "I think you're missing your family."

"I think it's none of your business, Red."

"You can confide in me, you know," I told her sincerely. "I can keep a secret."

"I bet you tell that cowboy everything," she spat as she hopped up on the counter across from me.

"I tell him some stuff, but I don't need to tell him everything. Sisters before misters, eh?"

That made her laugh. "If you say so."

We sat quietly, swinging our legs and lost in thought.

Finally, I looked up at her again. "Nothing to share?"

She shrugged.

"Okay, well, I'll share then. I'm frustrated with my brother."

Alba didn't look surprised. "Why is that?"

I shrugged. I didn't know if I should tell her what was really in my mind or if I should sugar coat it. Finally, I just said it. "Because he exists, I guess." Once I had spoken the words, I immediately regretted putting them out into the universe, but it was too late to take them back.

Alba gave me a half smile. "That's not really his fault, though."

I looked down at my shoes and then squeezed my eyes shut tightly to keep any tears away. "Yeah, I guess not."

"Look, Red. Family is family. They are really all we've got in the world. It's not Reign's fault that he didn't get to grow up with you and your mom. I bet if he could pick right now, he'd choose to have grown up with you. But he didn't get to pick. He didn't get to choose being born either. Now, I'm not Reign's biggest fan, but I feel like he really wants to get to know you. That's got to count for something, right?"

I nodded solemnly. Maybe she was right. Maybe I was just being a brat.

"Alright, so give the guy a chance. Get to know him. I think the fact that we had this whole murder surrounding your meeting has really skewed your opinion of him and that's not fair to Reign. I know you're confident he didn't kill Harper, but there's probably still got to be that lingering doubt."

"A little bit," I admitted. "I can't help it."

"Yeah, see there's the problem. If Reign had come to Aspen Falls, riding in on a white horse, I don't know if we'd be having this conversation right now. You'd probably have taken to him. But the fact that he came in under such mysterious circumstances has clouded your brain. Maybe you should give him a chance."

"Okay," I said quietly. "Thanks, Alba." I gave her a thankful little smile.

She nodded at me.

"How'd you get so smart?" I asked her.

She laughed. "I'm hardly smart, Red. I just have a bit of life experience."

"You do?" It hit me then that I knew very little about Alba's life before the Institute. "Tell me about your family."

"What's to tell?"

"I know your family has a furniture moving company. Who is in the business?"

"My pops started the business. My two older brothers, Jerry and Vinnie, work for him and this other guy, Tony. I used to work for Pops too until I moved here."

I noticed Alba's eyes shifting when she mentioned the other guy, Tony. My spidey senses went a little crazy and I thought maybe now would be a good time to answer some of my questions about Alba.

"What made you decide to go to college if you have a family business back home?"

"Pops said one of us needed to be able to run the business if we are ever going to let him retire. The boys didn't want to do it, so they volunteered me."

"What did your mom think of that?"

Alba shrugged. "I don't know. She didn't say much. My grandmother and my Aunt Gloria live with my parents too. I think Mom was just happy to have one less mouth to feed for awhile. When I move back to Jersey, I'll be moving out of the house."

I raised my eyebrows. "Really? You're going to live all by yourself in the city?"

She flinched. "I'll probably get a roommate."

"You've got girlfriends back home?"

She snorted at the thought. "No."

"So then who would you live with?" I pressed. I could tell there was something just underneath the surface of this conversation that I was missing.

Alba jumped off the counter and went to the cauldron to stir it. "Geez, Red. Nosy much?"

I pulled my legs up and sat on them pretzel style, then spun myself around to face Alba. "Sorry, I'm just wondering who you're planning to live with after college. Why's that such a big deal?"

"It's not a big deal."

"Well then who are you going to be living with?"

Alba paused for a moment before finally just saying it. "I'll probably live with Tony."

My mouth opened. "Why would you and Tony live together?"

"Geez, what's it to you?" she barked, meeting my eyes.

I just stared at her, waiting for her answer.

"Fine!" she hollered. "Because Tony's my husband!"

My jaw dropped again. "Alba, you're *married*?" My mind reeled. There was no way I would have ever guessed that in a million years. I'd thought she was going to tell me she was living with a girlfriend! No wonder she never had an interest in Reign or meeting any of the wizards next door.

"It's not a big deal," she said quietly.

"Yeah, it sort of is," I disagreed. "How long have you been married?"

After stirring the pot, she put the long handled spoon

down and shrugged. "I don't know. We got married when I turned sixteen."

"*Sixteen*? You're twenty-two. You've been married for *six years*?! Alba, this is crazy!"

Alba rushed me and threw a fist under my chin. "Red, so help me, I'll cream you if you tell the girls."

I pushed her fist away, "Okay, okay! Jeesh. I told you I can keep a secret."

"You can't tell Hugh either, or your brother," she said, pointing her finger at me.

I held up my right hand. "I swear! Why can't anyone know?"

"Because I don't want anyone to know," she jeered in a mock high voice.

"Whatever, Alba. It's your secret to keep. I won't tell. Gosh, I can't believe you're *married!* Are you and your husband in a fight or something? Is that why you're so grumpy lately?"

"You really don't know when to zip it, do ya, kid?"

I shrugged. "All this time I thought you were into girls and were crushing on Holly or something. I had no idea you were *married*."

Alba nearly spit out her gum. "You thought I was a *lesbian*?"

"Well, yeah."

"How many lesbian witches do you know?"

"Well, I thought I knew *one*!" I answered honestly.

"Yeah, well, I'm not a lesbian. And if I *were* a lesbian, I certainly wouldn't be interested in Holly. She's too – too – I don't know, HOLLY!"

My mind reeled; trying to catch up with all the new information it was being afforded. "So, what does your husband think of you going away to college?"

"I don't really know," she said quietly.

"Well, what did he say the last time you talked to him?" I asked her.

She shrugged. "He said, see you at Christmas."

"The last time you talked to your husband was before you left?" No wonder Alba was so moody lately!

She turned her back to me. I'd struck a nerve. I jumped off the counter, plucked Chesney up and sat him on my hip, and raced around to face Alba. "Oh, I'm sorry, Alba. I didn't know!"

Alba threw a stiff arm my way. "Nope, I'm good," she said, stifling back her emotion on the subject.

"It's my fault. I was digging around…" I began. I didn't know what to do to make her feel better.

She shook her head. "Can we not talk about this anymore?"

I nodded, biting my bottom lip anxiously. "Yeah."

"Oh, look, the potion is ready," she said, changing the subject.

I peered down into the pot. The water had turned into a creamy white substance, and the root was still intact. "So now what?"

"We light the candles in the circle," she said.

The lab was equipped with a large open area with a circle and star painted on the floor for spells to take place. There was a short table with a little cloth covering it in the center of the circle. Gingerly, I placed the candles on the table. Alba looked at them, snapped her fingers and blew. The candle's fire immediately sprang to life.

"I love that trick," I told Alba with a grin.

"Everyone does," she admitted. "Okay, kneel down in front of the candles with the dog."

I picked up Chesney and knelt down in front of the little

center table and waited for Alba. Chesney licked my ear, causing me to giggle.

"We're ready," I told her.

"Coming," she said as she grabbed the cauldron and the spell book.

She handed me the spell book which was opened to the Animal Enchantment spell we'd been reading and sat the cauldron down in the center of the little table. She pulled the ginger root from the pot and handed it to me. "I can't be in the circle for this," she said as she left the circle.

"But you can stay in the room, right?" I asked her nervously. I was mildly afraid something would go wrong with the spell, and I'd wind up with a tail or something.

"Yeah, I'll just wait over here," she said as she hopped up to sit on the counter top.

"Okay, so what do I do?"

"Use the root to smear the potion behind your ear and then Chesney's ear. Then encircle both of your eyes with it and both of Chesney's eyes and then encircle both your mouths and then do the chant."

"Okay, here goes," I said. My stomach was doing nervous flip flops as I used the root to do as Alba had instructed. Despite the fact that Chesney wanted to eat the root, I managed to get the potion in the correct spots on both of us.

"Now read the spell three times," Alba instructed. "Make sure to insert Chesney's name into the part at the end."

Holding Chesney tightly, I looked down at the book in front of me and began to read, focusing my energy on the words of the spell.

"Bind our eyes and our mouths as well.

Hear me while I speak this spell.
Show me what he sees and hears
Bind our tongues, bind our ears.
When I speak this sacred vow,
Show me what he sees right now.
And when I cross my arms at night,
End the spell with solemn might.
Call it back with gentle force,
Say Chesney Enchantment, but of course."

I chanted the spell two more times. Chesney studied my face closely as if I were hypnotizing him. When I finished, I gave him a hug, stood up and exited the circle.

"Now you just have to say 'Chesney Enchantment,' to invoke the spell."

"Do you think it worked?" I asked Alba.

"I guess we'll find out!"

Alba took a deep breath and blew towards the flickering candles on the little table as she snapped her fingers. The candles flickered for a moment before shutting off as if someone had flipped a switch. "Let's go," she said.

We shut the door behind us and headed back up the stairs to our dorm room. We'd barely made it halfway up the stairs when Jax came tearing around the corner. "Mercy! There you are, omigosh, I've been looking for you everywhere!"

CHAPTER 14

My heart leapt into my throat. "Jax! Slow down, what's going on? What happened? Are Sweets and Holly alright?" I asked her nervously.

"Yeah, they're fine. Nothing's wrong. Something just happened, and it's *great!*" she cooed and did a little pirouette on the top stair. "Reign just texted me. He wants to take me out on a date! I'm dying right now, ahh!"

"I'm glad you're already dying, so I don't have to kill you," Alba barked angrily. "You scared the crap out of me!"

"Me too, Jax!"

Jax looked down at her feet. "Oh, sorry. I was just so excited, and I wanted to share it with someone. I can't tell Holly because, well, I think she might have a crush on Reign too. Ahh! I can't believe Sweets came through!"

Jax gave me a quick squeeze around the shoulders and then plucked Chesney out of my arms and flew away like the little pesky mosquito that she was.

I groaned inwardly.

"Sweets did this?"

"No, my *brother* did this."

"Isn't Jax a little young for him?" Alba asked.

"Of course she is! You tell her!" I complained.

Alba had barely turned the doorknob to her room when it burst open, and Holly shot forward. *"Finally!"* she exclaimed. "I've been waiting forever for you to get back!"

My stomach flipped over. I could already guess what she was going to tell me.

"You'll never guess what just happened!"

Alba rolled her eyes as she pushed Holly aside and strutted past her. She fell onto the bottom bunk with a thud and put her arms over her face.

"What's *her* problem?" she asked me.

"I don't know. She's tired?" I offered.

"More like grumpy," said Holly.

"She's got ears," hollered Alba.

"Then what's your problem?"

"My problem is that I don't care about whatever it is you're about to say."

Holly rolled her eyes and turned back to me. Her enthusiasm had been squashed slightly, but I could see her quickly rebounding.

"Reign asked me out on a date!" she cooed. "Sweets made it happen. I owe her something big!"

"I suppose you do," I said flatly. I spun on my heel and headed back to my room leaving a long faced Holly with Alba.

I opened the door to my room and was thankful to discover that Jax wasn't inside. I dropped onto my bed and threw an arm over my face. I couldn't understand it. Harper's murder was solved, and yet it didn't make me feel better. It just didn't make sense. Something felt off.

I heard a noise at the window and quickly threw my

arm off of my face and cranked around to see Sneaks sitting on my windowsill. I quickly stood up and went to her.

"Finally! It's about time! What took you so long?" I ranted. "I have so much to tell you. I just don't even know where to begin! First of all, *your son* has asked out *two* of my girlfriends. Ugh! You need to talk to Reign, Mom. Tell him he's *not allowed* to date my friends!" I said to Sneaks while pacing back and forth on the carpet.

"Holly, Jax, and Sweets said I couldn't call girl code because Reign and I didn't grow up together. How dumb is that? And I just found out a *major* secret about Alba, but unfortunately, I can't even tell you. Which totally stinks because this secret is going to eat me alive! And on top of that, this whole murder thing has got me totally on edge! I'm just freaking out right now. I'm so stressed, that I can't focus on classes. Ugh. Mom! Tell me what to do?" I begged.

I stopped talking and stared at Sneaks. She just looked at me blankly.

"Hello? Where's all that unwanted advice now? I finally ask for your help, and you're speechless? Mark it on the calendar. The day my mother didn't have any advice!"

I looked at Sneaks again. "Hello?" I asked, bending over to look her in the face.

"Meow," she said plainly.

"Meow? Are you playing with me now?" I asked.

Sneaks began to purr and rubbed her body up against my face.

"Mom?"

"Meow," said Sneaks.

"Ugh!" I groaned out loud. I threw myself back onto my bed and pounded the mattress with my balled fists. Why couldn't my mother show up when I needed her? It felt like days since I'd last talked to her and I felt like my world was spinning crazily around me. I felt fragile and abandoned.

Then a thought occurred to me. It had been a really long time since my mom had visited. What if something happened to her? I pulled out my cell phone and dialed my mom's house, something I should have done earlier, but had been too busy. It rang six times before the answering machine picked up.

"This is Linda, and this is Mercy. We're not home right now, leave a message, beep…" The sound of my mom's voice widened a tiny crack inside the hard outer layer around my heart. I suddenly felt hot tears on my cheek, and before I knew it, I was crying myself to sleep.

SEEING JAX OUT OF HER WITCH UNIFORM THE NEXT AFTERNOON was a welcome change. I was starting to think the girl didn't own any other clothes. Reign had suggested that she dress casually, as they were just going to go for a jog together around the park and then go out for ice cream afterwards. The weather was unseasonably warm, so Jax had opted to wear only a sports bra, matching yoga capri pants and her jogging shoes. As usual, her petite waist and six-pack abs were on point. She looked positively adorable and almost like a normal person, aside from her hair which she had had Holly turn blue the night before with Holly's new favorite beauty spell. If the whole witch thing didn't work out for Holly, I was sure she had a career as a cosmetologist waiting for her somewhere.

Jax still hadn't told Holly that she and Reign were going out, and I was thankful that she hadn't. Reign had put us all in a position that could potentially pit friends against friends and against his sister, so I wanted to stay as far away from that messapalooza as possible. If asked about any of their date plans, I planned to plead the fifth.

Sweets met Jax in our dorm as Jax was finishing her makeup. I was lying on my bed, cuddled up with Chesney when she came to the room. She handed Jax a small box of confections tied up with a tiny pink ribbon.

"What's this?" Jax asked excitedly.

"It's your date potion," Sweets told her reverently. "They're chocolate truffles. You have to get him to eat one. Once he's eaten his piece, then you can eat yours."

Jax jumped up and down excitedly. "Eeee," she squealed. "That's all I have to do?"

Sweets winced. "Usually matchmaking spells work the best if they are sealed with a kiss."

Jax's eyes widened. "I have to kiss him?"

Sweets took a deep breath and sighed. "Typically that's what seals the spell, but sometimes things happen."

"Like what?"

"Mmm, like if you kiss him too soon before the potion has had time to take effect, then he might never want to see you again."

Jax's mouth fell open. "That would be *horrible!* What happens if I kiss him too late?"

"Nothing. It'll just be too late, and the spell will have worn off, and you'll miss your opportunity for him to love you forever."

"Well, how will I know when it's the perfect time?" Jax asked confused.

Sweets put a finger to her chin. "Mmm, he'll get a tickle in his throat. The minute he gets a tickle in his throat, that's when you need to swoop in on him. Got it? Tickle – swoop."

Jax nodded seriously. "Tickle – swoop. Yeah, I can remember that. Tickle – swoop."

I rolled my eyes as I twirled Chesney's soft fur around my fingers.

"Oh, Sweets, you're the best!" Jax gushed and threw her arms around Sweets's wide middle.

Just then there was a knock at the door. Jax looked positively petrified, so Sweets answered the door for her. Reign was dressed, like Jax, in work-out gear. A black Nike t-shirt, athletic shorts, and trainers. His thick black hair was perfectly coiffed, and he wore a pair of tinted sports sunglasses. "Hey, Sweets, how ya doin'? Is Jax here?"

Reign poked his head into our room, and when he saw me lying on the bed, he came over to greet me. "Hey, Mercy, it's too nice to be inside today, you alright?" he asked. His deep voice *sounded* caring, but I didn't truly feel like he cared about me.

"I'm fine," I said cryptically. Chesney gave a little bark as Reign reached down to pet him.

"This little guy is pretty adorable. What's his name again?"

"Chesney," Jax answered from behind Sweets.

"Jax!" Reign said. He pulled his sunglasses off of his face so he could get a better look at her. "You look amazing. You work out?"

Jax nodded excitedly. "Yeah, I'm a little OCD about working out," she admitted.

"I figured you would enjoy going for a jog, are you ready to go?"

Jax grabbed the little box of candy Sweets had given her. "Yeah, I'm ready!"

"What's that?" he asked.

"Sweets made us a surprise, we'll check it out when we

get to the park," Jax explained nervously bouncing around on her toes.

"You're full of energy," he noticed.

"She's *always* full of energy," I groaned from the bed.

"You want to come with us, sis?" he asked.

"Don't call me sis, and no, I don't want to come with. But you could take Chesney with you. I'm sure he'd like to go for a walk," I suggested, crossing my fingers at my sides.

Jax nodded excitedly. "Oh, yeah, that's a great idea. Do you mind, Reign?"

My brother shook his head. "Not at all, does he have a leash?"

I had the leash by my side, ready to go. I reached it out immediately. "Here ya go!"

Reign laughed. "That was a little convenient. Trying to get rid of all of us? Have a hot date yourself?"

I chuckled nervously and avoided making eye contact with my brother as Jax scooped up Chesney. "No, of course not. I just – need to study," I lied. "Now go, get out of here. I've got stuff to do. You too, Sweets."

"Okay, well, have fun studying," he said as he let Jax pull him out of the room. "Bye, Sweets, thanks for the treat."

"Bye, Mercy," Jax hollered without waiting for a reply.

Sweets was the last to leave. She eyed me suspiciously. "You're up to something," she said as she hovered near the door.

"As if you're not?" I asked her pointedly.

Her eyes widened like a deer caught in the headlights and like that, she was gone.

When the coast was clear, I leapt off my bed and peered out my door, checking both sides of the hallway. With the exception of Sweets swaying down the hallway towards her room, the coast was clear. I shut my dorm room door and locked the deadbolt. My pulse throbbed ferociously in my ears.

I sat down cross-legged on the plush carpet and let my arms fall naturally to my knees. I took several deep breaths and shook out my shoulders in an attempt to relax my body. I focused all of my energy and spirit on the task at hand. Then I began to chant. "Chesney Enchantment, Chesney Enchantment, Chesney Enchantment…." And just like that, I was seeing out of the eyes of Chesney as I walked beside Jax and Reign's feet. What a strange feeling it was to be all of eight inches off the ground and have four legs. It was as if I were inside of a virtual reality 3D video game. *How cool is this?*

I stumbled a bit on the cobblestone sidewalk as I tried to make Chesney's front legs and back legs work together as they should and got drug by the leash about twelve steps before Jax realized that I wasn't walking anymore. "Ow!" I hollered as the sidewalk scratched at my rump.

Jax and Reign immediately looked down at me curiously. "Did Chesney just say, *Ow*?" Reign asked Jax.

Jax peered at me oddly, and I panicked and immediately started howling to cover up my blunder. "Ow, ow, owwwwww."

Jax laughed. "He was howling, silly. He didn't say, *ow*."

Reign laughed too and then put an arm around Jax's shoulder. "You sure look hot today," he said, and I watched as the hand on her shoulder gently slid down to her hip and teetered dangerously close to her butt. I put the brakes on, tugged at the leash, and began to whimper.

"Aww, Ches, what's the matter, baby, are we walking too fast for you?" Jax asked, bending down to scoop me up and toss me over her shoulder.

I licked her face and squirmed about in her arms to show my appreciation. Reign put a hand on my head, and I growled immediately at him, baring my teeth for extra effect. That should show him how I felt about him putting his hand on my friend's butt. *Don't get too close, brother,* I thought.

"So, tell me about yourself! Where are you from?" Jax asked him.

This vantage point was *so* much better from Jax's shoulder. I could actually hear what they were talking about from up here.

"Oh, I –uh, grew up in a little town in Kansas. On a Christmas tree farm," he told her.

My ears perked up. *Liar!*

"Oh, a Christmas tree farm! Isn't that interesting!" Jax gushed.

Reign shrugged. "Not really. It was a lot of work and I was raised by a single dad, so that was tough."

I was *stunned* by what I was hearing. This was *not* the story Reign had given me!

"You had a single dad? *Oh my gosh*, I had a single mom! I can totally relate," Jax said and linked arms with him after finding out they had that in common. "Wasn't that hard?"

Reign swung his eyes down to the ground, "Yeah, it really was."

I wiggled around in Jax's arms until I could squint at Reign angrily. I wanted to rip him apart limb from limb for lying to me. Or lying to Jax. Or heck, probably both of us! What a scoundrel! What a liar! I wondered what lame story he had given my mother? If he lied to her too, I was going to be furious.

"So, I was thinking…" he began, "we could go drive down to the Aspen Falls park and start our jog there? I've been wanting to explore the town, but with the murder investigation lingering over my head, I'd been hesitant to show my face around town. I know how small towns can be. I assumed everyone thought I was guilty."

Jax's big blue eyes opened wide. "Oh, I never thought you were guilty. Not for a *second*! I'm just so glad we have proven your innocence."

I nipped at Jax's ear. She was making me want to vomit. "Oh, Chesney, stop," she chirped.

"Yeah, so we start at the park and then we can go from there? Sound okay?"

"That sounds amazing!" Jax gushed as they jumped into his shiny black sports car. Jax kept me on her lap as we drove and Reign sped off down the driveway like a crazy man.

At the park, we all unloaded and Jax and Reign stretched a bit. Then Jax pulled out the little box of treats that Sweets had sent with her.

"Isn't that nice of Sweets to make us a treat for our first date?" Jax asked as she pulled the little ribbon off.

Reign looked down at the box. "Yeah, she seems like a sweetheart, I guess that's why everyone calls her Sweets."

Jax laughed. "That and she *loves* sweets! Anyway, she made these just for our walk. I think they are like energy snacks. We should definitely eat them before we take off."

Reign chuckled. "Having chocolate before a workout seems kind of counterproductive, but hey, I like chocolate just as much as the next guy, so count me in!"

"Awesome," she said with a smile. "Here, this one's yours." Jax handed him a small ball of chocolate that he popped into his mouth immediately.

"Mmmm, so creamy, that Sweets is an *amazing* baker!" he gushed with his eyes closed.

Jax nodded as she popped her candy into her mouth next. I watched as they each let it melt away. Jax's eyes were trained on Reign, just waiting for him to so much as hiccup.

"How was yours?" Reign asked.

"Super delish!"

I barked at them. I didn't know exactly what game Sweets had been playing with that potion, but I certainly didn't want Jax to kiss him, and then they were suddenly a match for life. Jax was a nice girl, a good friend, and an okay roommate, but she was too young to be my sister-in-law. Especially after hearing Reign's lies, I knew he wasn't necessarily the best guy for her, anyway.

I barked again.

Reign knelt down to me. "You alright, lil guy? You want a treat too?"

I stuck my tongue out and panted. I wasn't really sure how a dog would react to a question like that, so I just went with what came naturally to me.

On one knee, Reign looked up at Jax. "I think he's hungry. Has he eaten lately?"

Jax shrugged. I could tell she was trying not to talk. She was just waiting for him to have a tickle so she could pounce.

Reign looked at me again and tousled my fur when all of a sudden his eyes looked kind of bulgy and his hand went to his throat. "Uh-hum!" he coughed. "Uh-uh-hum!"

"You alright?" Jax asked him nervously.

I could tell it was the tickle. I hurled myself into his arms to prevent Jax from getting there first. He stood up with me in one arm and his other hand at his throat. "Uh-hum," he coughed again.

"Tickle-swoop," I heard her whisper before launching herself at him. Her skinny little arms surrounded his neck, and her legs wrapped themselves around his waist. She squeezed the three of us together, turning me into a Chesney sandwich. I barked furiously, as Jax pressed her mouth against Reign's. It was too late. She'd managed to kiss him!

Reign's tickle was still there, though. "Uh-hum," he tried to cough despite Jax's mouth smashed against his. His cough couldn't go anywhere because Jax was covering his mouth and he began to choke. My barking continued.

Reign's face turned crimson red as he tried to unload Jax and me from his arms while he coughed. "Jax!" he managed to utter between choked coughs.

But Jax wouldn't let go. She clung to him for dear life.

"Jax! Get off!" he muttered.

Jax finally pulled her mouth off of his and jerked her head back, but yet her wiry frame was still firmly attached to his body.

"Jax! Can't breathe! Get off!" he muttered again.

She untangled herself from him and jumped down onto the pavement. Reign handed me to her and spun around to get the coughs out of his system. When he finally was able to compose himself again, his face was scarlet red, and he looked at Jax as if she were a crazy woman.

"What the hell was that? I was dying there!" he hollered at her.

Jax's face crumpled. She stuttered, "I – I, I'm sorry. I thought maybe I should give you mouth to mouth resuscitation."

"That wasn't mouth to mouth. That was a kiss. And a very inopportune kiss if I might add," he said angrily, wiping at his mouth with the back of his hand.

"I'm sorry, Reign. Sweets said to…" she began and then quickly covered her mouth with both hands.

"Sweets said to what?"

"Nothing," she said, pinching her lips together between her front teeth.

"You're acting strange," he commented. "Maybe we should just start walking."

Jax gave him a nervous smile. "Yeah, maybe," she said.

He tried to collect himself. "Okay, let's go." He jogged ahead of her. "Come on, Chesney," he called.

I ran behind him while Jax finally took off to catch up with the two of us. He ran faster than he had before and I had to work hard with my little legs to keep up with him. I sucked in a deep breath and ran harder. My asthma began to kick in, and I suddenly felt myself wheezing. It made me wonder if dogs could have asthma.

Jax breezed past me until she was caught up to Reign. "So, whatdidyadoafterhighschool," Jax rattled off a mile a minute.

Reign looked at her curiously. "Yeah, sorry, I didn't catch a word of that."

Jax smiled and tried again, "Whatdidyadoafterhigh-school," she speed talked again.

"I caught high school in there," he said with a nervous laugh.

Jax waved a hand in front of her face nervously. "Feelinkindaweird," she mumbled. It sounded like she had a swollen tongue.

"Are you okay? I can hardly understand a word out of your mouth."

Jax turned to give Reign a little smile, but the second she took her eyes off the sidewalk, her foot caught in a crack and down she went. Reign's reflexes were like magic, and in hindsight, perhaps they were magic, as he caught her before she hit the pavement.

"Are you alright, Jax?" he asked her, cradling her head inches away from the ground. I snuck under his arm and crawled up Jax's torso to peer into her eyes. She looked fine, just freaked out. I suddenly wondered if the chocolate potion had done this to her and this had been Sweets's plan all along to sabotage their date.

Jax sat upright. "OmigoshIamsoembarrassed." Her words blurred together. Even I had a hard time understanding her. She popped two hands over her mouth again as she heard how her words were coming out all jumbled together.

Reign helped her to her feet as I bounced around her ankles. "You talk really fast."

With her mouth still covered, Jax shook her head. Her eyes were wild from fear of not understanding what was going on. She jerked her head towards the sidewalk and began to jog again. He shrugged and followed along with her as well.

"So, what kind of witch are you?" he asked her, trying to make small talk.

Jax's face flushed bright red. Her least favorite topic. She shrugged. "Idoalittlebitofeverything," she lied.

"Are you feeling alright, Jax?" Reign asked, stopping on the path once again.

"I'mfeelinfineIjustdon'tknowwhat'sgoingon," she rattled. I tried hard not to laugh, despite the fact that my friend's date was going nowhere fast, it was quite the funny prank Sweets had pulled on her.

"Maybe I should just take you home then? It seems like maybe you're tired or something."

Jax nodded. "Okay," she whispered, clearly disappointed.

Despite the fact that my chest was tight from the asthma

attack, I bounced around on my toes, excited that Sweets's plan had worked. We were going home! *Yay!* I thought I was going to have to be the one to sabotage the date, but Sweets had managed to do it all on her own. I had to give the girl some credit!

Jax was silent on the way home. I watched as she bit down on her lips to keep from accidentally speaking. Reign told her it was alright and they'd do it again, but in guy speak, I knew that meant he wasn't going to call her. I felt bad for my friend, and I felt even worse that it was my brother crushing her, but I had warned her that I didn't want her dating my brother. When we got back to the dorm, Jax jumped onto her bed and promptly fell asleep in a ball of tears.

CHAPTER 15

Holly's dinner date was later in the evening. As she finished getting ready, I could barely look at her without blushing. Her dress was *that* revealing. Not only did the little black dress hug her curves perfectly, but the front also dipped low past her breasts, nearly touching her stomach.

"Why do you always have to shove those things in everyone's faces?" Alba asked her.

Holly looked down at her chest. "I'm not shoving them in your face."

"Why can't you cover them up?"

Holly primped her hair one last time and then looked at Alba. "We've had this conversation before." She turned to me. "Are you ready to go?"

I groaned. Even though I didn't want to go with her on a double date, it had been my idea. I needed to make sure that her date was properly botched and while the Chesney enchantment spell had worked great for disturbing Jax's date, I knew Holly wouldn't want to take Chesney out to a restaurant. Plus, the idea of getting to go out with Hugh again had secretly put a smile on my face.

"Why are you groaning? This double date was your idea! You better not be negative like that when we're with the boys," she said bluntly.

"I'm not going to be negative, I just really don't like the fact that you're going out with my brother."

Holly gave me a coy little grin. "I'm not just going out with your brother. I'm going to *marry* your brother," she asserted.

I rolled my eyes. "Sweets did the spell?"

Holly swiveled around and looked at the clock in her room. "She should be here any minute."

"What kind of spell is she doing?" Alba asked.

"A matchmaking spell. She's going to make sure that Reign and I are together forever!"

There was a knock at the door. I opened it to find Sweets standing before us with a little white paper sack sealed shut with a big pink bow.

"Hey, Sweets," I greeted her. "Come on in."

"Hi, Mercy. I brought Holly's love potion." With a wink, she held up the sack.

I hitched my thumb towards Holly. "Over there."

Holly rushed over and took the sack from Sweets. "This is it? What do we need to do? Just eat it?"

Sweets gave her a devilish smile. "Pretty much. He should eat his first, and then you eat yours next."

"That's it?" Holly asked.

"Yeah, doesn't she have to, like, *kiss him* or something?" I asked with a little chuckle.

Sweets's eyes grew larger, and she shot me a look that clearly read, *shut up, Mercy.* "Nope, this one is a no kissing required spell. In fact, I think kissing may reverse the effects of the spell, so no kissing until the second date."

Holly looked forlorn. "Really? Not even at the end of the date?"

I glared at Holly. "You're not supposed to kiss a boy on the first date anyway."

"Seriously, Mercy? It's not the 1940's. You can kiss a boy on the first date now."

I shrugged and plopped down on the saucer chair in their room. "I think you should wait anyway."

"Are you telling me you didn't kiss Hugh on the first date?" Holly asked.

By their long stare, I could tell Sweets and Alba were curious as well.

"I don't kiss and tell," I said quietly.

"You didn't!" Holly guessed. "You didn't kiss the cowboy on your first date."

"Well, we've only been on *two* dates," I asserted.

"Did you kiss him on the second date?" Holly pressed.

"Who shares this kind of information? Because I don't!"

Holly smacked herself on the forehead. "Oh my gosh! You haven't kissed him yet, have you?"

Sweets giggled.

"Holly, I'm not going to go with you if you make a big deal out of this," I told her angrily. I could feel my temperature rising.

"Okay, okay, I won't say another word. But gosh, I can't believe…"

"Not another word!" I cut her off.

"Fine," she mumbled.

"Okay, we should go," I said. "Do I look alright?" I spun around. I was wearing a pair of jeans, my Converse sneakers and a sweater that Holly had loaned me. Surprisingly it covered my chest, I couldn't believe Holly *owned* a shirt that did that, but it was tighter than I was used to and I thought at least Hugh would be reminded that I was indeed a female. I had unleashed my long red hair and brushed it out until it shone brightly around my shoulders. With my bangs pulled to one side, I was satisfied with how I looked. I just wanted a little validation from the girls.

"You should have worn a dress," Holly said disdainfully.

"I don't wear dresses."

"You wore one on your first date," Alba pointed out.

"That was, like, a one-time only occurrence."

"Hugh liked the dress, though, right?" Sweets asked.

I glared at the three of them. "Fine. I'll wear a dress on my wedding day, happy?"

Sweets giggled, and Holly rolled her eyes and put away her makeup case.

"Okay, I'm ready, let's go."

"Bye, girls, wish me luck!" Holly squealed excitedly, as she grabbed the little paper bag from the counter.

"Bye, good luck," Sweets said, but I could see her finger crossed by her side as we left the room.

THE RESTAURANT WAS CROWDED THAT EVENING, BUT WITH Hugh by our side, we got in right away.

"Booth please," he suggested to the waitress as she led us towards an empty table. With that request, she veered to the right and to the back corner and seated us at the only empty booth in the room.

Holly and Reign sat on one side of the table and Hugh

SON OF A WITCH

and I sat on the other side of the table. "I can't believe we got in right away," Holly said, bouncing on the seat.

"Hugh's *charmed* in that way," I shared. Hugh shot me a glare, and I wondered if that was perhaps supposed to have been between the two of us.

"You go to the Institute, Hugh?" Reign asked him.

"I do," Hugh acknowledged. I appreciated the fact that the two men in my life were trying to be civil with one another.

"And how long have you known my sister?"

Hugh squeezed my hand. "I've known this lovely lady since the beginning of school. She's quite the lil sweetheart, your sister."

Reign rolled his eyes. Thankfully Hugh didn't catch the little slight. "Yes, my sister is a sweetheart. As is my gorgeous date this evening. Doesn't Holly just look spectacular?"

Hugh and I both glanced at Holly. I noticed Hugh quickly averting his eyes like a true gentleman. That made me smile. I knew I was with the right guy. "She looks very lovely," Hugh answered politely.

Even though the boys were on their best behavior, tension at the table was high, and I was thankful when Holly pulled out the little bag that Sweets had given her and set it on the table.

"Sweets sent along a little treat for the evening," Holly shared.

I bit my lip hard to keep from laughing. Hugh felt my body jerk and looked at me. I squeezed his hand and tried to play it off.

"Did she now?" asked Reign. Considering the fact that he had just gotten one of Sweets's sweet treats earlier in the day, he did a good job of acting surprised. "That Sweets, she must really do a lot of baking."

Holly giggled. "Oh, I asked her to make us something special."

"Oh! Well then! What do you have?" Reign asked as he ran a hand through his thick hair.

Holly opened the sack and reached in and pulled out two small brownies.

"Brownies?" Reign asked with furrowed eyebrows. "These don't have pot in them or something?"

Holly laughed. "Of course not! They're just brownies, but, um, Sweets makes *the best* brownies, and I wanted you to try them."

Reign didn't know what to think. "Well, maybe we should save them for dessert?"

Holly shook her head. "Of course not! They are supposed to be good luck brownies. You eat them at the beginning of your date."

"Ahh, good luck brownies. Got it. Okay, well, there are only two here. Hand me your knife. I'll cut them in half so Mercy and Hugh can have a piece."

Holly's eyes opened wider. "No! They can't!" she admonished.

Reign looked around curiously. "Holly, we're being rude by not sharing."

I raised a hand in protest. "Oh, don't worry about us at all. We don't want to ruin our suppers. You guys go ahead and eat your brownies. Right, Hugh?"

"Well, I've got quite the sweet tooth myself, I don't mind having a little, ow!" he hollered as I kicked his leg.

"We're fine, Hugh!"

Hugh rubbed his leg. "Yes, ma'am, we're just fine," he said changing his mind.

"Okay, well, if you're sure," Reign said. He grabbed a brownie as did Holly. Reign held it out front of him and made a little toast. "To getting lucky."

Holly smiled broadly. "To getting lucky."

I rolled my eyes then let my head fall into my hands on the table. When I looked up, Holly and Reign had both devoured their brownies, and a waitress had come to bring us our drinks and take our orders. Once she'd gone, I looked at Holly again. I wasn't sure if it was just me, but the bodice of her skin tight dress appeared a little looser. It had been a long week. I was probably just getting tired. I took a sip of my soda.

"Mmm, that's a really great brownie. You're right. Sweets is a fantastic baker," Reign gushed.

Holly nodded emphatically, while she wiped at the corners of her mouth with her napkin.

"So, Holly, where are you from originally?" Reign asked her.

"I'm from California," she said. "How about you?"

Reign looked at me. "Umm, I'm from a small town. Nowhere exciting."

The hairs prickled at the back of my neck. I declared then and there that the minute I got home I was going to Google my brother and find out everything there was to know about Reign Alexander.

"Holly, you've got a little somethin', on your chin right there," Hugh drawled and pointed at a little dark spot on her chin.

Holly wiped at it, but it didn't disappear. "Did I get it?"

I shook my head and reached my arm out across the table to wipe it for her. But it didn't move. "Must be a little blemish."

Holly laughed nervously. "That's funny, Mercy. You know, I don't get blemishes."

I shrugged, and the conversation continued.

"So what are your magic specialties, Holly?" Reign asked her.

"Well, I'm a bit psychic, I have a lot of premonitions either through touching objects or through dreams. I'm also learning a lot about glamour spells."

"Glamour spells?" Reign shook his head.

"You know, like beauty spells, vanity spells…I just did Jax's hair coloring the other day, no dyes necessary!"

"Oh, I see," Reign said, nodding his head. "Like a beautician."

"Yeah, but with magic."

I squinted my eyes as I looked closer at Holly. She was starting to get dark circles under her eyes, and the dark spot on her chin had evolved into a full-blown zit. "Holly, I think you and I should make a trip to the ladies' room," I suggested. Hugh squeezed my hand as if to say *do not leave me alone with this guy.* I squeezed it back but got up out of the booth.

"It's okay, I don't need to use the restroom," she objected with a sugar sweet smile.

"Yeah, but I do. And you know, girls go together, right?"

"Fine," she grumbled.

When I had her safely in the bathroom, I took her by the shoulders and moved her in front of the mirror. "You're breaking out!" I told her.

"Oh my gosh!" she hollered. A second pimple had formed on her nose. "This one is HUGE!"

She was right, the one on her chin was ginormous, but the pimple on her nose was twice as big. Holly was meticulous about her beauty regime, she always took her makeup off before bed and was careful to use moisturizers and creams to keep her skin soft, supple, and blemish free and now she was getting two zits on her first date with Reign.

"Must be the stress," I offered to her as a suggestion.

She shook her head. "I don't get pimples. EVER! And *look* at these bags under my eyes!"

Suddenly it hit me, the brownies. This was Sweets's doing. Of course! It had to be! I tried to suppress my laugh.

"Okay, well, there's nothing you can do about it now, let's just go back to the table. I'm sure Reign won't notice," I told her.

She fidgeted in front of the mirror and spun around sideways. "My dress doesn't feel as tight as it did before. That's weird," she commented.

"I hate to say it, Holl, but your boobs look way smaller," I told her earnestly.

"They do?" she asked and turned sideways to peer into the mirror.

"Yeah. Did your bra deflate?" I asked her, trying hard not to burst out in laughter.

"I will have you know that these are one hundred percent natural," she said and grabbed her chest. She looked in the mirror curiously. "Wait, they *do* feel smaller." She looked at herself more closely in the mirror. "Do you really think they look smaller?"

I shrugged. "Yeah, they really do, and they look like they're shrinking even more now."

Holly panicked. "What is happening, Mercy?"

"I have no idea, but our dates are waiting for us, we should probably go back out there."

"I can't go out there like this! My boobs are shrinking, and I'm getting acne!"

"I'm sure far worse things have happened on a date

than that," I assured her. Though I couldn't think of what those things would be. Boobs shrinking and sudden onset acne seemed pretty high on my list of material for a date gone wrong.

"Maybe we should just go home," she suggested.

"Now? We just got here! We haven't even eaten yet!"

"Look at me!" she cried as another pimple sprung up on her forehead.

I linked arms with her and pulled her out of the bathroom. "There's nothing we can do about it. You'll just have to buck up and put on a brave face. Let's go."

The two of us walked back to our table, and by the time we were back to our dates, three more zits had sprung up on Holly's face, and her boobs had shrunken a bit more. She looked almost as developed as a thirteen-year-old girl, causing her dress to hang on her limply.

Reign and Hugh gave us a funny look when we came back to the table. Holly tried to let her hair cover her face, but it was too late.

"Holly, are you feeling – oh!" Reign said with surprise when he saw her pimple covered face. "Are you allergic to something?"

"Noooo," she cried. "I don't think so. I don't know what is happening."

"Maybe it was those brownies," Hugh suggested plainly.

Something in Reign's brain finally clicked. "Maybe it *was* the brownies. I wonder if Sweets got a bad batch of flour or something."

Holly thought about it for a second. When it occurred to her that Reign might be on to something, she balled up her napkin and threw it down onto the table. "Ugh! Sweets!"

CHAPTER 16

J ax and Chesney were alone in our room when Holly and I got back from our short double date. Thanks to Holly's "allergic reaction," we ended the date early and just grabbed a slice of pizza from the cafeteria when we got back.

"What happened to you?!" Jax asked in shock.

"Bad shellfish," Holly grumbled.

"Tell her," I ordered. "We're going to fix this right now."

"Tell me what?" Jax asked curiously.

"Tell her who you really went out with tonight."

Holly shot me an evil look. "I don't want to."

"You mean you didn't go out with Hugh's roommate?" Jax asked, confused.

"Holly!" I warned.

"What?!"

"Tell her."

"Ugh, fine. I went out with Reign!" Holly declared as she slumped down in the chair she'd just pulled up.

"Reign! But..." Jax looked at me for help. I could tell she

didn't know if she should admit that she'd also been out on a date with Reign earlier in the day.

I nodded my head at her.

Jax hung her head. "I went out on a date with Reign earlier today, too," she admitted grudgingly.

Holly's eyes grew huge and her face filled with blood. "But! We said we weren't going to go after him!"

Jax stood up angrily. "Ugh! You went out with him!"

"So, that's because you're a terrible friend. You broke our deal."

"Holly!" I said sternly. "You broke whatever deal you had with Jax too. Neither one of you is in the right. And I didn't want *either* of you to go out with my brother anyway. He's *my brother,* and I'd like a chance to get to know him before either of you do anyway. This is what you both get for going out with him when I specifically asked you not to."

"So *you* did this to me?" Holly asked, training her eyes on me.

"*You* sabotaged my date this afternoon?" Jax asked at the same time.

"Wait a minute. Your date got sabotaged too?" Holly looked at Jax curiously.

Jax nodded. "Yes! My words got all jumbled up, and I tripped and fell. I couldn't speak coherently at all. And Sweets told me I had to kiss Reign, and when I did I just about killed him!"

"Wait a minute, Sweets told you? What does Sweets have to do with this?"

Jax covered her mouth. She had revealed more than she had intended to. "Nothing."

"No, not nothing. What does Sweets have to do with this?"

Jax groaned with frustration. "She did a matchmaking spell on us for me. She told me after Reign ate the candy potion then I was supposed to kiss him. But don't worry, it didn't work." Jax's eyes swung downward, and she fell back down on the bed next to Chesney.

"Sweets did a matchmaking spell for me too, and then *this* happened!" Holly said angrily, pointing to her face. "I bet she did all of this on purpose. I bet Sweets *sabotaged* us intentionally!"

"I can't believe her!" Jax sighed.

"Regardless of why this happened, I feel like Reign has been lying to me about his past," I told the girls. I scooped Chesney up and plopped him down on my lap in front of the computer. I typed in Reign Alexander and did a little nosing around on Google. It didn't take long to find Reign's criminal record in black and white. He'd been in trouble for theft, aggravated assault and battery, and criminal mischief. Since he turned eighteen, he'd been in and out of jail on numerous occasions. My jaw, as well as my heart, dropped.

"Jax, you were on a date with him, did he tell you anything about his past?" I asked her even though I already knew what he had told her.

Jax thought back in her head for a moment. "Umm, not much. He did say he grew up on a Christmas tree farm in Kansas though and he was raised by a single dad."

"He told me he grew up in a small town in Nebraska with a mom who was the lunch lady at a school and a dad who was a banker. He lied to one of us or both of us. I really wish Mom would contact me again. I'm dying to know what he told her, because if he lied to *my mother*…" I trailed off, not knowing what I'd do to him, but I did know it would really push my buttons. "Has either of you seen

Sneaks tonight? She was here earlier, but it wasn't Mom, it was just Sneaks. I'm starting to get worried."

The girls shook their heads. "Nope, sorry," Jax said.

I stood up and handed Chesney to Jax. "I've gotta go, I need to go see my brother," I said and grabbed my purse off the desk. "I wish I had a car. I'm so tired of bumming rides off of people."

Jax shrugged. "I told you we should have signed up for broomstick riding lessons in the quad."

Twenty minutes later I waved goodbye to Hugh as he dropped me off at my brother's rented room. He hadn't wanted to let me go in alone, but I convinced him that I needed some one on one time with my brother.

"I'll just wait here in the truck for ya," Hugh hollered out the window as I walked up the sidewalk. "I can be there in five shakes of a lamb's tail if you need me."

"I'll be fine," I hollered back.

"We're going out for ice cream when you're done," he yelled back. "So don't dilly dally."

I waved my hand behind my back as I opened the door and quietly slid up the stairs. Reign was waiting for me. "Your message seemed urgent. You worried me, are you alright?" The worry in his eyes was apparent and appeared genuine.

I shook my head, biting back tears. He'd lied to me! He was a criminal and I'd just practically thrown the book at another man for killing Harper Bradshaw. What if that was all a lie. What if Vaughn had nothing to do with her death, and what if my brother had done it after all? The thought made me nauseous.

"No, I'm not alright," I admitted. My knees were weak and felt like they might buckle at any moment. "I need to sit down."

Reign gestured for me to take a seat on his bed while he pulled a chair up close to me.

"Reign, I know you've been lying to me. You didn't grow up in a small town in Nebraska or on a Christmas tree farm in Kansas. What else have you been lying to me about?"

Reign took a deep breath and leaned back in his seat. "My life is complicated, Mercy."

"Does my mom know the truth about you? Or did you lie to her too?"

He shifted in his seat. "I probably wasn't completely honest with her either."

"Did you tell her about your criminal history?"

Reign's cheeks filled with blood, and he swallowed hard. "You looked me up?"

"I did a little digging when I found out you were lying to me about your past."

"Ugh," Reign groaned as he slumped forward with his head in his hands. He rubbed his face with frustration.

"I need to know something, Reign." I tried looking him in the face, but he wouldn't make eye contact. "Did you kill Harper? And don't lie to me, because the truth will come out sooner or later and I'd rather hear it from you than to hear it from Detective Whitman when he pieces this whole puzzle together."

Reign's head snapped up, and he finally made eye contact. "I didn't kill Harper, Mercy. I swear. I truly didn't."

A large piece of me felt like I could believe him, but I decided to stay silent and let him explain his lies to me.

"I *did* lie to you about where I came from. But I only did

that because I didn't grow up like you, with a mom that loved you. I had a rough childhood," Reign admitted.

"Reign, I want to get to know *you*. I don't want some made for TV movie about your perfect life on a Christmas tree farm in Kansas with your single dad father. I want the truth. I want to know you and understand you, and if that means that you tell me the hard truth, then that's what it means. My opinion of you isn't going to change because of how you were raised, although it might help me to understand you better."

Reign took a deep breath and leaned back in his seat, stretching his long thin legs out before him. "Okay," he whispered. "After I was born, our dear old granny dropped me off at an orphanage in a rough part of Chicago. It didn't take long before I was adopted by a couple. From the stories I hear, things were good for the first two years. Then my adoptive parents divorced. That was when the fun began," he said with a little laugh.

I reached out and put a hand on his knee. "You don't have to make light of it for me, Reign."

He nodded and blinked several times. "My adoptive father took off. I haven't seen him since I was two. My adoptive mother took the split kind of hard. She moved us to Nevada where her sister was living at the time. She started drinking. People tell me she dated quite a bit, but I really don't remember any of the men. By the time I was five, she was an alcoholic and had married Paul. Paul was a plumber with anger issues. He used to get so angry with me, and my mom," Reign added. His face was transforming while he spoke. His jaw clenched, and his eyes appeared to be in a trance, as he recalled his troubled past.

"Paul was abusive, to say the least. He used to knock my mom and me around from as far back as I can remember. My mom was too scared to leave of course. She didn't have enough money for us to go anywhere far enough away from Paul and on his good days, she'd decide he wasn't that bad, she could stick it out, he'd get better. Paul would buy me a bike or a football, and he'd promise he was sorry for smacking us around, but then the next week, a switch would flip inside of him, and he'd break his promise to me."

Reign's eyes glossed over as he looked up at me. "I used to pray, Mercy. I'd pray to a God that I didn't even know that he'd help us and he'd make Paul disappear. For years nothing happened. Mom stayed with Paul, and I couldn't just run off and leave my mom alone with him when I became old enough to go out on my own. I was her protector. By the time I turned sixteen, I was able to, at the very least, keep her safe. If he came home in the mood to fight, I let him take it out on me. Sometimes I would fight back, but Paul was bigger and stronger. And then I turned eighteen. And something happened to me. It was like something inside of me that had been sleeping for eighteen years woke up."

"The next time Paul came home in one of his moods, it happened. I fought back, but it wasn't just me fighting back anymore. It was my powers, Mercy. I didn't know I had powers. I had never known I had powers. I didn't know who my birth parents were, or what my lineage was. I had discovered I was adopted a few years earlier, but I didn't know about Linda or my father. And so my powers took me by surprise, and they took Paul by surprise too. I unleashed them on him. I nearly killed him. I had so much pent up rage inside of me that once I had him down on the ground, I just couldn't stop hitting him."

Tears were falling freely down Reign's cheeks as he

spoke. I didn't know if the tears were from the recollection of what he had done or the recollection of what he had been through or that he was admitting it to me, but my heart went out to him. It crushed me to realize that my brother, my own flesh and blood, had grown up in such miserable circumstances. I slid over on the bed, right next to his chair, and put my arms around him.

"I put him in the hospital, and it took him months to get out. He's got some permanent damage, to his body, he's got some brain damage and his knee is messed up. He'll live out his life in an assisted care home for the rest of his life. And you know what, I have a hard time regretting what I did, Mercy. I'm sure it's wrong that I don't, but mom and I were his punching bag for thirteen years! He deserved everything he got! And I paid for my actions. The criminal record you found was a result of that. Then when I got out of jail, I had a few anger issues I had to work through myself, and I got in a bit more trouble. I finally feel like I'm in a place to move past all of that and move forward."

"That's why you decided to come find Mom and me?" I asked him quietly.

He nodded and took both of my hands. "Yes. I need to have good people in my life, and I need to know about my powers and my family and where I come from. I need to feel like I have a purpose."

I wiped away the tears that I hadn't even noticed I was shedding. Finally, I had what I had been longing for. I felt like my brother was telling me the truth. I felt like I was actually hearing the true him. While I was happy to feel like my brother was finally being real with me, it broke my heart to hear about what his life had been like without my mother and I. "If my mother had known for a second what was going on with you…" I began.

He stopped me. "No, Mercy, she had no way of knowing. I understand she didn't give me away. I *was taken* from her. I know things would have been different if I had been raised in the same home that you were, but I can't be angry at her for that, and I can't be angry at you."

"I'm so sorry my grandmother did this to you," I told him, choking back the lump in my throat. I didn't want to hate my granny, but after Reign's story, it was hard not to be upset with her.

"What our grandmother did to Linda and you and me was in no way your fault, so you have nothing to apologize for. Someday, she and I will have to come to terms with what happened as a result of her actions, but we'll save that for another day."

I nodded and blotted my tears with the sleeves of Holly's sweater as Reign stood up. "I know you're not much of a hugger, but can I hug you?"

I managed a shy smile as I stood up and Reign wrapped his strong arms around my shoulders. For the first time, I felt like he was my brother. I hugged him around the middle tightly and felt him kiss the top of my forehead. I'd always imagined having a brother, and that's what he'd do, kiss my forehead just like that. The thought made me smile, and I hugged Reign tighter. It suddenly felt good to have a big brother.

"I'm glad you told me everything," I said as we finally parted.

He gave me a megawatt smile. "I'm glad too. I was scared to tell you, and I haven't told Linda any of this. I didn't want her to feel bad in any way that all of that happened. It wasn't her fault, and I certainly don't blame her, but I could see how she might have some bad feelings about it."

"Yeah, Mom won't like it. Unfortunately, I haven't been able to talk to her for a couple of days now. For a while there, I was talking to her a couple of times a day, but then she just disappeared. I tried calling the house phone too and nothing."

"Linda's missing?" he asked nervously.

"I don't know if she's missing, she just doesn't answer the phone at the house and I haven't been able to communicate with her. Which is so weird, especially now, you'd think she'd be super worried about you with the murder investigation going on and all."

Reign's face showed panic. "Should we call the Dubbsburg police and have them go check the house?"

I shook my head. "We'll give her another day, if she doesn't show up by tomorrow we'll do that, okay?"

He nodded. "Mercy, I have some other things to tell you that are really important. It involves Linda."

I shook my head and held up a flattened palm. "Reign, we just had a good talk. Good talk." I clapped my hands in a staccato. "Let's not go throwing a bunch of other hidden family secrets into this right now. I can't handle it right now. There's just too much going on, and I'm exhausted. Plus, Hugh's waiting for me in the car. We're going to go have ice cream. You want to come?"

"I don't think Hugh wants me to tag along," he said with a little chuckle. "I can tell he doesn't care for me."

"Exactly why the two of you should get to know each other better!" I insisted. "Come on. Let's go."

WITH OUR ICE CREAM CONES IN HAND, HUGH, REIGN, AND I left the Dairy Diva ice cream parlor. It was a beautiful evening, and I was feeling buoyant for the first time in a long time. Hugh and Reign were both on their best behavior and pretending to like each other, even if just for me.

"Hey, do you guys mind if I go across the street to Jimmy's? I should check on Harper. I haven't talked to her since her falling out with Elena yesterday," I said.

"I'll go with you," said Hugh.

"Me too," agreed Reign.

"Oh, no, silly boys, I'll be fine, it will just be a minute!" I said and ran across the street. I threw open the door to Jimmy's and was surprised to find the bar completely empty with the door unlocked. "Jimmy?" I called.

When no one answered, I dashed upstairs and found Harper sitting in the closet of Reign's old room. "Harper! There you are. Is everything okay?"

Harper nodded sadly. "Mercy, why am I still here? I'm tired of being a ghost. Every little noise scares me."

I knelt down in front of her. "Spirits usually stick around until their Earthly issues have been resolved. Your issue is resolved, maybe you need to go say goodbye to your parents or something," I suggested. "I can take you to them."

Harper shook her head. "I've been giving this a lot of thought. I don't think Vaughn would do this to me. I'm shocked that my sister was cheating on me with Vaughn, but I don't feel like either of them would have killed me. Vaughn loved me, despite everything."

"Who else would have done this to you, though? I've talked to my brother, and I don't think he did this. If it wasn't Vaughn and it wasn't Reign, who else would it be?"

"Mercy!" I heard hollered from the first floor. "Mercy, where are you?"

I shot to the door and looked over the railing. "Up here, I told you two to wait for me outside. Jimmy doesn't want you in here, Reign," I hollered downstairs.

"Mercy, is there anyone up there?" Hugh asked nervously.

"Harper's up here. I haven't seen anyone else, why?"

"Stay up there," Hugh instructed.

I ran back to talk to Harper. "Something's going on downstairs, Harper. I have to go. I'll talk to you more about this in a little bit, okay?"

She nodded. I took off down the stairs, "What's going on?"

"I told you to stay up there," Hugh said.

"Why? Where's Reign?" I asked.

"We've got a problem," I heard Reign say from behind the bar.

"Why are you behind the bar? Jimmy's not going to like that," I told him.

"Jimmy's not going to care," Reign assured me.

"Yeah, he is. He doesn't want his bar associated with you, at least until your cleared anyway," I told him. "That's why I asked you two to wait outside. I didn't want there to be a scene. Where's Jimmy?" I asked, finally looking around.

"Darlin', something's happened to Jimmy," said Hugh.

"Something's happened? I don't understand, what do you mean?" I asked as I walked over to the bar and crawled up on a barstool. I leaned over the counter where Reign was standing looking at the ground. There, sprawled out behind the counter was Jimmy.

"Oh, my gosh!" I screamed. "Is he?"

Reign nodded. "Yeah, I just checked for a pulse. He's dead."

CHAPTER 17

"So Detective Whitman thinks it was another poisoning?" Alba asked while we picked at our breakfast the next morning.

"Yeah, he said there was no sign of trauma, he's fairly confident it was another poisoning," I told the girls with another yawn. The night before had been a long evening, and I was exhausted. Finding Jimmy Spencer's body had been quite a shock to my already fatigued system.

"Who do they think did it?" Jax asked.

I shrugged as I took a long sip of my double caramel macchiato. "I assume it was Harper's killer."

"Where were Vaughn and Elena when the murder happened?" Holly asked.

"In police custody," I said sadly. The whole night had been a blur, but the one thing we couldn't get over was the fact that Vaughn and Elena had both been in custody when Jimmy was killed.

"Well, then they probably didn't kill Harper either," rationalized Jax. "Where was Reign?"

"With me," I told them. "And he was with both of you

all day. I really don't think it was Reign. He and I had a long talk last night, and he opened up to me. I've changed my opinion of him."

"So what do we know about Jimmy Spencer?" Alba asked, throwing her fork down onto her nearly empty plate.

"Very little. He's from Aspen Falls originally. He owns the tavern. That's all I know."

"Have you looked him up online?" she asked.

I shook my head. "No, I thought we could do that after breakfast."

"Well, then what are we waiting for, let's go do some digging," said Alba, standing up with her tray.

Five minutes later the five of us were back in my dorm room scouring the internet for any information on Jimmy Spencer that we could find.

"Says here he's owned Jimmy's Bed and Brew since 2001. It was his father's tavern before that," I said. "It's on his website."

"Oh, look, click on that Aspen Falls Observer page," Alba said, pointing at the computer screen.

I clicked the link, and an Aspen Falls Daily Record Arrests page opened up. "Look, Jimmy Spencer, 35, Aspen Falls, PA was arrested Tuesday for theft by insufficient funds check/second degree."

"What's the date on that?" Alba asked.

"Mmm," I scrolled to the top of the page. "This is from August."

"That's interesting. Keep looking," Alba instructed.

I flipped back over to my Google search results and found another page. "Oh my gosh, guys, look at this!" I hollered and pointed at another link.

Jax, Sweets, and Holly sucked in their breath as they saw what I was seeing. "What's it say?" Alba asked.

"Jimmy's bar is in foreclosure!" I told her, tapping the screen.

"He needed money," Alba said knowingly.

"I wonder if Detective Whitman knows?" I asked the girls.

"We've got to tell him!" Jax admonished.

"Yeah, he needs to know," Alba agreed. "What if he owed money to someone and that's who killed him! Maybe that same person killed Harper too!"

"I'll call him," I said and stood up, pulling out my cell phone from my back pocket. Alba slid into my spot and began scrolling through the links while I paced around the room waiting for Detective Whitman to answer.

Jax and Holly jumped up to sit on Jax's desk while Sweets sat on the bed.

"Detective Whitman," said his deep voice on the other end of the phone.

"Detective! This is Mercy Habernackle," I said excitedly.

"Mercy, do you have new information for me?" he asked.

"The girls and I have been doing some digging, and we just found out that Jimmy Spencer's bar was in foreclosure."

"I just found that out myself," Detective Whitman said. "Anything else?"

I looked at the girls sheepishly. "No, I just thought that sounded like an important part of the puzzle. What if he owed money to someone else and they are the ones who killed him?"

"It's possible," Detective Whitman said. "Listen, call me

if you get any psychic information. I've got to go, lots going on at the station right now."

"Okay, bye," I said and hung up the phone. I looked at the girls. "He already knew about Jimmy's financial problems. That was embarrassing."

Jax leaned backwards on her desk. Her hand bumped an object on her desk, sending a glass rolling to the floor. Holly shot forward and caught it with one hand. "Nice reflexes, Cosmo," Alba muttered with a little laugh.

With the glass still clutched in her hand, Holly's body stiffened, and she crumpled to the floor. "Hurry, get her," I hollered. No one was fast enough, and she landed with a thud on the floor.

"Holly!" Jax screamed as she leapt off the desk to her friend's side. "Holly! Is she breathing?"

I held a hand over her mouth and discovered she was breathing. "Yeah, I think she's in a trance."

"What did she touch?" Alba asked.

We looked down at her hand to see the object that had rolled off of Jax's desk. It was the shot glass that Jax had stolen from Jimmy's bar the day after Harper's murder. "It's a shot glass. It was Jimmy's."

"Don't touch it! Let her have a vision. Maybe she'll see something important," Alba ordered.

Crouched down around her, we allowed Holly to have her vision. Her breathing became shallow as her mind moved through whatever scene it was watching. Finally, her eyes shot open, as if she'd just come out of a terrible nightmare. "Ahh!" she hollered.

"Holly, are you alright?" Sweets asked her.

"Let's get her up," Alba instructed.

Her hands and arms trembled as we lifted her from the

floor and sat her down on the desk chair. "You okay, Holly?" I asked her.

"My head," she cried and reached back to hold the base of her skull.

"You hit it on the way down. Thankfully we've got this nice carpet that broke your fall a bit," Jax said and shot me a haughty grin.

"Shaky," she managed to utter.

Sweets rose a hand up. "I got this. Her blood sugar is low. It happens to me all the time. Jax, you have any more orange juice in your fridge?" Without waiting for a reply, Sweets rummaged through our mini fridge. "Ah-ha! Found one! Here, Holly, drink this."

Holly took several long gulps of the juice until it was gone. We all trained our eyes on her until she began to move in her seat. "I feel a little better."

"Take some deep breaths," Jax instructed her. "Inhale....exhale."

"This isn't yoga class, Shorty," Alba barked.

"It'll help her relax! She needs to relax."

"I'm okay, I'm doing better," Holly said shaking her head.

"What did you see?" Sweets asked her excitedly.

"You're *never* in a million years going to guess," said Holly.

"You saw who poisoned Harper?" Alba asked flatly.

Holly's bottom lip pouted out. "Boo. That was no fun."

Jax clapped her hands excitedly. "You saw who poisoned Harper? Awesome!"

Holly glared at Alba. "But you'll *never* in a million years guess who did it!" Holly clapped at her exciting secret.

"Jimmy Spencer," Alba guessed.

Holly spun around in her seat and threw her arms on her hips angrily. "Alba! You're no fun at all!"

Alba shrugged. "I get that from time to time."

I stared at Holly, stunned. "Are you telling us that Jimmy Spencer poisoned Harper Bradshaw?! Wait, what?! How in the world did you guess?" I asked Alba.

Alba gave a little smile. "I dabble in mind reading, in case you forgot."

"Ugh," Holly groaned.

"I'm shocked. I cannot believe Jimmy killed Harper!"

"I know, I couldn't believe it either," Holly said. "But I *saw* him pour the poison into her drink."

"Why would Jimmy Spencer want to kill Harper Bradshaw? That doesn't make any sense!" Sweets asked.

I shoved my glasses further back up onto my nose. "I have no idea. It *doesn't* make any sense. And now *he's* been poisoned. None of this makes any sense."

"Maybe he couldn't live with the guilt, so he poisoned himself," Jax suggested with a shrug.

Alba shook her head. "I doubt it. That guy didn't seem to be the guilty conscience kind of person."

"I agree. The only way Jimmy would have killed himself was if it was unintentional," I said. "Maybe he accidentally drank the poison that he gave Harper."

"Seriously? There's no way he did that, he was a bartender, he wasn't stupid," Alba disagreed.

"So now what? Jimmy killed Harper. What do we do with that information?" Holly asked.

"Well, I think we've got to go down to the station and let Detective Whitman know what we've discovered."

Suddenly my cell phone rang. I looked at it curiously. It wasn't a phone number that I recognized. "Hello?"

"Mercy?" said a timid voice on the other end of the phone.

"Yes? Who is this?"

"It's Elena. Elena Bradshaw."

THE WITCH SQUAD RUSHED DOWN TO JIMMY'S WHERE ELENA, Reign, and Detective Whitman were already parked outside waiting for us when we got there. We needed to tell them all what we had discovered, and I had a few questions I wanted to ask Elena and Harper.

With Chesney slung over one shoulder, I looked at Detective Whitman. "I know it's a crime scene, but can we go inside?"

"Yes, I've got the keys, come on," he said and led the group inside. He flicked the light switch by the front door and illuminated the empty bar.

"What's this meeting about, Mercy?" Reign asked.

"Should we sit down?" Detective Whitman asked.

"This won't take long," I assured him.

"We know who killed Harper," Alba revealed to him.

Detective Whitman's face seemed unimpressed as did Elena's. "You thought you knew it was Vaughn and Elena earlier. What happened to that theory?"

Elena held up her hands to plead her innocence. "It wasn't me, honest!"

"We know that it wasn't you now," I said with a pang of regret. Perhaps we'd jumped on the Vaughn and Elena train a little too quickly.

"Good!" she admonished.

"I'm dying to hear who you think killed Harper Bradshaw *this* time," Detective Whitman said with a huff.

"I'm dying to know who you think killed Harper Bradshaw too!" said a familiar voice from the doorway.

I spun around in my seat and leapt off the chair I was perched on. "Mom!" I exclaimed as I lunged at her. My arms encircled her waist as I wrapped her in a huge bear hug.

"Mercy!" she said with a laugh. "Wow, I guess you missed me then?"

"Mom! Of course, I missed you. And I've been worried about you. Sneaks wasn't talking to me anymore, and I tried calling the house, but you didn't answer!"

My mom sighed. I took a good look at her face. She was almost like a carbon copy of me, but her hair was peppered with white strands, and she had a few new wrinkles around her temples. "Mercy, when you told me that your brother was in trouble, I jumped in that old rickety car of yours and hopped on over here as fast as I could. Of course, wouldn't you know, about an hour outside of Akron the alternator went out on the darned thing. Do you think I could find a parts store close by? Of course not!" she took a deep breath and looked around the room.

"Are we having a party?" she asked casually, as she took in each face one by one. Finally, her eyes settled on Reign. "Oh! Reign! My son!"

"Hi, Linda," he said with a wide smile. "I'm sorry all this happened, and you had to come all the way out to Pennsylvania. That's a long drive!"

My mom's face, which had lit up at the sight of my brother, scrunched up into a dumping ground of tears. She reached her arms out in front of her, "Oh, son! Come over here and give your mother a hug!"

Reign's eyes smiled before his mouth did, but when they caught up to each other, it just about made *me* cry. He stood up and threw his arms around my mother's shoulders. The minute I heard her choking back a happy sob, my tears broke out too.

"Uh-hum," Detective Whitman cleared his throat.

"Oh, sorry. I know you've got a lot going on. Detective Whitman, this is my mother, Linda Habernackle. Mom, this is Detective Whitman."

Mom wiped her eyes with the sleeve of her shirt and looked at Detective Whitman with interest. "Well hello," she said as she patted at her cheeks. "It's so nice to meet you."

Detective Whitman stood up and straightened his khaki sports coat. Then he leaned forward and shook her hand. "Nice to meet you as well. Your daughter has been very helpful on the last two of our murder investigations."

"I'm so glad to hear that," Mom said without taking her eyes off of the detective.

"And, Mom, you know the girls," I said and pointed at the rest of the Witch Squad.

"Jax and I have formally met," she began. That's all it took, and Jax launched herself at my mother.

"Hi, Mom!" she cooed excitedly.

"Hi, Jax, it's a pleasure to see you too," she said with a little laugh as she looked down at the elf hugging her middle. "Now I've only met Alba, Holly, and Sweets through Sneaks. Hello, ladies, I'm Mercy's mom, Linda," she said with a little wave at the rest of the girls.

"And this is Elena," I said and gestured towards the blond girl sitting quietly next to Detective Whitman. "She is Harper Bradshaw's sister. Harper is the girl that passed away recently."

"Oh, Elena, I'm so very sorry for your loss," my mom

said quietly as Jax disengaged herself from my mother's waist.

"Thank you," she whispered.

"And who is this little guy?" Mom asked, petting the top of Chesney's head.

"Oh, this is Chesney, he's mine. He's new," I said excitedly.

"I see. You think you have room for a puppy in your dorm room?" Mom asked skeptically.

"Mom! You can't come to college and start in on me. Can't you just let me be happy that you're here for five minutes before getting on my nerves?"

Mom held up her hands in defeat. "Fine, fine. Your business. I'll stay out of it. So, what's going on here today?"

"Wait, how did you know we were here?" I asked her with narrowed eyes.

Mom shifted her weight onto one leg and put her hand on her hip. "Mercy. You know I've got strong powers of intuition. I could just *feel* where you were."

"Yeah right, Mom, how did you know?"

She shrugged. "Eh, I was pulling into town and just happened to see you and the girls crossing the street. Jax's witch hat was a dead giveaway. I flipped a U-turn and came back."

"Figures," I said with a little laugh.

"So, what's going on?" she asked.

Holly stood up. "I'll tell you what's going on. I had a vision. I saw who killed Harper."

"Alright, out with it," Detective Whitman prompted.

"Jimmy Spencer," Holly said with gusto.

Detective Whitman looked around at all of our faces. "Really? You're gonna pin it on the dead guy?"

SON OF A WITCH

Mom's eyes opened wide. "There's another dead person?"

"The owner. Jimmy Spencer. Your son and daughter just found him last night. He was dead behind the counter," Detective Whitman told my mother.

"That's terrible!" she said as a hand fluttered to her mouth.

"And now we're pinning Harper's murder on him?" he asked.

"I know, positively, Jimmy did it," Holly asserted. "I *saw* him in my vision. I was holding one of his shot glasses, and I saw him pouring the poison into Harper's drink, and I saw him give it to her. I also saw him drug Reign."

Reign's face lit up. "So that's why I don't remember what happened, I was drugged."

"Did anything show up in your vision about how Jimmy ended up dead?" he asked us.

Alba and I looked at each other. "No, we don't know how Jimmy died. We were going to go talk to Harper about that and see if she could help us."

Detective Whitman stood up. "Okay, I have a lot to do to follow up with this. I'll do some digging. If Harper remembers anything, give me a call." He headed towards the door. "Lock up when you leave, please. And, Linda, it was so nice meeting you."

My mom gave him a coy smile. "It was nice meeting you as well."

"Mom, the girls and I have some work to do also. Reign, can you watch Mom for me while we go do a little more digging?"

"Watch Mom? I need a babysitter all of a sudden?" Mom looked at me like I was crazy.

"Fine. Mom, will you watch Reign for the rest of the

afternoon? And Chesney, can you guys watch him too?" I asked and handed him to Reign.

Reign's dark eyes shone happily. "I'd be happy to take Linda and Chesney for the day."

"Linda? Son, I told you, I'd love for you to call me Mom."

Reign's face lit up again, and after hearing his story about his less than stellar childhood, his sheepish smile tugged at my heartstrings. "Of course, *Mom*."

CHAPTER 18

With the Witch Squad and Elena in tow, we made our way up the stairs to check on Harper. Elena had asked to be able to talk to her sister again, and after discovering that Jimmy was dead, I knew we needed to see if Harper had seen or heard anything that might help in figuring out how that happened.

"Harper?" I called as we came in the small room. The hardwood floors creaked as we all shuffled about. I pulled back the closet doors to find Harper's ghost huddled on the floor, as usual. When the light flooded her sanctuary, she looked up me.

"Harper, are you alright?" I asked her.

She nodded. "This place has been a madhouse of activity lately. What happened?"

"Jimmy Spencer is dead," I told her.

Alba and Sweets took a seat around the little table in front of the window while Jax and Holly tossed themselves onto the bed. Only Elena looked uneasy in the situation.

"Jimmy Spencer? He was the bartender?" Harper asked.

"Yes."

"You brought Elena with you I see. I'm still not speaking to her," Harper told me.

I turned to Elena. "Harper said she's still not speaking to you."

"But I want her to know how sorry I am about Vaughn and me," Elena cried as tears began to slide down her cheeks easily.

"I don't want to hear any more apologies," Harper said and crossed her arms across her chest.

"There's something you need to know, Harper," I began uneasily. "We know who killed you."

Harper's head snapped back to look up at me. "Was it my sister?"

I gave her a gentle little smile and shook my head. "No, it wasn't Elena. And it wasn't Vaughn."

"Then it was your brother?" Harper asked in surprise. "Wow, I'm shocked, I didn't think it was going to be him."

"No, thankfully it wasn't my brother. It was Jimmy."

"The guy that just died? Why would he have wanted to kill me?"

"That's what we're trying to figure out. We have no idea. The only thing we know is that Jimmy Spencer was having financial troubles. This building just went into foreclosure."

"What's foreclosure?" Harper asked.

"He must not be making the payments on it. Foreclosure means the bank is trying to take it away from him to settle his debts with them," I explained to her.

"So you think he killed me for *money*?" she asked me incredulously.

Elena's eyes widened when she heard about his money problems. "The Bed & Brew is in foreclosure? I had no idea!"

"I don't know if he killed you for money," I told Harper.

"My parents are worth a fortune," she admitted.

I turned to the girls. "Harper asked if we think Jimmy killed her for money. She said her parents are worth a fortune."

Elena shook her head. "But how would he get any of their money by killing her?"

"Maybe he was only going to drug her enough to abduct her," Jax suggested. "And then he would hold her for ransom."

"That seems kind of unlikely," I said. "Wouldn't it be too obvious? I mean if the cops started digging around and found out that Jimmy was broke and losing the bar, wouldn't they immediately suspect him?"

"Maybe someone offered to pay Jimmy to kill Harper," Holly suggested.

"But the only person that knew I was coming to town was Elena," Harper told me.

I repeated Harper's rebuttal to the girls.

Elena visibly winced, and Alba caught it.

"What aren't you telling us, Elena?" she asked.

Elena looked uncomfortable. "Well, I guess I did tell one other person that Harper was coming to town."

My jaw dropped as I turned to look at her squarely. "You told us that you didn't tell anyone."

"Well, I didn't think that this person mattered. There's no way he would hurt Harper. Not in a million years."

"Who?" Sweets asked as we all hung in the air anxiously.

Elena pinched her cheeks up into her eyes nervously. "My dad?"

"Dad knew I was coming?" Harper asked, jumping off the floor. She marched right up in front of her sister's face.

"You told *Dad* I was coming? I told you not to tell anyone! So much for confiding in my sister! You know, you're the worst sister *ever!* First, you sleep with my boyfriend and then, you tell *Dad* I was coming to town when I specifically asked you not to," Harper ranted at Elena.

I shot Elena a nervous little look. "Harper's not very happy with you."

"Yeah, I figured she wouldn't be. She wanted to surprise him," she admitted to me. Then she looked down at her hands. "I'm really sorry, Harp. It was an accident. I was over at the house, borrowing some money because I bounced a check and they were going to shut off my lights and Dad asked me if I'd heard from you lately and, well, it just slipped. I swear. I didn't mean to."

Harper crossed her arms across her chest again and harrumphed with her back towards Elena.

"She's taking a minute," I whispered to Elena.

"So, let's think this out," Alba said calmly. "Harper came to town. Jimmy needed money. Harper's parents *have* money. Harper's dad knew she was coming to town. There are so many pieces of that puzzle missing. It just doesn't make sense. I mean, did Jimmy even *know* your dad?"

Elena shook her head. "I've literally never heard my dad talk about Jimmy Spencer."

Harper spun around. "Wait! Jimmy *does* know my dad! The night I was killed, Jimmy mentioned that Daddy and his friends have been coming to the Bed & Brew for coffee every morning. He said he'd known Daddy for years!"

"Harper says that Jimmy and Sergeant Bradshaw did know each other. She said that the Sergeant had coffee with the guys here every morning," I repeated.

Elena looked surprised. "I didn't know that. I knew he

had coffee with his friends in the mornings, but I guess I never even thought to ask where they had it at."

"Okay, so Harper came to town. Jimmy needed money. Sergeant Bradshaw has money, and he knew Harper was coming to town. And now we know that Sergeant Bradshaw and Jimmy knew each other," Alba recited, adding that last piece to the puzzle.

"Did Jimmy think that if he killed Harper, he could extort money from my father in some way?" Elena asked, puzzled.

"Maybe he was planning to harm you too if the Sergeant didn't pay up?" I suggested.

Elena shrugged. "You'd think Daddy would have been keeping a closer eye on me since Harper's murder then. He's been grieving so much. I don't even think he's even given me a second thought!"

"And you don't think your father would have hurt your sister?" I asked her.

Elena shook her head emphatically. "Absolutely not! Daddy thought Harper hung the moon. There's no way he would hurt her."

"Besides, that would have taken *a lot* of planning. Elena and Harper's father would have had to know where Harper was staying, gotten in contact with Jimmy in advance and worked out some kind of deal. Did Harper make reservations at Jimmy's?" Holly asked.

I looked at Harper, she looked relieved. "No, we didn't make reservations."

"She didn't make reservations," I repeated to the girls. Then I caught sight of Elena, gnawing on her bottom lip ferociously. "What is it, Elena?"

"Nothing," she chirped.

"What does she know?" I asked Harper.

Harper's eyes widened. "I just remembered. We stayed at Jimmy's because Elena suggested it."

I swiveled around to look at Elena. "You suggested that Harper and Vaughn stay at Jimmy's? Did you know Jimmy?"

"Wait, *what?*" Alba asked. "It was Elena's idea for Harper to stay here?"

"That's what Harper says."

All eyes were on Elena. "I don't know Jimmy at all," she assured us. Then she sighed heavily. "My *dad* suggested Harper stay at Jimmy's."

"WHAT?!" I asked, shocked.

"When I accidentally mentioned to Dad that Harper was coming to town, he asked me when. I told him, and I said they'd probably be rolling into town late that night because they were driving in from Connecticut. He suggested it would be easier on them both if Harper and her boyfriend stayed somewhere that night and came to the house in the morning. He said there was a little bed and breakfast type place downtown that he knew of – Jimmy's Bed & Brew. I relayed that to Harper."

"This just keeps getting more and more interesting," Sweets said as she readjusted herself in her chair.

"Most definitely!" I agreed. "So what do we do with this information? Harper's father could have had something to do with this."

Harper wrung her hands. "There's no way Daddy would do this to me. Just no way. I thought he loved me!"

"We don't know anything for sure yet, Harper, relax," I said to her. My heart went out to her. She was probably better off believing that her sister had done this to her than her own father! "Harper's upset. She doesn't want to believe that her father did this."

Elena wrung her hands just as Harper did. "I don't believe it either. Daddy would never hurt either of us."

"Well, there's only one way to find out," Alba said knowingly.

"We've got to go talk to Sergeant Bradshaw," I agreed.

Sweets looked surprised. "Like he's really just going to tell us that he did it?"

"Maybe he'll need a little convincing!" I said to Sweets. "Looks like your potion making might come in handy today, Sweets. Are you up for it?"

CHAPTER 19

J ax, Holly, Sweets, Alba and I parked Sweets's car outside of the Bradshaw house. Even though Elena hadn't wanted to, we'd convinced her to invite Sergeant and Mrs. Bradshaw out for lunch to make sure that they were out of the house so we could do a little nosing around. As it turned out, Sergeant Bradshaw had some last-minute funeral arrangements to iron out and would be tied up until later in the day, but Louise Bradshaw had been available for lunch.

"Where did Elena say they hide their spare key?" I asked as the five of us approached the sprawling brick ranch style house in an established neighborhood in Aspen Falls.

"Under the flower pot on the patio," said Jax.

When we got to the front of the house a little dog inside began yipping like crazy. "Shhh," I hissed at the dog.

"Like he understands what that means?" Holly whispered back.

"He might."

"Which flower pot?" Alba asked, looking around the patio. A wide assortment of potted plants covered the patio.

"I have no idea, I guess we check them all," I said with frustration.

Each of us began hurriedly looking underneath the pots for a key. "Someone is going to see us," Jax whispered nervously.

"There's no key here," Holly said. "We've checked them all."

"Maybe she meant the patio in the back of the house," Sweets suggested.

"Oh, that's probably what she meant," I agreed. "Let's run around back."

Both sides of the house had a tall wooden fence enclosing the backyard. The right side of the house had a hinged wooden gate which was locked from the inside, and the fence was too tall to jump over.

"Give me a boost," I suggested.

"The neighbors are going to call the police," Jax hissed at me.

"Then hurry up," I said to her.

Alba rolled her at eyes at us. "Hello? We're witches?" she growled at us. "Ugh. Watch out."

We all stepped back as Alba bounced around on the balls of her feet lightly. She rolled her head around on her shoulders as her arms hung loosely by her sides, like a boxer loosening up for a fight. Then, just like that, she stopped bouncing and focused on the door. She closed her eyes as her arms raised out straight in front of her. Slowly, she flattened her palms so that they were perpendicular to the door and when she had enough energy built up in her body, she unleashed a bolt of blue and green electric energy towards the wooden gate. It made an intense crackling noise as it struck the wooden door and blasted it off of its hinges and into the backyard.

With our mouths hanging open, we all peered through the break in the fence. The wooden door lay splintered forty feet away in the backyard, and the fence itself was shredded where the hinge had been pulled out by the screws.

"Well that was a bit of overkill, don't ya think?" I asked Alba testily. "I offered to scale the fence!"

Jax looked around. "I'm sure the neighbors heard that one! Now they're definitely going to call the police. We better hurry."

"I just hope that if the neighbors *did* see it, they didn't get it on video. I don't want someone to post it on YouTube or something. I mean something like this would go viral. My mom would *kill* me if she saw me breaking and entering like this!" Sweets commented nervously.

"You guys are a bunch of worrywarts," Alba commented. "It's the middle of the day. All these people are probably at work right now."

"Come on," I groaned. "We need to find that key!"

"You're paying for that, by the way," Jax snapped at Alba as we walked past the broken gate in the backyard.

"Zip it, Shorty," Alba retorted.

In the back of the house, the Bradshaw's had a wooden deck with patio furniture on it. There were two potted plants on the deck. We made quick work of checking for the key and were disappointed to find it not there either.

"Now what are we going to do?" Holly whined.

"We'll have to go in through a window," I suggested. "There's got to be an open window around here some-where. Spread out and start looking."

The girls all jumped off the deck and began looking for

an open window. I went around the side we'd just come from and looked up when I heard the little yippy dog barking at me again. It sounded like he was right in front of me. He was standing in front of an open window with a screen on it. "Girls!" I hissed excitedly. I raced back around to the backyard. "Girls! I found an open window!"

As they all tore around the corner to where I was, we looked up at the window. It was a good ten feet off the ground.

"How are we supposed to get up there?" Sweets asked.

"I'm going to climb up there. You guys will have to give me a boost," I told her.

"There's a screen on the window, though," she argued.

"I'll take it off. Come on, lift me up!"

Alba grabbed hold of my waist and tried to lift me that way. My legs floundered as they searched for something to grab onto. "Put me down, Alba, that won't work. I'll need to stand on you."

Alba and Sweets each crouched down and put out a knee for me to stand on while Jax and Holly steadied me by holding onto my hands. I was still about four feet too short to look into the open window, and the little dog was getting even more and more annoyed with my attempts. "Shut up!" I hollered at the dog.

"Mercy! That's not very nice!" Sweets cried. "How would Chesney feel if you told *him* to shut up like that!"

I rolled my eyes at Sweets. "They don't speak English, Sweets. Now boost me up higher!"

Alba and Sweets each took hold of a foot and tried to lift me up higher towards the window. My fingertips caught hold of the screen, but I wasn't high enough to budge it.

"Okay, put me down, we'll have to make a pyramid," I finally sighed.

The girls let me down and we all stood around looking at one another. "I think we need to send Jax up first," I told the girls. "She's the lightest."

"Sweets, Alba, you two will have to get down on your hands and knees and form a base. Holly and I will stand on your backs, and Jax can climb on us."

"This is the dumbest plan ever, Red."

"No, it's not. It'll work, trust me," I retorted.

"But we'd be kneeling on rocks!" Sweets complained. "That's going to hurt our hands and knees."

"Fine, we need something to put down on the rocks to kneel on," I said, looking around. "Oh! The gate! We'll use what's left of the gate for a flat surface to kneel on."

I walked over to the beat-up wooden gate and tried to lift a corner. "It's heavy, come give me a hand."

Alba came over and together we carried the gate and set it down underneath the window. "There. Are we ready?"

"What am I supposed to do when I get up there?" Jax asked nervously.

"Pull the screen off, and then we'll push you up higher, and you'll climb in and go around and unlock the doors for us," I told her.

"Alright, let's go," she said.

Sweets and Alba got down on all fours while Holly and I climbed up on their backs. "Geez, Red, lay off the treats, huh?" Alba hollered at me as I climbed on her back.

When Holly and I were steadily on our feet on their backs, Jax climbed up between us and carefully we eased her up onto our bent legs. "Can you see inside?" I asked her.

"Yeah, the dog is growling at me, Mercy," she cried. "He's gonna bite me if I go in there."

"He's a tiny little thing. He won't bite you. Start talking to him," Alba hollered up from the ground.

"Hey, little guy," Jax cooed as she began working on the screen. "This screen won't come off!"

"You have to shove it up first, and then you should be able to get your fingers underneath the bottom, and you can pull it out that way," Holly instructed.

I looked at Holly with a little grin. "Moonlight as a cat burglar?"

"I had a boyfriend that locked me out of his house once," she retorted.

"I need something flat to slip under the screen. I can't get my fingers in there," Jax hollered down at us.

"Would keys work?" Sweets asked from the bottom of the unstable pyramid.

"Yeah, I think they might," Jax called down to her.

Sweets managed to lift one arm and grabbed her keys from her pocket. "Holly, can you reach?"

"Hang on, Jax," Holly called and reached down to grab Sweets' keys. "Got em! Here, Jaxie."

Jax reached down and got the keys, and within a matter of seconds, she had the window screen popped out. The little dog jumped right towards her face, growling at her. "Nice puppy," she cooed. "Lift me up, hurry!"

Holly and I each took a foot and lifted Jax as high as we could. She was able to grab a hold of the inside of the window and pull herself up through the frame. From below we could hear the dog going crazy.

"Jax, are you alright?" Sweets hollered to her as we all dismounted and Sweets was able to stand up.

"Ahhh!" Jax screamed. We could see the top of her head running past the window crazily. Then we heard a door slam, and the house went silent.

"Jax?" I hollered.

She didn't respond.

"Jaxie?" Holly hollered after an extended silence. And then just like that, we heard Jax's voice from the backyard.

"Door's open, ladies!"

"Jax! You did it!" Sweets called out excitedly. "Good job, sister!"

Alba walked past Jax, tousling her hair as she walked by. "Way to go, Shorty."

Jax beamed.

"How'd you get Barky to zip it?" Alba asked.

"He chased me into a bedroom, and I slammed the door behind me as I ran out," Jax said with a little laugh.

"Nice, way to go," I told her. "Now, let's hurry. Someone could show up any minute after all of that."

We all filed up the deck steps and into the back, sliding door which led us into the kitchen and breakfast nook area.

"Nice house!" Holly said, admiring their meticulously decorated interior.

"It's kind of chilly in here," I told the girls, putting a hand up around my shoulders.

"It doesn't feel that bad," Sweets commented. "It's probably just the breeze coming in through that open window. I'll go get the screen from the back yard so we can close the window."

"Thanks, Sweets," I told her gratefully. "I'm going to go this way," I told the rest of the girls.

Alba nodded. "Holly and I will go this way. Holler if you find anything interesting."

"Okay, you do the same." I rubbed my arms to warm them up and make my pebbled flesh disappear while I began my investigation of the Bradshaw house. Their living room was very formal. Everything was in its place, very neat and tidy. It hardly looked like anyone even lived there.

Just off the living room was a study, closed off by double sliding doors. Bookshelves packed full of books lined one entire wall. Obviously, someone in the house liked to read.

Jax was right behind me, looking around as well. "Wow, they have a lot of books," said Jax, standing back as she admired the extensive collection.

"Yeah, they do," I agreed.

The wall opposite the bookshelves faced the street side of the house. I peeked outside to make sure that Sergeant Bradshaw wasn't pulling into the driveway or that the neighbors weren't looking across the street at us. When the coast looked clear, I pulled out some drawers in the dark mahogany desk.

"What are you looking for?" Jax asked me.

"I have no idea. Proof that Sergeant Bradshaw paid Jimmy to kill Harper, I guess."

"You really think her father killed her?"

It pained me to think that way. How could a father possibly pay someone to kill his own daughter? The thought sickened me. "I really hope he didn't, Jax."

"Girls! Look at this!" Alba hollered from the other doorway in the study.

Jax and I looked up to see Holly and Alba rushing in with a small packet.

"What is it?" I asked Alba.

"It's arsenic!" she said excitedly.

"You're kidding? How in the world did you find it so fast?"

Alba pointed at Holly. "She's like a bloodhound."

"My senses are extra strong right now. I had a premonition that it was hiding under some clothing in the master bedroom closet and I was right," she said with a little shrug.

"Holly, this is major!" Jax gushed.

"Yeah, it is. Good job, Holly!" I agreed. "Detective Whitman said that the latest signs in the toxicology report were showing arsenic poisoning."

The realization of the case we were putting together was daunting. To accuse Harper's father of the murder of his own daughter just wasn't sitting right with me. But now we had the murder weapon in our hands. "We need to get that in a Ziploc baggie," I said as the thought occurred to me that it likely had fingerprints on it from the murderer.

Holly nodded. "I'll take it to the kitchen and find one."

"What are we going to do now?" I asked Alba and Jax. "How are we supposed to accuse Sergeant Bradshaw of killing his own daughter? Detective Whitman would eat us alive!"

"Did you just say you want to accuse me of killing my own daughter?" said a voice from the living room. Our heads swiveled up to see Sergeant Bradshaw at the double doors adjoining the study to the living room.

CHAPTER 20

"Sergeant Bradshaw!" I gasped. My heart practically leapt out of my chest, and my feet felt heavy, like they were anchored in concrete blocks.

"What are you girls doing in my house? I'm calling the police!" he said right away as he entered the room.

"Sweets!" Alba called immediately.

"Sergeant Bradshaw, we can explain," I began slowly, holding my arms up in front of me in a defensive position. My stomach dropped almost immediately triggering my pulse to shoot out of control in my ears.

"Sweets!" Alba called again.

"Fine, then you can explain to Detective Whitman why you busted my gate, broke into my house, and are snooping around in my personal desk drawer!"

"Sweets!" Alba yelled once again.

Sergeant Bradshaw turned to Alba with annoyance and anger. "Why does she keep yelling Sweets?" he asked as he pulled his cell phone out of his back pocket.

"Tourette's," I told him chastely.

Jax suppressed a giggle.

Finally, Sweets appeared from behind Sergeant Bradshaw. She took one deep breath, held her hands out in front of her and blew the sparkling dust she held, right into Sergeant Bradshaw's face. It stunned him momentarily, but before he could react, the five of us began to chant in unison,

> *"Magic and powers so deeply bound,*
> *We seek the truth that's not yet found.*
> *Show us what we need to know,*
> *With Verity dust, we humbly blow.*
> *His lips shall part with truths untold,*
> *We ask for him to be so bold.*
> *And when the time's not on our side,*
> *Pause your anger. You must abide."*

When the chant was over, and the truth dust had settled like dandruff flakes on his suit coat shoulders, Sergeant Bradshaw appeared stunned. "What did you just do?" he asked calmly.

"It was a truth spell," I answered as I rubbed my arms.

"Hogwash," he spat.

"Did you know Harper was coming home for the weekend?" Alba asked him.

"Yes, I did," he responded plainly. When he realized what he had just said, so simply, he winced. "But that doesn't mean I killed my daughter!"

"It doesn't mean that you didn't either," I reversed as another pang of chills zipped down my spine.

"Did you kill your daughter, Sergeant?" Alba asked him.

"I did no such thing! I loved my daughter very much," he told us.

Alba's eyes narrowed. "Did you pay someone to kill your daughter?"

"No!" he contended. "I most certainly did not!"

I slumped down. I was nearly positive he was going to admit it, though if I were being honest with myself, I was thankful that he didn't admit it. That would have been too much for me and the girls to handle.

"Do you know who killed your daughter?" Alba asked.

"I do not," he said matter-of-factly.

"Did you know Jimmy Spencer?" I asked him.

"Yes, I did."

"Did you know that Jimmy Spencer was found dead in his bar yesterday?"

"It's a small town, dear. Everyone heard that Jimmy Spencer was found dead in his bar."

"Did you have anything to do with his death?" I asked him pointedly.

"I did not have anything to do with the death of Jimmy Spencer. I was quite fond of Jimmy. He ran a clean bar and made a decent cup of coffee."

"Did you suggest to Harper that she stay overnight at Jimmy's Bed & Brew?" Alba asked.

Sergeant Bradshaw nodded sadly. "That was my suggestion, yes. I told Elena to suggest it to Harper. I thought if Harper came out to the house too late in the evening, she might upset my wife. Louise is rather delicate in nature, and she doesn't care for surprises. I was just trying to keep peace in the house."

"Why did you suggest that Harper stay at Jimmy's specifically, though? You could have just suggested that she come the next day, but you made sure to tell Elena to suggest Harper stay at Jimmy's," I pointed out.

Sergeant Bradshaw sighed. "I only suggested Jimmy's

because I knew I could trust him to keep my daughter's whereabouts to himself. He's not one for gossip. I didn't want word to get back to Louise that Harper and her boyfriend were in town. I wanted to save that little surprise for the next day when my wife would be fresh and at her best."

"Your wife is that fragile?" I asked him.

He tipped his head to the side and rose a shoulder. "Something like that," he said.

Jax stepped forward. "I notice that you have a lot of books on your shelves about mental conditions. You've got several books on bipolar disorders, a few on personality disorders, some on depression and schizophrenia."

Sergeant Bradshaw nodded. "I do have an extensive collection of those types of books, yes."

"Does someone in your family struggle with a mental disorder?" Jax asked.

He rubbed his hand across the back of his neck but answered honestly. "Yes."

"Is it your wife?" Jax asked.

He gritted his teeth and muttered. "Yes."

"I can tell that it bothers you to admit that. Why?" I asked.

"My wife is embarrassed about the fact that she's got those mental problems. It's not something she likes people to know about her. We've been able to hide it from our friends and neighbors for all these years. She keeps up on her medication, and she's very strict with her dosage. She's able to keep her episodes under control."

"What kinds of episodes does she have?" Alba asked.

"It varies," he admitted. "She can be temperamental at times. Sometimes it's sadness, sometimes anger. But we have it under control."

"Do you have any arsenic in the house, Sergeant Bradshaw," I asked him.

"Arsenic?" he scoffed. "Of course not."

"Is there any reason that your wife might have arsenic in the house?"

He shook his head in confusion. "No. No reason at all. We don't have arsenic in the house."

I rubbed my pebbled arms as I walked around the desk. "I see. Then you might tell us why we found arsenic in your master bedroom closet underneath some clothes." I motioned for Holly to show the Sergeant what she'd found.

"You planted that!" he exclaimed. His mind was reeling now. We could see it on his face.

"We didn't," said Holly. "We did put it in a baggie so that they can test it for fingerprints. I'm sure Detective Whitman has his ways to prove that it was touched by someone in your household."

Sergeant Bradshaw's eyes became frantic. "That's not possible. Why would my wife have arsenic in the house?"

"I don't know," I said calmly. "Is there anyone else in and out of your house on a frequent basis? A housekeeper, a family member or friend, or anyone else that would have had access to your bedroom?"

He shook his head in bewilderment. "No, no one. Just my wife and I. We don't have a housekeeper, there are no family members in town besides Elena, and she rarely comes to visit. Our friends only come over for suppers, and we always keep our bedroom door closed. We have a restroom off of the dining room for guests to use."

"Detective Whitman is pretty sure that Harper was killed by arsenic poisoning," I told him quietly.

He shook his head wildly. "I know, he told me."

"If this isn't yours, it's got to be your wife's," I suggested.

"Why would Louise have arsenic? She just *wouldn't*," he said as his voice choked off.

"Sergeant, did your wife know that Harper was in town? Did you tell her?"

He shook his head as if that was his saving grace. "No! I didn't tell her. She didn't know! When we found out that Harper had died, she was shocked that Harper was even in town."

"That could have been an act," Alba pointed out skeptically.

"I think it's time we get your wife and Elena home. They are out to lunch right now," I told him. "I think you should call Louise."

He nodded crazily. His hands shook as he lifted his phone. He looked down at it in a daze.

"He doesn't look so good, Mercy," Sweets whispered. "Maybe he should sit down."

Sweets was right. The white-haired man was falling apart right before our eyes. "Sergeant Bradshaw, let's get you to the living room, I think you need to sit down."

"We could call Elena," Holly suggested, following us to the living room as we helped him sit down on the formal sofa.

Alba nodded as she whispered to me. "It might be too much for him to call his wife. If she's behind this, he could tip her off."

I sat down next to the Sergeant. He stared at the wall opposite him in a daze. "We'll call Elena and have her bring Louise back. Okay? You just sit here and relax." He didn't flinch. It worried me that perhaps he had fallen into a state of shock.

I pulled my cell phone out of my back pocket and dialed Elena's number. It rang, and it rang with no answer until finally, it went to her voicemail. I hung up the phone. "She's not answering. They've got to come back eventually. I mean she was only taking Louise out for lunch."

"Speaking of lunch," Sweets began. "I'm getting really hungry. Sergeant Bradshaw, do you mind if I check your fridge for something to snack on?"

"Sweets!" Alba admonished. "How can you think of your stomach at a time like this?"

Sweets looked around innocently. "A time like what? Lunch time? Easy. My stomach reminds me that it's lunch time."

Sergeant Bradshaw didn't move or make any other signal that he had heard Sweets's request.

"I'm sure it's fine, Sweets. I'm going to go find a sweater myself. It's freezing in here!"

"I put the screen back and shut the window."

"I know you did, thanks, Sweets. I'm still freezing."

"I'll help you look," said Holly. "I saw a couple of sweaters in the master bedroom closet."

I laughed. "I'm not going to wear one of Mrs. Bradshaw's expensive cardigans. Elena has got to have an old bedroom here."

"I did see a spare bedroom down the hall, come on, I'll show you."

Holly led me down the hallway behind the study and to a bedroom painted lavender with white bedroom furniture and a lavender quilt atop the bed. "This looks like a girl's bedroom to me," I told her as we entered.

"Look, it's a picture of Elena and Harper," said Holly as she held up one of the photographs on the dresser.

I peered over her shoulder at the photograph. "Oh, they

look like teenagers in that picture," I said with a smile. They looked almost identical at that age.

"Such a shame that Harper's gone now," said Holly wistfully. "She was a beautiful girl."

"Yeah," I said sadly. "We've got to bring her killer to justice!"

Holly opened the closet and reached in to grab a sweater, and as she pulled it off of the hanger just like that, her body locked up. I'd seen that vacant expression enough to know that she was having a vision.

"Holly!" I exclaimed as I caught her before she fell to the ground. I pulled her limp body to the bed and managed to get her up onto her back.

Her eyes were closed, but I could see her eyes darting about frantically behind her eyelids. I rushed to the hallway. "Girls!" I hollered. "It's Holly, hurry!"

Jax and Alba came running immediately. Sweets followed seconds later with a butter knife covered in peanut butter.

"What's going on?" she asked nervously.

"Holly's having a vision. She touched one of Elena's sweaters and then just collapsed."

All eyes riveted to Holly. Her body convulsed slightly and then finally, it went slack as if she'd fallen asleep. "Holly?" Jax asked tentatively.

Holly's eyes shot open. She stared straight ahead of her at the ceiling. The four of us bent over her nervously, and gradually her eyes wandered to scan each of our faces.

"Are you alright?" Sweets asked her.

Holly's eyes widened. "Elena," she whispered, and then before promptly fainting, she added breathlessly. "In danger."

CHAPTER 21

After she snapped out of it, it took a glass of apple juice and a couple of bites of Sweets's peanut butter and jelly sandwich before Holly felt strong enough to talk.

"She was in a car with a blond woman with gold jewelry," she began before taking another drink of her juice.

"That's her mother," I told the girls, remembering what Louise Bradshaw looked like from the night Harper had been discovered dead.

"Her mother had a gun pointed at her," Holly exclaimed. Fear covered her face. "Elena asked her where she was taking her. Her mother said 'To our special place.'"

"What?!" Jax shrieked.

I was equally in a state of shock. The faint possibility that Louise had killed her daughter, Harper, existed, but to think of her killing her other daughter now too? What in the world was going on?

"Where were they?" I asked Holly.

Holly shook her head. "I'm not sure. They were in Elena's car. I couldn't see anything else."

"Where would Mrs. Bradshaw be taking her? Where is their special place?" Jax asked nervously.

"I have no idea, but we've got to find out. Let's pack up the Sergeant and go find Harper. Maybe she'll know where to look!" I suggested.

Alba looked at Holly. "Holly, you can stay here and rest. We'll come back and pick you up."

Holly shook her head. "No, I'm fine. I feel a lot better now. I can make it."

"Shorty, you and Sweets help Holly get to the car. Red and I will get Sergeant Bradshaw."

"Is there room for all of us?" Sweets asked.

"We'll make room," I assured them.

"Should we call Detective Whitman?" Jax asked.

"We don't know where we're going yet. We have to find Harper."

"Okay," she agreed and helped Holly get her arm around her shoulder.

Alba and I dashed to the living room to get Sergeant Bradshaw to his feet. "Come on, Sarge. We've got to go save Elena."

"Elena?" he asked vaguely, as if he were caught up in a dream.

"Yes, Elena. Your daughter. She's …" my voice trailed off. I didn't know what to say. I didn't want to tell him that his daughter was being held at gunpoint by his wife. He was already in a precarious mental state.

"She needs your help," Alba finished. "We've got to go. Come on. We're going to drive you to her."

"To Elena? Elena needs me?" he asked, coming out of his foggy mental state little by little.

"Yes, but we have to go, right now."

Sergeant Bradshaw looked more lively than he had

moments earlier. He stood of his own free will and followed us out to Sweets's car where Jax was sitting on Holly's lap in the back seat and Sweets was in the driver's seat.

"Get in!" Sweets ordered.

Alba and I helped the Sergeant into the front seat, and she and I crammed ourselves into the backseat.

"Okay, all in. Let's go!" Alba hollered.

Sweets squealed the tires as she pulled away from the curb and then whipped around the corner, knocking Jax's head against the door frame of the car. "Oww!" Jax shrieked.

"Sorry," Sweets called out.

Aspen Falls was a very small town, so it didn't take long to get to Jimmy's Bed & Brew. "You guys stay in here," I asserted. "I'll go get her."

"I'll come with you," Alba offered. "In case you need any help."

I nodded as I ducked out of the car and sprinted to the front door, which sure enough, was locked. "It's locked."

"Stand back," Alba ordered, raising her flattened palms.

I put a hand on her arm. "Alba, you'd make a terrible cat burglar. You can't just go around blowing doors off their hinges. There's got to be a subtler way to do this."

"It would be handy if you learned to summon ghosts," Alba scoffed. "Then you could just call Harper down here, and we wouldn't have to go up."

"I realize that, but I've been a little busy solving murders lately to put much time into studying!" I barked at her. My nerves were more than a little shot. I was worried that Elena was going to be harmed before we had time to get to her.

Suddenly a thought hit me. There was a window in Harper's room. We'd looked out it a dozen times. It faced the alleyway, and I was almost positive there was a fire escape up to the window. "Let's go to the alley," I suggested.

We ran around to the back, and there it was, the fire escape that went all the way up to Harper's window. When we got to the top, I let out a sigh of relief that the window wasn't locked. Carefully we slid it open and climbed into the room. I pulled open the closet doors to find Harper in her usual fetal position.

"You really should get out more, Harp," I quipped. "You're getting a little pale."

Alba slugged me. "Nice, Red."

"Well that was rude," Harper grimaced. "I can't help that I'm dead!"

"I'm sorry, I was kidding. Look, we need you to go with us. It's Elena, she's being held at gunpoint, but we don't know where she is."

"Elena's being held at gunpoint?" she asked as she quickly got to her feet.

"Yeah, we need your help finding her."

Harper's eyes opened wide, and she splayed her hands out in front of her. "How in the world can I help? I'm just a ghost!"

"Your mother is the one holding her," I told her.

"What?!"

"We'll explain it all later, but we think that your mother is the one that paid Jimmy to poison your drink."

"Ugh! That witch!" Harper cried angrily.

"Hey! Watch it!" I snapped. "You say, *witch,* like it's a bad thing!"

"Oh, sorry, girls," Harper said, covering her mouth.

"What did she say?" Alba asked.

SON OF A WITCH

"Nothing, she just called her mother a witch," I said with a chuckle.

"We've got to go," Alba said hurriedly.

"Let's go. We can talk about it in the car."

"Can I ride in a car? I'm a ghost."

"Of course you can, I hear about haunted cars all the time," I told her seriously.

"Really?" Harper asked.

"Yeah, absolutely."

"Our car's pretty full, though," I told her.

"Like she's going to take up a lot of space?" Alba asked.

"True. Okay, you can sit on my lap," I suggested.

"Oh, one more thing," Alba said quickly. "We've got your dad with us."

"Daddy?" Harper's eyes lit up at the mention of her father.

"Yeah, we should probably save the reunion for after we've found Elena, okay? We'll have to keep your presence on the down low," I told her.

"Okay," she said quietly.

"Let's go. We're running out of time."

Alba and I climbed out of the window first. Harper trepidatiously let herself float out of the window. She pulled her head back to soak in the sunshine. "It feels so good to be outside!"

"See, you should have left earlier," I told her.

Quickly we descended the stairs and made our way back to the car. Alba and I climbed in first, and Harper stuffed herself on top of me. Her presence made my chills worse, and I hugged Elena's sweater tighter around my arms.

"Daddy!" she cooed excitedly.

"Relax," I whispered. "Down low, remember?"

"Where are we going?" Sweets asked immediately.

Alba looked at me. "I don't know, *Mercy*," she enunciated my name in a funny way. I was so used to her calling me Red, that hearing her say Mercy sounded foreign to me. "Where would their special place be?"

"Hmm, let me think if there is anywhere that maybe she'd have gone in her childhood, maybe somewhere her mother would have taken her to hide out?" I asked aloud.

Jax and Holly looked at me as if I were crazy. "Why do you two sound like zombies?" Jax asked hesitantly.

Alba elbowed Jax's leg. "Oh!" Jax hollered.

Harper thought carefully. "Well, there's this creek that wanders through town to the waterfall. But if you follow it up the creek there's an old cabin that we used to walk to when we were little girls. Our mother used to do tea parties in the cabin with us. She said tea parties would teach us manners and make us well behaved society girls," Harper said with a little laugh. "I guess that blew up in her face."

Sweets caught my eye in her rear-view mirror. "There's a creek that runs through town, Sweets. We can follow it from the waterfall in the center of town. Start there and follow it upstream."

"Okay," she said.

It took only a minute before we were following the stream. We followed it to a country road just outside of town. "There!" Harper pointed. "See that little grove of Hemlock trees? The cabin is over there."

"There!" I shouted at Sweets. "That grove of trees."

"Is there a road?" Sweets asked.

"There's an old country road, keep going, and this road will fork, take a right," Harper added.

"Yeah, keep going. There's a fork in the road up ahead, yeah, there!" I pointed. "Stay to the right."

We followed the road as it veered off I could see the cabin through a break in the trees. "There," I pointed. "Turn off here!"

Our car bustled over the bumpy terrain until we got to the cabin's driveway. "I see a car," Holly hollered from her side of the car.

"We should call Detective Whitman," Jax said nervously.

"And tell him what address?" I asked.

"I don't know, a cabin along the creek," Jax responded.

"Fine, you call him," I said and handed her my phone as we pulled into the cabin's parking area. "We're going in."

The girls all started to pile out, but Sergeant Bradshaw remained seated. "Sergeant Bradshaw. We need you to help us. Elena might be in there."

"Elena?" he asked again. I was starting to think that was the only word he knew anymore.

"Yes, your daughter. She needs your help, remember. She's in that cabin. She's in danger."

His eyes perked up again. "What are we waiting for? Let's go!"

I smiled at him, glad to see that he was coming out of the coma he had been in. I jumped out of the car and met him as he was getting out. The girls were all waiting for us beside the front of the car. Jax had stayed back to call Detective Whitman and fill him in and ask for police backup.

Trepidatiously we approached the house. As we passed the other car, my arm rubbed up against the hood. It was still warm. I hoped that we had gotten there soon enough to save Elena.

We converged on the house. Nervously I knocked on the front door as I waved at the other girls and Sergeant

Bradshaw to hide around the corner. Harper stood bravely by my side as I waited for someone to answer the door.

I heard a scuffle inside, and then the door cracked open a sliver. "Yes?" I heard a woman's voice call out from the inside.

"I'm selling Girl Scout cookies. I was wondering if you wanted to buy any?" I asked facetiously.

The woman peered at me through the crack in the door. I was fairly confident it was Louise Bradshaw, but not completely, the crack was too narrow for me to see anything more than one eye and a spot of blonde hair.

"We don't want any," she said. "Wait, aren't you...?" she began again before nearly slamming the door in my face.

"Yup!" I cried, and with all the force in my body, I slammed against the door, sending her reeling backwards. The door flew open, and I ran in, the girls and Sergeant Bradshaw came running in behind me. It was Louise alright, and she had Elena by a fistful of blond hair with a gun to her head.

Harper sucked in a breath.

"Louise! Elena!" Sergeant Bradshaw cried when he saw the two of them entangled in such a way inside the cabin.

"Daddy!" Elena screamed. "Help!"

"Hello, Henry," Louise smirked as she shuffled to her feet with Elena's hair still in her grip.

"Louise, what in the world are you doing?"

Alba, Holly, and Sweets stood by anxiously, not knowing what to do. Sergeant Bradshaw began slowly inching his way towards Louise. She pulled Elena's head back farther and pointed the gun at her husband. "Stop right there! Not another muscle, Henry. Or I'll shoot both of you."

"Louise! What in the world has gotten into you? Are you off of your meds?" he asked, appalled.

"I'm just fed up, Henry."

"Fed up? Fed up with what?"

"Your daughters," she spat at him.

"My-my daughters?" he stuttered, looking at Elena shiftily. "Don't you mean *our* daughters?"

"No you fool!" she screamed at him. "I mean *your* daughters! We both know that they aren't *our* daughters."

"Louise, you've got to be off of your meds. You can't possibly know what you're saying here."

"Oh, I know exactly what I'm saying! For *years* I've pretended that your daughters were my own. I treated them like my own. And what did it get me? Humiliation and disappointment! That's what it got me! Both of those girls turned into nothing more than the town harlots. Neither one of them made a single decent grade in school. They didn't go to college. They didn't marry into a good family. They sleep around with whatever man will have them. They've been a drain on us financially, and don't think I don't know that you've been supporting both of them since high school! Just because you handle our finances, doesn't mean that I'm an idiot!"

"Louise! The girls might have some issues, but they are good girls," Sergeant Bradshaw pleaded to his wife.

"No, they aren't! They act just like their dead mother, Marjory was a harlot too. Right up until the day she died. She was cheating on you, you know."

He shook his head frantically.

"She was. After she died, I took pity on you, raising two little girls on your own. Even though I never wanted children of my own, I fell in love with you, and I promised to be a good mother to those girls. And I was too! So when we moved to Aspen Falls, I thought it would be a clean break from our old lives. Everyone would think they were our daughters together and life would be good. But then they began to take after Marjory, whoring it up all over town. Every single one of my friends talks about them, you know. They gossip behind my back about them. I know it! Those girls are an embarrassment to the Bradshaw name! I just wanted them gone from our lives. I'm tired of being second to your bratty girls and the memory of your dead wife. You've always loved them more than me! I know you have."

"Louise, tell me you didn't have Jimmy kill Harper, please?" he begged.

"Are you an idiot Henry? Really. Isn't it obvious? Of course, I paid your dear old buddy Jimmy to kill Harper! I overheard you talking to Elena the day that she came home to *beg* for yet *more money.* You told Elena to ask Harper to come to the house in the morning. You suggested that she stay at Jimmy's because you trusted him so much with your *precious Harper!*"

She gave Elena's hair another solid yank causing the young woman to scream out.

"But what you didn't realize is, Jimmy was bankrupt. I read it in the paper not that long ago. Jimmy Spencer's building was in foreclosure. How easy would it be just to offer him the money that you were going to give to your daughters anyway and have him end our misery permanently?"

"Misery? I can't believe what you're saying, Louise," he cried.

"Believe it, Henry. It was easy. It hardly took any convincing at all. Jimmy was going to get his bar paid for free and clear, and I was going to get the bane of my existence out of my life for good. Of course, Jimmy made things hard for me. He decided he needed to blackmail me for more money. I don't take too kindly to blackmailers," she scoffed. "So Jimmy had to go."

"Louise!" Sergeant Bradshaw said in shock.

"What? Elena's next you know," Louise cackled. "I've had just about all that I can take from this one." Louise pushed the gun against Elena's temple. Elena winced, as did Sergeant Bradshaw. He held his hands up in front of him.

"No, Louise. Don't do this. Please. I'll give you whatever you want," he promised her as the sound of sirens racing up the dusty dirt road could be heard in the distance.

"Who called the police?" Louise asked with surprise as she looked between all of us girls and Sergeant Bradshaw.

I eyed Alba, Holly, and Sweets out of the corner of my eyes. None of them moved. Then I saw Alba look at me out of the corner of her eyes. I gave her a little nod, and she nodded back as a tiny smile lifted the sides of her mouth.

"We did!" I smirked.

Louise loosened her grip on Elena's hair and took the gun off of her temple and aimed it at me. "Well then, you deserve everything you're about to get."

"Louise, no!" Sergeant Bradshaw hollered.

Alba inhaled a deep breath, raised her arms up in front of her, closed her eyes and took no time in discharging her pent up energy from the palms of her hands. It shot forth in bright blue and green streaks of electrical energy, powering Louise Bradshaw straight through the side wall of the cabin and out into the field. Elena's eyes widened as she watched her stepmother fly past her. Sergeant Bradshaw rushed to Elena's side immediately and held her tightly to his chest.

"Daddy!" Elena cried.

"Oh, sweetheart, I'm so sorry!"

Harper rushed to be by her father and sister's side while Alba, Holly, Sweets and I rushed outside to make sure Louise Bradshaw was down for the count.

Outside she was still lying on her back on top of the wooden section of wall that Alba had blown clear off of the cabin. She groaned, holding her back as she struggled to get up. I walked over to her and kicked the gun out of her hand before she could think of using it to harm anyone.

"Alba, I'm going to start calling you the Hulk! You smash everything that gets in your way!" I quipped.

Police officers descended upon the small house with Detective Whitman leading the pack.

"Mercy! What kind of trouble have you gotten yourself into now?" he asked, as his gaze covered the destruction of the cabin.

"We found your killer, sir," I told him proudly, pointing towards Louise Bradshaw who was being lifted to her feet by a team of police officers.

"Another murder suspect, Miss Habernackle? How am I ever supposed to believe you? You are constantly changing your mind!"

"She confessed! Her husband heard the confession and everything," I argued.

Sergeant Bradshaw and Elena walked out of the cabin. He glanced over at Detective Whitman and nodded. "These young women saved the day, Detective. My wife paid Jimmy Spencer to kill my daughter and then she killed Jimmy Spencer herself. If it wasn't for these girls..." he trailed off as the immensity of the situation hit him and tears began to fall down his cheeks.

"You mean the Witch Squad?" Detective Whitman asked with a chuckle.

SON OF A WITCH

"Yes," Sergeant Bradshaw agreed with a sniffle. "If it weren't for them, my Elena would be dead right now. They are to be commended!"

Detective Whitman threw his shoulders back and grinned at the five of us, like a proud father. "Very good. Very good indeed. Sorceress Stone will be happy to hear this!"

Sweets's eyes shot open as did Holly's. "Why do you have to tell *her* everything?"

"Yeah," I agreed. "I think we can keep this one to ourselves, can't we?"

"I suppose," Detective Whitman agreed.

CHAPTER 22

S everal days later, Sergeant Bradshaw gathered the lot of us together - everyone that had had an impact on solving his daughter's murder. Detective Whitman and several of the officers from the Aspen Falls Police Department, the Witch Squad and Hugh, of course, Mom, Reign and Chesney, and Harper and Elena all gathered together in Jimmy Spencer's Bed & Brew.

Sergeant Bradshaw had a meal catered to show his thanks for all of the work we'd done. With his daughters flanking either side of him, he raised a glass to the crowd. "I'd like to make a toast," he began. His thick, heavy voice filled the room. "To Detective Whitman and his officers at the Aspen Falls PD and to the girls here today from the Paranormal Institute. Without you, I can't even imagine what my life would be like right now without my dear, sweet, Elena. I'm still reeling from the loss of my beautiful Harper. May she rest in peace." His voice lowered as he spoke her name.

Harper rested her head on her father's shoulder, causing a lump to form in my throat and tears to well up in my eyes. I only wished that I had the power to allow a ghost one last opportunity to say goodbye to their loved ones.

"I would like to offer my sincerest apologies to the family of Reign Alexander, as he was falsely accused of committing this horrible crime. Stand up, son," he said to my brother.

Reign stood up quietly.

"Reign, I understand that you're new to Aspen Falls. You came here to meet your sister. The very woman who helped solve my daughter's murder. I'd like to do something for your family, son."

Reign shook his head, waving one hand slightly in front of his face. "No, no. That's quite alright."

"No, I insist. My wife, who I'd like to mention was indeed off of her medication for at least the last month, if her prescription history is any indication, gave Jimmy Spencer a large amount of money to pay off his debts. When his apartment was searched, it was discovered that he hadn't yet cashed the check from my wife. Perhaps they had agreed to wait until things died down so as not to alert anyone about their involvement together. In any regard, his property is still in foreclosure, and I have made arrangements with the bank to purchase this building and subsequent business."

Whispers of excitement swirled through the bar.

"And I have decided that I would like to gift the building and business to you and your sister to show my sincere appreciation and apologies for everything you have all been through."

My eyes widened as did Reign's. "You want to give us this bar?" Reign asked in shock.

"Yes, son. I enjoyed coming down here for coffee every morning, and I'd like to be able to continue my morning ritual. The place needs a young person to have the energy to keep such a thing in business. I'd like to keep you around Aspen Falls while you get to know your family. And, when you decide it's time for your journey to move on, it's yours to sell as you please."

"Sir, you don't have to do this! I could never repay you," Reign argued as his eyes met our mother's. She beamed at him proudly.

"No, no. It's a done deal. And no thanks necessary. I'd just be thrilled to have a free cup of coffee in the mornings."

Reign smiled from ear to ear. "Of course, yeah, definitely!"

"Very good," he asserted. "Now, enjoy your meal, everyone." With that, he sat back down.

I stood up and walked towards the head of the table. "Sergeant Bradshaw, Elena, I was wondering if I might have a word with you? Privately?" I asked them.

They exchanged curious glances before standing up. "Of course," he said.

I led them upstairs to the room that Harper had been killed in. Harper followed closely behind. When we got into the room, I closed the door and offered them a seat at the little table overlooking the fire escape and alley.

"First of all," I began quietly. "I'd like to thank you, Sergeant, for the generous gift you've given my brother. I look forward to keeping him around and getting to know him better. That was very kind of you."

Sergeant Bradshaw nodded and gave me a pleasant smile. "Of course, it's the least I could do."

"Now, the reason I asked you both up here, is there is one last order of business before I'm able to put this case behind me. That issue is that of your daughter, Harper."

"Harper?" he asked.

"Yes. I don't know if you realize this, sir, but Harper has appeared to me as a ghost," I began gently.

He nodded. "Yes. Elena has filled me in on some of the details."

Harper sat down on the bed in front of her father and sister.

"She's here with us, right now. Until she can say goodbye to you both, I don't think she'll be able to be at peace."

"Harper's here?" he choked out, as his eyes filled with tears.

"Yes."

"Hi, Daddy," Harper whispered. I could tell she wanted to cry but knew she couldn't.

"She said, 'Hi, Daddy,'" I told him.

"Hi, darling, I love you so much, and I'll miss you."

"I'll miss you too, Daddy. And Elena," Harper said sadly.

"She said she'll miss you and Elena too."

Elena looked heartbroken. "Tell her I'm sorry I wasn't a better sister."

Harper shook her head. "No, tell her *I'm* sorry that I told her she was a horrible sister. She wasn't a horrible sister. She was a great sister, and I'll miss her forever."

I smiled gently, as Harper's words tugged at my heart. "She said no, she's sorry that she said you were a horrible sister. She said you were a great sister and she's going to miss you forever."

Elena wiped at her wet cheeks with the pads of her fingertips. "Harper, I love you."

"I love you too, Lena," Harper croaked out.

"Me too Harper, sweetheart. I love you!"

"I love you too, Daddy!"

ing to keep my tears from falling.
"She said she loves you both," I whispered.

The outline of Harper's body began to flicker, like the fire atop a candle when it's caught a breeze. "Thank you, Mercy," she called out.

"Goodbye, Harper," I called back to her until finally, she flickered away into nothingness.

"She's gone," I whispered to her family. "She's at peace now."

"Thank you, Mercy," Elena whispered back.

"Yes, thank you, dear," her father agreed.

I nodded at them both. "I'll let you two have time together. I'm going to go downstairs."

With that I left the room, closing the door behind me and descended the stairs where Hugh was standing at the bottom of the stairs waiting for me.

"Hey there, darlin', you alright?" he asked me sweetly.

I nodded and swallowed hard again. "Yeah," I whispered. Then I mustered up a smile for him. "Thank you for being there for me this week. It's been a tough week."

"I know it has. Now that we're finally putting all of this behind us, there's something that I've meant to do all week," he said quietly.

"What's that?" I asked as the skin on my arms rippled.

"This," he said and gently bent his head down to lay his lips atop mine. It was sweet and tender, a true kiss of a gentleman. My heart raced inside my chest.

I smiled as he lifted his lips off mine. Leaning my head onto his broad shoulder, I linked arms with him.

"Let's go sit down," he suggested.

"Yeah," I agreed happily.

I followed him back to the table where Mom was

259

holding Chesney. "I've sure fallen in love with this little guy," she said as he nuzzled her neck.

"Mom and I were just talking, Mercy, I think we're both going to move in here. For awhile anyway. Mom's going to help me get this business off its feet."

I smiled at them both as I slid into my chair and took Chesney from my mother, "That's *awesome!*"

"Yeah, it'll give us a chance to get to know each other better," said Mom. "You know, Mercy, a dorm room is no place for a puppy. He needs to be able to have room to run around and play."

I rolled my eyes as I played with Chesney's ears.

"I'm not kidding. I know your heart was in the right place when you adopted Ches, but until you've left the dorms, I think you should consider letting me take care of him. He will have so much more room to run and play here."

I looked at Chesney sadly. I knew Mom was probably right. I stuck out my bottom lip as I patted the top of Chesney's head. "But he'd miss me!"

"You can come and see him anytime you want. It would give me an opportunity to see you more, too."

"Fine," I grumbled. "I suppose." I hugged Chesney close before handing him back to my mom.

My mom squeezed Chesney close to her before pulling her navy-blue cardigan tighter over her shoulders. "Brr, it's freezing in here," she commented. "Aren't you girls cold?"

Alba, Sweets, Holly and Jax looked at me nervously. "Your mom's cold, Mercy," Holly stated nervously.

As if on cue, Reign cleared his throat. "Umm, Mercy, I know you wanted to wait for any big new surprises," my brother began. "But there's really something I need to tell you and Mom."

From across the table, Hugh's eyes met mine.

I raised a hand to stop my brother. "Reign, no! I said this before. Give me a week off. Or maybe two before dropping bombs on me! I need a break!"

Mom looked at him curiously. "What is it, Reign?"

He looked at me, unsure of what to do. "Mercy?"

"No, Reign," I growled.

"Mercy! Let your brother tell us."

"Mom, it's going to be bad, I can just feel it. The girls and I have just been through three murder investigations. We are exhausted. *I'm* exhausted! I need a break. He can tell us next week."

"Mercy Mae Habernackle! You stop, this instant!" she cried.

I sighed, feeling defeated. "Fine. Spill your guts, Reign."

"Sorry, sis. This was going to come out soon anyway," he said looking nervously between Mom and I. "You weren't the only reason I came to Aspen Falls."

I looked at Mom curiously. Her confused expression told me she obviously had no idea what he was talking about either.

"Oh-kayyyy?" I drug out. He had piqued my curiosity.

Reign looked down at his hands. "I came to Aspen Falls to meet someone else."

"Who else do you know in Aspen Falls?" Mom asked in surprise.

Reign played nervously with his hands. "My father."

Mom's head jarred backwards. "Excuse me?"

The girls all looked at each other in confusion. I was sure they were thinking exactly what I was thinking. How in the world does he know who his father is?

"You can't possibly…" Mom began.

"My grandmother told me," he said quietly. "I went to see her."

"You talked to granny?" I was shocked.

"Yeah," he whispered.

"Why didn't you tell me?" I demanded.

He cocked his head to the side and gave me a sly smile. "Mercy, I tried. You know that."

"So, who is it? Who's your father?" Jax asked from across the table.

"Yeah! We're dying over here," Holly added. "Tell us!"

Reign chuckled. "I'd love to tell you who ladies, but first, I need to introduce myself to my father. I don't think he even knows that he has a son."

I furtively glanced at my mother. A dark shadow seemed to have crossed over her face. That's when I knew that the relaxing break I had dreamed about was only the beginning of troubled days to come.

∼

…

THANKS FOR READING! I HOPE YOU ENJOYED THE SECOND BOOK in the Witch Squad series. If you did, I'd really appreciate it if you left a review. Reviews are the best way to tell the author if you'd like them to keep writing the characters you love!

Would you like to receive an email when new books in the series are released? Join my newsletter! I promise not to spam you, I send newsletters only when I have a new release or something important to share.

Other Books Set in Aspen Falls in Reading Order

Witch Squad Book #1 - The Witch Squad - Season 1

Witch Squad Book #2 - Son of a Witch

Witch Squad Book #3 - Witch Degrees of Separation

Witch Squad Book #4 - Witch Pie

Witch Squad Book #5 - A Very Mercy Christmas

Witch Squad Book #6 - Where Witches Lie

Witch Squad Book #7 - Witch School Dropout

The Coffee Coven #1 - That Old Witch!

The Coffee Coven #2 - Hazel Raises the Stakes

Witch Squad Book #7.5 - Witch, Please!

The Coffee Coven #3 - That Crazy Witch!

Witch Squad Book #8 - The Witch Within

Witch Squad Book #9 - Road Trippin' with my Witches

The Coffee Coven #4 - That Broke Witch!

Witch Squad Book #10 - Welcome Back Witches - Season 2

The Mystic Snow Globe Mystery Series

Deal or Snow Deal: A Prequel

Snow Cold Case: Book 1

Snow Way Out: Book 2

The Witch Island Series

Behind the Black Veil: Book 1

ABOUT THE AUTHOR

Hello! I'm M. I live in the Midwest. I enjoy my house full of family, including my wonderfully amazing husband, four beautiful daughters, two handsome sons, and an amazing sidekick cat, who keeps me company all day while I dream up my crazy and exciting stories!

I love writing, gardening, football games, and DIY projects. I love chatting with fans, so feel free catch up with me on Facebook or Twitter.

If you'd like to be the first notified when the next Witch Squad Cozy Mystery comes out, you can sign up for my newsletter. Finally, if you enjoyed the book, **I would really appreciate you leaving a review!**

All the best,
XOXO - M

For more information:
www.mzandrews.com
mzandrews@mzandrews.com